A SUDDEN PROPOSAL ...

"I think you ought to marry me," Lord Brooke said.

"What?" Jane looked shocked. "Why should I do that, my lord?"

"Because you need to be rescued from this lunatic asylum, that is why. Since your father isn't here to save you, it appears that I'll have to be the one to do it."

"I still don't see why you feel responsible for me," Jane replied. "Why is it up to you to 'save' me?"

"Oh, well, for my sister's sake, I suppose. You are her dearest friend."

Jane stared down at her hands, then carefully raised her head. "But I am not yours, Lord Brooke. Therefore, thank you, but no thank you."

His Lordship looked as though she had struck him. "What? Do you mean that you are denying my suit? You can't do that."

"Oh, can't I?" She stood up and glowered at him. "Why can't I?"

He rose as well. "Because you need me."

Jane laughed humorlessly. "In case you haven't noticed, I *don't* need you. I am perfectly capable of managing my own life."

A Larcenous Affair
Ellen Rawlings

DIAMOND BOOKS, NEW YORK

A LARCENOUS AFFAIR

A Diamond Book / published by arrangement with the author

PRINTING HISTORY
Diamond edition / October 1991

All rights reserved.
Copyright © 1991 by Ellen Rawlings.
This book may not be reproduced in whole or in part,
by mimeograph or any other means, without permission.
For information address: The Berkley Publishing Group,
200 Madison Avenue, New York, New York 10016.

ISBN: 1-55773-599-9

Diamond Books are published by The Berkley Publishing Group,
200 Madison Avenue, New York, New York 10016.
The name "DIAMOND" and its logo are trademarks
belonging to Charter Communications, Inc.

PRINTED IN THE UNITED STATES OF AMERICA

10 9 8 7 6 5 4 3 2 1

**TO BELLE AND DAN ROSE,
MY BELOVED PARENTS**

CHAPTER

1

ALTHOUGH it was just the third week of the Season, people were saying that the Mannings' ball couldn't possibly be exceeded for brilliance. The beauty of the surroundings, no doubt, influenced this opinion. Three Irish crystal chandeliers sparkled like diamonds under the ornate coved ceilings, the plasterwork walls were newly washed and regilded, and arbors of hothouse flowers crowned the festive ballroom.

Even more glittering than the decor, however, was the guest list. Everyone who mattered had come to the Mannings' huge Berkeley Square town house, including the entirety of Almack's Ladies' Committee and the Prince Regent himself, who stayed for more than an hour playing whist.

Surely, Lady Jane Ashworth should have been pleased to have been invited to such a splendid, dazzling affair. It was so much more stimulating than the prosy local balls and assembly dances she attended in her neighborhood in Lincolnshire. And, indeed, she *had* been pleased—but that had been before she'd found out what her aunt, Lady Lettice, had done. The discovery ruined all of Jane's enjoyment.

"You must return it at once," she informed her aunt with such emphasis that two silky yellow strands of hair fell either side Jane's beautiful oval face. "If nothing else, think of the disgrace if you are discovered."

Lady Lettice looked up fondly, though with a hint of impatience, at her disapproving niece. "Pish-tosh. None of the Mannings will miss it tonight. It is too small."

"But, Aunt, what you did is wrong, not to say foolish and dangerous." Lady Jane accompanied her words with a poke of a graceful, long-fingered hand at her aunt's green reticule. "You should not have taken it, even if Lady Manning *never* discovers her loss. Promise me that you will put it back as quickly as possible."

Lady Lettice frowned, deepening the wrinkles on her narrow face, which was thin almost to the point of gauntness. Then her expression relaxed. "Oh, very well, my dear," she said agreeably, "if it means that much to you. I don't believe I want it anyway." So saying she removed from her reticule a small ivory carving of a Chinese peasant balancing two water buckets on a long pole. "Ugly little thing, isn't it? I don't know why the Mannings ever bought it."

Quick as a cat, Lady Jane grabbed the carving and thrust it back into her aunt's reticule, then looked about with large, uneasy blue eyes to see if anyone had observed her action. To her relief, no horrified hordes stared accusingly in her direction. Then Jane slumped against the back of the spindly gilt armchair she perched on. "Why did you?" she asked in a strained voice.

"Why did I what, dear?"

Jane sighed. "Why did you take the carving, Aunt? As you said, you do not even want it. I fear I do not understand you at all."

Lady Lettice chuckled indulgently. "It should be obvious, you silly goose. It was the only object in the library that would fit into my reticule. I never, ever, take anything larger than a reticule. That is my rule."

"Your rule," Jane said faintly. She fought off an inappropriate urge to laugh.

Lady Lettice stroked her flat bosom in an unconscious gesture of self-approval. "Yes, although I won't deny that I've been sorely tempted now and again. There was a very pretty malachite box I saw one time at the Prime Minister's—well, the point is that I left it. Because of my standards, you see. To take something large like that would have been dishonest."

Lady Lettice's explanation, which she delivered with obvious if inexplicable sincerity, made Jane lift her shapely arms in a gesture of helplessness, a gesture she rarely permitted herself. At five feet and ten inches in her silk stockings, she felt she was too big for helplessness. What she'd chosen for herself, instead, was to be capable and independent.

This was not to say that now and again she didn't wonder if she might have enjoyed being a bit shorter and a tinge dependent. But then she'd remember how her father always attempted to dominate those who were small and meek—like her late, dear mother—and she'd be glad once more of her size and nature. Let other females give in to ineffectual flutterings; she took matters into her own large but attractive white hands.

Yet neither her height, nor her nature, nor even her great age of three and twenty, had prepared her to deal with a relative who made off with other people's possessions and lived happily in a household that was the closest thing to bedlam that Jane had ever encountered. Why, if her papa had been in England rather than in Jamaica seeing to their holdings, she might almost have been tempted to return home—almost.

She shook her blonde head once again. "Don't forget, Aunt, you gave me your word that you would put that piece back as soon as possible."

The plumes in Lady Lettice's yellow turban appeared to bristle for an instant. "Did I? Then I suppose I shall have to." When Jane's white teeth flashed in an encouraging smile, her unrepentant aunt added, "You do make a fuss over nothing, though, don't you? You're more like your father than I thought."

This remark, which Lady Lettice well knew was an insult, demanded a reply. Before Jane could think of one, however, the young man who had signed her card for the boulanger came to claim her and she was taken off. "Don't forget," she called over her shoulder as she went. "You promised."

As Jane danced down the length of the room with her partner, her host, Lord Freddy Manning, stood to one side watching the crowd with a pleased expression on his round, young-looking face. Having finished his scrutiny, Freddy turned to speak to Lord Marcus Brooke, the gentleman next to him, who was Freddy's oldest and dearest friend.

Marcus Brooke was a handsome, very tall man of nine and twenty whose handsomeness came more from his height and strong aura of masculinity than any particular beauty of feature. Three weeks earlier he had returned from Portugal, where he'd served as an aide-de-camp to Lord Wellington. His military training showed in his fine posture and easy air of command.

At the moment, though, he looked out-of-sorts. In fact, he was scowling. The effect of this expression was to drive from Freddy Manning's mind the idle comment he had been about to make.

"What is it, Marcus?" he said in a concerned voice. "You have the fiercest look on your face. Has something happened to displease you?"

Lord Brooke's scowl lightened. "If you mean here, at your ball, then, no; nothing has happened."

"I didn't think it could have," said Freddy with a relieved, cheerful smile. "Certainly, there are quite a lot of pretty girls here tonight, don't you agree? Even enough to satisfy a man of the world like you. Remind me to commend my mother for having collected so many."

Lord Brooke moved slightly away from the pillar he'd been leaning against and straightened to his full six feet, four inches. He looked cross-tempered again. "Are there many? I fear I haven't noticed."

Lord Manning's blue eyes lifted upward as though seeking inspiration from the ceiling's cavorting gods and goddesses. "You didn't used to be oblivious when it came to women, Marcus," he rebuked mildly. "I may not have seen you for several years, but I remember that. Now you seem unaware of them most of the time and also not especially to like them when you do notice them." He paused and reddened. "That is not to say that I think you're a . . . Dash it, Marcus, what I mean is, I believe you're becoming a misogynist."

"I am a soldier," Marcus said, flexing his long fingers, "or was until a few weeks ago. I'm not a dancing partner for silly women who have nothing to do but be on the catch for a husband—or get into trouble and force me to sell out."

"Oh, yes; I keep forgetting that you would be in Portugal still if it weren't for your mother's and sister's . . . that is, if you weren't needed at home to provide guidance to the women in your family. The word is that Wellington insisted you sell out when someone wrote to inform him that your ladies were wading into ever-deeper waters."

This time Marcus's scowl was fierce indeed. "You are mistaken," he said in a cold, offended voice. "It was I who told him about my mother and sister and begged permission to return home."

Freddy seemed unprepared to comment on this statement. "Probably, I should have gone to him sooner," Marcus said more neutrally, "when I got the letter from my man of business saying that my mother was losing increasingly larger sums at the gambling houses. And almost certainly I should have done so when I received the letters, mostly anonymous, describing my sister's various antics. However, I wasn't yet convinced."

He paused to give his friend a wry, self-mocking grin. "When the last letter arrived, however, I knew I had no alternative."

"Umm." Freddy put his finger to his lower lip. "I remember hearing something about your sister causing a to-do at the Arlingtons', but I can't recall it clearly. It had to do with pets, didn't it?"

For the first time during their conversation, Lord

Brooke's brown eyes lit with laughter. "Not pets," he said. "Bats."

"Bats?"

"Yes, that's what I said. My darling sister released three bats into the Arlingtons' dining room when the guests were about to take their places for dinner. You can imagine the havoc that was created. According to my informant, all the women ran about covering their hairdos and screaming—as did Lord Arlington."

Lord Manning found this information so entertaining that he had to choke off the sounds of his amusement with his handkerchief. When he could finally speak, he said, "I always suspected that Arlington wore a toupee; now I'm convinced of it. But tell me, where could Susan have found the creatures? I'm sure they aren't the sorts of things one can just buy in a shop."

"I'm sure they aren't to be found in shops, either," Lord Brooke agreed with a chuckle. He reflected for a few seconds, then said with a renewed frown, "It wouldn't surprise me to learn that she'd gone to some cave and collected them herself. She's an enterprising chit.

"On second thought," he said more grimly, "given her ability to enmesh others in her schemes, it's likely that she convinced some stupid young person to collect the beasts for her." He turned his head to stare at the dancers, saying with a grimace, "I think you must be right about my becoming a misogynist. In my opinion, women aren't worth a great deal. In fact, if they were men, I wouldn't have a thing to do with them."

"Ah, but fortunately for us they aren't men." Lord Manning accompanied his words with a happy tug at his cravat that would have caused apoplexy in Needham, his valet. "I see females in every direction I'd be more than willing to stand up with. That one over there, for example"—he gestured toward Jane as she danced gracefully by—"has a lovely face and a quite wonderful figure. Remarkably fine eyes, too. I don't know why you've been glaring at her. Is she in partnership with your sister?"

"What the devil are you talking about? I have not been

glaring—" He broke off to look more closely at the spot to which Freddy pointed. "I've never seen that young woman before; I'm sure I would remember the height and the bosom if I had. In any case, I wasn't glaring at her."

"Well, you seemed to me as though you were," Freddy said amiably.

Lord Brooke took another peek at the object of his friend's admiration. "Beautiful, but a bit long in the tooth," he said, refusing to be pleased.

Freddy stared up at his friend. "How can you say so? I'll wager she's no more than two or three and twenty, which hardly makes her doddering."

"I would not care if she were just out of the schoolroom and a Pocket Venus instead of an Amazon. I'm no fit companion right now for any female, Freddy, so I suggest you stubble it." He gave Jane one last look. Then he relapsed against the pillar.

Lord Brooke's scrutiny had not escaped Jane. Thus, she took in his frowning glance and decided that she had been judged and found wanting. To her annoyance, she felt the hot color rise in her cheeks.

Of course, she told herself, she was being absurd. Why should she care what that great oaf over there thought of her? He was not the sort she would have chosen to attract if she could have done so. Heaven forbid! True, he was handsome in a rough sort of way, with a look of latent power that stirred something in her. And he was certainly tall enough to suit her. Nevertheless, he seemed—*difficult*, maybe even a bit of a bully like her father. She already had difficulties enough and to spare.

Still, she felt some curiosity about him. A further, surreptitious, glance revealed a man with a square chin, brown eyes, and thick, light brown hair worn fashionably in a Brutus. He was dressed in a blue coat and black breeches which, though superbly cut, seemed somehow out-of-place on such a strong-looking frame. In fact, he looked to her as though he'd be more at home dressed for the hunting field or attendance at a mill than a ball.

She supposed he might be thought quite an eligible *parti*

by those who did not object to his commanding, unfriendly manner. Even his narrow Roman nose, with a bump that proclaimed it had once been broken, looked proud and forceful.

The dark-haired gentleman beside him she recognized as her host. He had put himself down for a set of country dances later in the evening. She was grateful that the tall man had not written on her card, although if he had she would at least have had the advantage of knowing his name. Despite herself, she wished very much to know it.

When the dance ended, instead of promenading with her partner, she excused herself and went to stand beside her friend Lady Susan, who was beautifully garbed in a white muslin tunic over a pink silk underdress. Jane discreetly indicated the tall man. "Do you know who that is?"

Susan's pretty face, crowned with a topknot of straight, dark hair, took on an interested expression. "Who? Oh, that one? Why do you ask?"

"Because, although we've never even been introduced, I think he hates me."

Lady Susan laughed. "It wouldn't surprise me. He's been as cross as a bear since he came back from Portugal."

"Is that so? Is he a soldier, then?" When Susan nodded, Jane said obscurely, "I'm not surprised. He seems the rudest thing."

Again, Susan laughed. "I quite agree, and I ought to know. He is my brother."

"Oh, dear!" Jane ran an uncomfortable finger inside the neck of her beaded white sarcenet gown. "I'm sorry. I had no idea, of course. He is so large, and you are . . . ah . . . small."

"Yes, as is the rest of my family. That's why I'm convinced that Marcus is a changeling. If I could find the evil fairy who brought him, I'd make her take him back immediately."

Her dark eyes lit with curiosity. "What was it that he did to put you out of countenance? Oh, never mind. Here comes the ogre now."

Susan greeted her brother with an airy "Hello, Marcus," then gave him her cheek to kiss. Without a second's hesitation, he refused it.

Not seeming to care, she laughed and said, "Lady Jane Ashworth, may I present my brother, Lord Brooke. Marcus, this is my dear friend, Lady Jane. We attended Miss Wortham's together."

Jane and Lord Brooke gazed at each other with thinly veiled hostility. She felt that she had good reason for her dislike, of course, but why he continued to look at her with such displeasure she could not imagine.

She knew that there were men who did not find tall women appealing. Nevertheless, she could not see how anyone Lord Brooke's height could hold with such an idea. Compared to him, she was almost short. In addition, although she never dwelled on it, she was aware that she had a beautiful face. Given people's reactions to her, she could hardly be other than aware. Then why was this man staring down at her as though her very existence was an insult to polite society?

Lord Brooke was now looking disapprovingly at his sister. "Am I correct in assuming that this is the young woman who was with you on your scandalous ride in Hyde Park today?"

Lady Susan grinned. "Oh, you know about that. I rather hoped you wouldn't just yet."

"Of course, I know," his Lordship snapped. "Everyone must by now. When two gentlewomen ride through the park in a donkey cart pulled by mongrel dogs, that is hardly an event not to be noted and commented upon."

"But . . ." said Jane, who hadn't been near the park that day.

Lord Brooke gave her a withering look, then returned his attention to his sister. "You never fail to find some foolish female to follow your lead, do you? Tell me, did she supply the bats, too?"

"Who in particular told you about me this time?" said Lady Susan, ignoring the last part of his remark. "I'll wager it was that old cat Lady Brandon."

"So you admit it?"

"Just a minute—" A red-faced Jane tried once more to intervene, but the brother and sister ignored her.

Well, why should she care if she were unable to defend herself? She was very fond of Susan, but the abominable Lord Brooke was nothing to her. Besides, she thought he might be touched in his upper works. Bats, indeed!

Thinking about being *touched* made her remember her aunt. Hopefully, her Ladyship had already returned the ivory carving, but Jane wouldn't have wagered on it. Worrying again, she started to excuse herself.

Instantly, Lord Brooke's fingers clamped about her wrist. "You shan't leave just yet," he said in a commanding tone. "I haven't finished with you, my lady—I fear I've forgotten . . . What is your name?"

Odious man! He had not even bothered to recall it. How many insults did that make? Jane had an urge to bite his Lordship's warm, imprisoning fingers.

Perhaps she unconsciously bared her teeth, because Lord Brooke removed his hand rather quickly. He did not give over on his attack, however. "I must insist that you two stay away from each other, do you hear? Susan, you are going to behave yourself this year if I have to lock you up, and you, too, Lady—what the devil is your name?" he said, now clearly exasperated.

"Melisande. Don't you remember?" said Susan with a giggle, and Jane, picturing the just-mentioned tale-bearer whom everyone at Miss Wortham's loathed, could not help but laugh as well.

Lord Brooke, his jaw jutting out dangerously, practically growled. "Oh, you find this funny, do you? May I offer you some advice, Lady Melisande? Do not be too amused. I am in deadly earnest. And as for you, Susan—Susan!" But Lady Susan, seeing her next partner approach, waved her hand merrily and walked forward to meet him.

Left alone with a glowering, ill-natured giant, Jane hastily decided that the farce had gone on long enough. "There has been a mistake, my lord," she said in a quiet voice. "Several, in fact."

"Yes, and you and my sister have made all of them," said Lord Brooke. "She is a hoyden who apparently uses animals to play her tricks upon society, and you, Lady Melisande, for all you look as though you should know better, are another hoyden."

"Thank you very much!" said Jane, resisting a strong impulse to slap him. "You are mistaken about me, you know. Oh, and I . . . that is, my name is not Lady Melisande; it is Jane."

This admission seemed to irritate Lord Brooke more than anything that had gone before. His straight brows drew down menacingly over his eyes. "Then why did you say that it was Melisande?" he barked.

But she hadn't said it. Susan had. Unlike the real Lady Melisande, though, Jane did not tell tales. So what was she to reply to this irate gentleman?

It was at that fortuitous moment that Jane saw her next partner approach. She was unable to keep the smug satisfaction from her voice. "I'm afraid you'll have to excuse me, my lord. I am bespoken for this dance."

Before she quite realized what was happening, Lord Brooke whirled Jane around to face him. "If I must dance with you in order to finish what I want to say," he told her, "then, as distasteful as it is to me, I shall do it." With that, he drew her in among the dancers making up the lines. He took such wide steps that Jane, for all her length of limb, felt obliged to skip in order to keep up.

What a dreadful, horrible man. She was sorry that she had ever laid eyes upon him. She licked her suddenly dry lips with the point of her tongue.

Lord Brooke bent his head a little so that his face was close to hers. His thin nostrils flared slightly as his nose took in the sweet-sharp odor of her lime-scented cologne. His hand tightened on hers, and his intense gaze scrutinized her as though he were truly seeing her for the first time. For a moment, he looked surprised. Then he shook his head and said, "No."

"No?"

"No, Lady Jane, I am afraid we cannot overlook your escapade today. Something will have to be done."

Jane stared at Lord Brooke's forbidding expression. Her blue eyes widened a little. "Wh . . . what . . . ?" She blushed to hear herself stutter. "What do you mean?"

Before he could answer, they changed partners.

"Don't play the fool with me," his Lordship said grimly when they came together again. "I am talking about your disgraceful behavior in Hyde Park today. What would your family think if I told them what you had been up to?"

Although normally an excellent dancer, Jane stumbled over one of his Lordship's black leather-shod feet. Embarrassment deepened her anger. "But I wasn't in Hyde Park," she said resentfully, turning red. "I was at home all day with my aunt."

Again, Lord Brooke had to wait to make his reply. This did not improve his temper. "Are you asking me to believe that you didn't accompany my sister on her outrageous ride through the park? The person described to me fits your image exactly. After all, there can't be many other young women in London as tall as you."

Jane's gloved hand twitched in irritation within his. "I am not asking you to believe anything, Lord Brooke. I am telling you that I was not with Susan, as, indeed, I was not. You may believe what you wish. However, I assure you that I do not lie—at least not usually," she said with complete, though probably unnecessary, candor.

Lord Brooke's brown eyes examined her intently. "I must apologize," he said at last. "I appear to have made a mistake."

All at once, Lady Jane felt confused. She knew that she should dislike his Lordship for his treatment of her, not to mention his behavior toward Susan. And she did. Yet there was something about being his partner that, for all of his offensive behavior, she found exhilarating.

It appeared to have mainly to do with Lord Brooke's size and emphatic masculinity. She could not help but respond to those things. The admission made her uncomfortable because it suggested that she harbored something elemental and uncivilized within her chaste, white bosom. It was a lowering thought.

The music stopped, and the two drew away from each other. Lord Brooke started to say something, but just then they were joined by their grinning host. "There you are," said Lord Manning. "Dancing with the young lady, are you? You dog in the manger," he added so low that Jane was not certain that she heard him.

"It's not what you think," replied Lord Brooke.

Jane looked from one gentleman to the other. Could she be the butt of a secret joke between them? Along with her unwelcome reaction to Lord Brooke, the thought of being an object of amusement to him and Lord Manning was more than she felt able to tolerate. Abruptly excusing herself, she fled.

What an evening this had been, she thought, pressing a palm to her smooth cheek. During most of it, she'd felt as though she were in a madhouse.

This last thought naturally made her remember her aunt again. She had best seek out Lady Lettice at once and discover what she had been doing all of this time.

When she did not see Lady Lettice sitting with the other chaperons, Jane began to worry. She knew her aunt wasn't much for cards, so she doubted she'd find her at the whist table. A horrifying thought struck her. Suppose she'd gone to return the carving and been apprehended? Suppose she had replaced it in her reticule with something else that did not belong to her?

Jane was about to search through the various rooms when she saw Lady Lettice. Her face animated, her Ladyship was talking to a swarthy man with a peg leg. He was wearing black trousers instead of the more acceptable pantaloons, one leg of which was pinned up neatly. He looked like an illustration Jane had once seen of a particularly unsavory pirate.

If it were anywhere but this tonnish ball, she might have suspected the man was a pirate. She knew from several rather startling experiences that Lady Lettice would talk to anyone, and did—servants, sailors, even a prostitute outside Covent Garden.

Her Ladyship was not content merely to talk to unacceptable people. She invited them to her home to visit her. Just a week before, an Irish revolutionary her aunt had met on a street corner had accepted her invitation to dine. After the fish course he'd practically come to blows with the bishop seated beside him. Living with Lady Lettice was quite an education, thought Jane with a grimace.

"Jane," said her aunt, breaking into her niece's unpleasant thoughts, "I want you to meet Mr. Leger. Mr. Leger is an explorer. He means to go to Africa shortly to look for the source of the Nile."

"How nice," said Lady Jane, looking pointedly at her aunt's reticule. Did it seem flatter? Jane didn't believe so.

Lady Lettice patted the chair next to her in invitation to her newly acquired companion. "Mr. Leger will be glad to tell you about his plans, Jane. Won't you, Mr. Leger?" At his sinister nod, she added, "And tomorrow he means to come to the house to show us his maps. Isn't that thrilling?"

"Thrilling," repeated Jane. "Will you excuse us, Mr. Leger?" Without waiting for permission, she took her aunt by the hand and led her to a secluded corner of the room. "Have you done it?" she asked without preamble.

Lady Lettice adjusted the neckline of her *eau de nil* gown, then raptly studied her chicken skin fan. "What?"

"You know perfectly well what I'm referring to," said Jane, her normally calm blue eyes fiery. "Have you returned the carving you—" She hesitated, unwilling to say it, but strong measures were called for. "—that you stole from the library, Aunt?"

Lady Lettice looked both insulted and astonished. "My dear child, how can you speak so to me? I thought I explained to you that I never—"

"This is not the time for you to expound upon your theory of what constitutes a theft, Aunt. This is the time for you to return the Mannings' property if you have not already done so. Please?"

Lady Lettice's faded brown eyes softened. "Does it truly mean so much to you, my dear? Very well, then. I'll return it."

Jane relaxed her rigidly held shoulders. "Thank you, Aunt. And, now, if you'll just promise not to take anything else."

"Oh, I can't do that. In fact, there was the sweetest gold box on the same table." She looked at Jane doubtfully. "It seemed a bit large, which was why I did not avail myself of it the first time, but if I emptied my reticule of my smelling salts and deer's foot brush, it's possible I could fit it in."

"Give me the carving," said Jane, tearing the green reticule from her aunt's bony wrist. "I shall return it to the library for you."

"Really? I must say you've managed to surprise me, Jane, since you've never appeared the sort to like to do dangerous, illicit things. You must promise me that you will be careful, child, and not let anyone see you; that might cause difficulties for you."

Jane hesitated. Then she patted her aunt's narrow shoulder. "Don't worry," she said more bravely than she felt. "Everything will go splendidly."

CHAPTER 2

TRUTHFULLY no one could have been more surprised than Jane that she had made her offer. She was sure that she had not meant to do so. The very idea of replacing the Mannings' stolen property put her in a quake.

The library was empty when she entered it. For a few seconds she indulged herself by looking about. The place seemed welcoming, with its blazing applewood fire and shelf upon shelf of books bound in beautiful Morocco leather. At any other time she would have been delighted to be in such a lovely room, but not now.

Without realizing it, she spoke aloud. "Now where does the Chinese carving go? Didn't Aunt say it had been next to a gold box?"

Uncertainly, she looked around. "Put it anywhere, Jane," she finally commanded herself, "and leave." First, however, she peered over her shoulder toward the entrance. One of the wide double doors stood open.

She needed to hurry before anyone peered in and saw her at her illicit work. With hasty fingers, she opened the reticule and tugged at the little figure, but, alas, it would

A LARCENOUS AFFAIR

not come free. The water pails had become entangled in the strings.

And someone was coming through the door! Guiltily, Jane thrust the incriminating tangle behind her. Then she took a close look at the rapidly advancing intruder.

"Oh, no," she cried. "It's you."

"And why should that concern you?" Lord Brooke asked suspiciously. "What are you up to?" He reached around her, found and took hold of her burden, and brought it into view.

Jane attempted a smile. "I know what you must be thinking, my lord, but I assure you, you are wrong."

Lord Brooke examined the ivory object caught in the purse strings. "Am I, little thief?" he said harshly. "And to think you'd finally convinced me that you were all propriety."

Though perversely fascinated by being called "little," Jane was horrified to hear herself accused. "Little thief!" she echoed. "How dare you!"

Lord Brooke placed the carving upon the table. "Naturally, you have an explanation for this," he said with a faint sneer.

"Naturally," Jane replied, then fell silent. What was she to tell him? That her aunt found it amusing to take other people's possessions? She could not.

She watched as Lord Brooke folded his arms across his beautifully tailored coat, noticing, even in her distress, how well it fit his muscular form. He smelled good, too, of bayberry, she thought; she had detected it earlier, when they were dancing.

She shook her head as if to get rid of these sensations. This was hardly the time to be aware of Lord Brooke's sartorial splendor, his manly figure, or his cologne.

"I am waiting."

His nearness was unnerving. "There is a good explanation," she said with as much self-assurance as she could manage. "If I told it to you, it would clear up your mistaken impression immediately." She paused, turning her graceful hands outward, then gave him a rueful smile.

"Unfortunately, however, I am not at liberty to provide it."

"Let me help you," Lord Brooke said smoothly. "You weren't taking the carving. Someone else took it and you were merely returning it. Am I correct? Ah, I see from the fact that the high color is beginning to recede from your face that I have discovered your secret."

Jane tilted her chin to take in more of his expression. Her blue eyes were wary. Was it possible that she had so easily convinced this man of her innocence? Somehow, she doubted it.

"We had a sergeant once who told us a similar story when he was found hiding one of our unit's gold bars. We shot him."

"Ooh," said Jane, giving a violent twist to the silver ribbons that fell from under her bosom, "what a horrid thing to say to me. And so unnecessary, my lord. As I already told you, I did not take the carving." When he did not reply but merely looked down his disdainful nose at her, she added, "You may believe me, you know. I rarely lie."

Lord Brooke shifted impatiently. "You already tried that speech on me, Lady Jane. It will not work again, since I make an effort not to be stupid more than once an evening. I do not believe you, and neither will your parents when I tell them what you have done."

"Tell my—you cannot."

His Lordship's lips tightened. "If I could believe that you would not repeat this unfortunate behavior, I might be willing to forgo that dubious honor."

"What I meant," Jane explained, "was that you can't tell them because my mother is deceased and my father is in Jamaica. I am in London with my aunt. Not that you need to tell her, either," she added hastily. "You may be assured that I will not repeat what you think I did, particularly since I did not do it the first time."

"You are incorrigible." Lord Brooke shook his handsome head at her. "I shall certainly call upon your aunt tomorrow."

"Oh, what is the use?" Jane cried, running a hand through her upswept blonde locks in exasperation. "You've made up your mind about me, and nothing I say will change it."

"Bravo!" His Lordship accompanied the word with a mocking bow. "I am all admiration for your theatrical talents: injured innocence pleading her cause." He paused before saying, "Unhappily for you, it won't wash."

Instead of replying, Jane stepped backward a few paces toward the white marble fireplace. Being close to his Lordship discomposed her, and not just because of his threats and disapproval. There was that unfortunate effect he had on her senses.

With a single step Lord Brooke closed the gap between them. "I must insist that you stay away from my sister, Lady Jane. As wild as she is, she does not *steal*."

Jane wanted to lash out at him, to make him pay for the humiliation he was causing her. But more urgently, she wanted to get away from him. She was almost ready to promise what he asked—almost, but not quite. "I will take your wishes into consideration," she said with as much dignity as she could contrive. "I have no desire to quarrel with you." Her fingers fluttered like trapped birds. "May I go now?"

"No, wait." His Lordship's big hands worked with surprising deftness among the reticule's strings until he freed the ivory carving. Then he threw the reticule toward Jane.

"There you are," said a cheerful Lady Lettice, walking briskly into the room just as Jane caught it. "And there is my reticule."

Lord Brooke stared at her in obvious confusion. "Your reticule? Am I to understand—?"

Jane cut him off. "Certainly not. You understand nothing."

"Then I will need to learn, won't I?" his Lordship said coldly. "Am I correct in assuming that this lady is your aunt? I shall take the liberty of calling upon you both tomorrow."

"Why?" asked Lady Lettice pleasantly. "Am I keeping anything of yours?"

Lord Brooke's brows drew together in puzzlement. "I fear I do not take your meaning."

"It does not matter." Lady Lettice made a jaunty adjustment to her feather-bedecked yellow turban. "Tell me, do you do anything interesting?"

"No," Jane snapped, her blue eyes sparkling. "He does not."

Lord Brooke gave her an affronted look. "I am a soldier, madam, or, at least, I was. But if you mean do I do such things as burn and pillage, then, no, I don't."

"That is too bad. But I suppose it will be all right for you to pay a call upon us, if you insist."

Despite himself, his Lordship was insulted by this strange, skinny woman's lack of interest in him. A former aide-de-camp, an earl—wealthy and not unpersonable—and this horse-faced person with a thief for a niece was reluctant to invite him into her home. "I do insist," he said with quite a bit less than his usual *savoir faire*. "Otherwise, I would not."

"Would not what?" said Lady Lettice before Jane could maneuver her out of the room.

Finally, they withdrew—with Lady Jane all stiff and straight as though she had been falsely charged, and her aunt chatting quite amiably.

His Lordship sighed. He was rather sorry that he had discovered Lady Jane Ashworth's secret. She was spirited. And beautiful. Under other circumstances, becoming better acquainted with her might have been interesting.

There was the rub, of course. Because she was a thief, no other circumstances mattered. Therefore, if she insisted upon remaining friends with his sister, he would have to intervene.

Again, he sighed. He did not want to deal with a bevy of females, not even his own. He did not want to snoop around looking for traitors, either, which was his new assignment. He wanted to be back in Portugal with Lord

Wellington, acting as a man was supposed to act. Unconsciously, he flexed the large muscles in his arms and back.

Suddenly, his Lordship's lips spread in a self-mocking grin. He should stop complaining. Things could be worse.

"Marcus, you are just the one to help me out of my difficulty," said his mother, providing proof, if he'd needed any, that matters could, indeed, deteriorate. "I seem to have spent all of my money playing Loo. Isn't it odd how money just disappears?"

She stopped speaking to take in a breath and looked around. "Oh, what a lovely room. I wish we had wallpaper like this. At any rate," she went on with a cheery smile, "I need to have more—more guineas, that is."

Lord Brooke jammed his fists into his coattails pockets so forcefully that only Weston's expert tailoring saved his garment from destruction. "I told you yesterday, Mother, that I would no longer frank you in your incessant gaming. Nothing has happened to make me change my mind."

"But I was sure that you could not mean it." Lady Rebecca stared up at her firstborn in indignation. "If I do not have funds, I will be unable to continue to play."

Despite himself, Lord Brooke laughed. "That is the idea, Mother. No, do not look at me as though I've suddenly grown an extra head. I did tell you that you must stop." Before she could remonstrate, he demanded, "Where is Susan? I mean to take both of you home now."

Lady Rebecca tipped her head up toward him once more, almost piercing his eye with one of the brilliantly colored Bird of Paradise feathers in her turban. "I'd really rather have the money. Oh, very well. Take me home, then. However, you needn't bother about Susan. She has already gone."

"Gone? Gone with whom?"

"With Lord Portman," Lady Rebecca said agreeably. "He had his carriage brought up."

Her son's face flushed deep red with temper. "And you let her go? With that loose screw? How could you, Mother?"

Her Ladyship looked abashed for a second, but she

quickly rallied. "I couldn't leave with her, you silly boy. I was in the midst of a most critical hand. It wouldn't have been at all the thing for me to have put down my cards and left. You do understand that, don't you?" she asked anxiously.

"We shall have another talk tomorrow, Mother. I fear that I have not made myself quite clear."

"Oh, Marcus, not another talk. I still feel dyspeptic from the last one."

Marcus groaned. What was he going to do with her? And what was he going to do with Susan? Grimly, he propelled his mother into their carriage. He wouldn't be defeated; he was going to make his female relations behave as they ought. No matter what it took!

It was not until well past noon the next day that he finally confronted Susan. He found her in the red dining room at the small rosewood table they used for all but their evening meal. She was sipping, reflectively, on her hot chocolate and nibbling at a slice of toast thickly covered with honey. Already a few strands of straight, dark hair had come loose from her topknot.

Marcus pulled out the red needlepoint chair across from her and seated himself with an economy of motion impressive in so large a man. "How thoughtful of you to come downstairs to join the family," he said by way of greeting, eyeing her sheer, clinging pink muslin with disfavor.

Susan's response was a barely concealed yawn.

"I suppose that breaking the rules is rather wearing," Marcus said, extending his long, booted legs out before him. "It must take a certain amount of energy to think of ways to thwart me and the whole of society."

Susan lifted her dark eyes to his scowling face. "Not at all," she said placidly. "Apparently, it comes naturally to me."

"Blast it, Susan." Lord Brooke pushed back his chair with a single violent thrust and rose to his full height. "You are going to behave yourself, you know. Otherwise,

I shall send you into the country to vegetate and think on your sins—which are undoubtedly far more numerous than I am aware."

"I should run away." She stared up at him defiantly. "Would you like that, Marcus?"

He stood quite still. "No, I shouldn't like it. And yet I cannot wink at your unconventional behavior, either, can I? Why do you do it?"

Susan looked steadily at him for a moment; then she shrugged. "You wouldn't understand, not being confined to skirts and sidesaddles and other restrictive, boring things." She stood up to join her brother. "The subject does not interest me at present, Marcus."

Marcus put a restraining hand on her shoulder. "I fear that it must interest me; I am responsible for you and Mother. Don't try me, Susan. I assure you that you will not like the consequences. And one thing more," he said as she pushed away his hand and made as if to leave the room. "You are not to see Jane Ashworth. She does not make an acceptable companion."

"Not see Jane?" All suggestion of disinterest was gone. "I will! Only the most unreasonable tyrant would demand that I stop seeing her."

"Do not exaggerate," Marcus said coolly. "It does not become you."

One of Susan's pink kid half boots kicked aside the embroidered fire screen as though it were the cause of all her difficulties. "Do you still believe that she accompanied me in the park, Marcus? I swear to you that she did not."

"No, I do not think she accompanied you." Marcus's brown eyes looked measuringly into hers. "I mean to find out who did, however."

"Then, why—?"

Marcus shook his head. He would not tell her about her friend's larcenous behavior. He would not degrade Jane. In addition, there should be no need. It was Susan's duty to obey him, wasn't it? The men under him always did, and without questions and arguments, either. "Stay away from her," he repeated, "or I shall see to it that you do. Otherwise, she will get you into trouble."

"Jane Ashworth?" Susan's voice rose. "That is absurd."

"There are troublemakers—and troublemakers," her brother answered enigmatically.

"Well, Jane is not one of them. What could you have against her?" Susan now sounded more puzzled than provoked. "She is a thoroughly nice girl, Marcus."

Her brother laughed derisively.

"She is, I tell you. In fact, she is the nicest girl—well, she's not precisely a girl anymore, of course—at any rate, she is the nicest person I know."

At his disbelieving look, she added, "It's true. She's never petty like other females one meets or tries to blacken anyone's name."

In Marcus's mind it took more than yellow hair, cornflower blue eyes, and an unwillingness to engage in gossip to equal goodness. A still more essential element was a steadfast refusal to help oneself to one's hostess's possessions. "A veritable saint." Marcus's voice dripped with sarcasm. "Idolize her if you must, Susan, but find another friend."

Susan's hand flexed as though it ached to slap him. "No, this is too much. I most certainly won't."

Brother and sister glared at each other. It was apparent that their quarrel was about to escalate past all redemption. Thus, it was a stroke of good fortune that Lady Rebecca chose to enter the room at that moment, even if she did not attempt to leave it almost immediately thereafter. "I can come back later," she said, eyeing the two, especially Marcus, warily.

"No, Mother, come in now," said Susan, with a mischievous glint in her eye. "Marcus has been reading me a scold, so your interruption is more than welcome."

Lady Rebecca tugged absently at a graying brown curl that peeped out from her lace-trimmed cap. "Oh, dear, is it because of last night? I suppose I should not have let you go off with Lord Portman—but, then, it did not matter, did it? You're safe and sound. You are, aren't you?" she queried optimistically.

"I might be if Marcus wouldn't malign Jane Ashworth."

"Malign Jane? How could you, Marcus? She's such a dear, sweet thing. I am hoping that you will marry her."

Although his Lordship had seemed calm, even distant, during the exchange between his mother and sister, all traces of serenity vanished. "What foolishness is this?" he exploded. "Marry Lady Jane? I'd as soon marry that wretched Caroline Lamb."

Lady Rebecca gave her firstborn a pitying look. "You can't, dear. She is already married. Besides, I think she favors poets, not soldiers. No, you must marry, for Susan won't. She finds everyone too fat or too dull or too—" Lady Rebecca wrung her hands. "That is why you must marry Jane."

Marcus thrust his thumbs under the lapels of his immaculate blue Bath cloth coat. "This should be amusing. Why is that, Mother?"

"So that I can become a grandmother, of course. I'll never keep from gambling if I am not a grandmother."

Marcus could not make up his mind whether to frown or smile at Lady Rebecca's explanation. He settled the contest by chuckling. "I'm afraid you'll have to stop without such inducements, for I have no intention of marrying soon, and I certainly do not mean to wed the person you mentioned."

"There. He is doing it again," said Susan angrily.

Lady Rebecca shook her head. "I don't know what is wrong with you, Marcus. You were never like this when you were small."

Susan's gaze traveled from the top of her brother's wavy brown hair to his richly polished black boots. "He was never small," she said dryly, "but at least he used to be amiable."

"If you both did not show such a want of conduct, I could be amiable again. Now, if none of us has anything further to say, I shall go to my office. I have reams of papers to read through."

He strode out of the room, but a minute later abruptly returned. "Remember," Marcus again addressed himself to Susan, "have nothing to do with Jane Ashworth."

The two women bided their time until they heard his footsteps fade. "What has Jane done to be in Marcus's bad graces?" Lady Rebecca asked. "I'm sure I've never heard that she is devoted to cards, and she's not a madcap like you. No one is."

"Thank you, Mother. As for your question, I do not know. It is one of Marcus's mad starts."

"Your brother does not have mad starts."

"Whether he does or not, I don't mean to heed him. I shall pay Jane a visit this afternoon." She accompanied her words with a defiant smile.

Lady Rebecca picked up a napkin from the rosewood table and nervously dabbed at her lips. "My dear, is that wise?"

"I do not care if it isn't, but, in any case, you need not fret yourself. Marcus will never know. He is busy with his papers."

"Oh, yes, his papers. Why does he have so many papers? I'm sure your father never did."

Susan shrugged. "It's something to do with the Foreign Office, but don't ask him about it because he will not tell you."

"Very well, then; I shan't. But now you must let me advise you." She gazed gravely into her daughter's dark sparkling eyes. "Do wear your new lilac gown when you go to visit Jane. It is vastly becoming. And the pink bonnet with the lilac trim."

"Done!" said Susan.

Lady Rebecca's suggestions proved to be good ones. The lilac gown, accented by pearl buttons that marched from neckline to scalloped hem, and the bonnet were, indeed, vastly becoming to Susan. She added a pink parasol and reticule; then, accompanied by her maid, entered the town carriage and had Tom Coachman deposit her at Lady Lettice's house in Upper Grosvenor Street.

Because she'd visited before, she wasn't surprised that the first two stories of the large stucco house were a beehive of activity—very little of it conventional, however. She moved past pink rooms and yellow rooms and blue rooms harboring, among other individuals no less flamboyant, a man polishing a sword, a lady with suspiciously bright orange hair, and a very sinister-looking man with one leg who was holding what seemed to be a collection of maps.

At last she found Jane, sitting tucked up on a window seat in the small but elegant first floor music room. With its dark green leather-covered walls and wooden chair rail replete with carvings of fruit and flowers in the style of Grinling Gibbons, it was one of Susan's favorites.

Ignoring the other occupant of the room, a monkey wearing a red fez, she bent forward to give Jane a kiss. Then she seated herself on the green and pink chintz cushion beside her friend. "Listen, my love," she said, "you must tell me what happened between you and my brother last night. It's made him a brute! He has forbidden me to visit you."

Jane, though charmingly appareled in a blue muslin round gown trimmed in blonde lace, was not especially in looks that afternoon. "Dear me. Did he? What reason did he give?"

"None. He was arbitrary and nasty—very military in his manner. It was all I could do not to leap to attention—or take up one of his pistols and shoot him."

Jane laughed, but the effort was transparently halfhearted.

"I am waiting to hear," Susan persisted. "What did you do to him?"

"I did nothing!" This disclaimer was accompanied by a shrug of Jane's shapely shoulders. "Your brother has a mistaken notion about me, and it seems that there is no way I can change it. You and I may have to stop going about together, at least for a while."

Susan rose to her full five feet, two inches. Her dark eyes flashed. She looked magnificent, thought her appreciative friend, like a miniature valkyrie. "Never!" the warrior maiden enunciated emphatically.

"I beg your pardon, milady?" said Miles, Lady Lettice's small, red-faced butler, who had entered the room in time to hear Susan's ringing last word. "Is there something I can get for you?"

When the two females, somewhat flushed with embarrassment, shook their heads, the butler said in a voice filled with doubt, "There is a man below who calls himself Lord Brooke. He says that he must talk to you."

"To me?" asked Jane, casting a worried glance in Susan's direction.

Miles looked surprised, as though Lady Lettice's niece should have realized he had no interest in delivering messages to other than family members. "To you, milady."

"Oh, dear. You had better go while you can, Susan. Miles will spirit you away."

Susan grabbed a corner of an elaborately carved teakwood desk as though she foresaw an imminent attempt to remove her by force. "I shan't leave." She frowned at Jane. "We will face the monster together."

Jane shook her blonde head. "No, Susan, I will face the monster alone. You will be somewhere else. It's best, I assure you."

"Oh, very well, if you insist." Susan scooped up her pink reticule, then, accompanied by the butler, flounced out of the room.

A short while later, Miles led Lord Brooke, now dressed in a fawn coat and yellow pantaloons, into the music room. Bowing to Jane, his lordship critically scanned his surroundings. He clearly appreciated the handsome decor.

Then he saw the monkey. "What is that creature?"

"It is a monkey, my lord."

Lord Brooke scowled. "I know that."

She started to ask why he had posed the question if he already knew the answer, but after considering the look on his face, she determined to forgo that pleasure.

A LARCENOUS AFFAIR 29

"What is he doing here?" Lord Brooke demanded.

Why did she feel that he expected her to stand at attention? Well, she would not. Instead, this time she would say one of the several witty but rude things that had just crossed her mind.

Lord Brooke *loomed* over Jane, thereby providing her with a novel experience. "Well?"

No need to stir hot coals, she decided, once more opting for self-control. "He is waiting for his master," she said mildly. "Signor Petrucchi is a very fine musician. He comes here several times a week to practice on my aunt's pianoforte."

Lord Brooke looked with some disbelief at the beautiful, expensive Broadwood piano that graced one corner of the room; it could not have cost a shilling less than twenty-five guineas. "This monkey looks like those one sees with organ grinders. Surely, you do not mean that its master is an organ grinder?" Jane nodded. "Are you saying that your aunt lets an organ grinder man play on that superb instrument?"

"It is the only one she has," replied Jane pertly, too annoyed to watch her tongue.

His Lordship flushed. "You live in an unusual household, Lady Jane—although why that should surprise me I cannot imagine."

If it had been anyone but Lord Brooke, Jane would have considered the term "unusual" as the height of diplomacy. However, since everything about Susan's large, domineering brother annoyed her, she took umbrage at the term. "I see nothing *unusual* about it. Why do you use that word?"

Before Lord Brooke could answer, the door opened and Lady Lettice came in accompanied by a rather dark-skinned man dressed in faded, shabby clothing. Behind them was Lady Susan.

Jane was amused despite her apprehensions for her friend. Lord Brooke's attention would no longer be on Signor Petrucchi and his monkey. Instead, he could vent his spleen upon his sister.

Jane was wrong. As soon as Lord Brooke uttered his first words to his sister, which though innocuous enough were voiced in a tone a commanding officer might have used to a deserter, the monkey seemed to take offense. Screeching madly, he careened about the room, finally landing on top of the pianoforte's keyboard. The resulting racket was only a little better than the screeches.

"*Bella; bella,*" said the signor in a soothing voice. "But now you must let me try." Ignoring everyone else in the room, he walked to the shining instrument and, after first removing his pet, sat down to play a piece by Bach. The room soon was filled with glorious sound.

Jane looked over at Lord Brooke. The effect was amazing. His eyes half-closed, he was obviously caught up in the wonderful sounds that poured forth from the pianoforte. Congreve was correct, she thought. Music did have charms to soothe a savage breast, and she did not mean the monkey's. But Signor Petrucchi could not play forever. What would happen when he stopped?

CHAPTER 3

THE answer to Jane's speculation was not long in coming. As the last beautiful notes of the piece died away, Lord Brooke straightened and his brown eyes lost their absorbed look. "Well done," he said, once more sounding crisp and impatient.

A moment later, to his obvious surprise, Lady Lettice unceremoniously ushered him and everyone else but the pianist and his monkey from the room. "The signor must practice," Jane explained. "We do not want to disturb him."

His Lordship, of course, had come to Upper Grosvenor Street to attend to matters that needed his attention, not to listen to music, even any as marvelous as that he had just heard. Nor had he come to be moved about like a chess piece.

He bent his head toward Jane to protest his summary expulsion from the room. As he did so, a strand of her silky blonde hair touched his chin. It brought with it a whiff of the lime perfume she seemed to favor, making his nostrils flare to take in the delectable scent. "We will go somewhere else and talk," he said more mildly than even he had anticipated. He followed up his words by taking Jane and Susan by the arm.

For her part, Jane felt like a lamb being herded by an excessively determined sheep dog. He annoyed her, she told herself. He had no right to order them about as though they were in his house instead of her aunt's. He needed to be shown that he was not in charge here and could not always have things his way.

"If you insist, my lord," she murmured, an impish glint lighting her large, expressive blue eyes. Quietly, she placed herself at the head of their little group and led Lord Brooke and Susan down the exquisite free-standing staircase to the ground floor Yellow Room.

This room, one among several of Lady Lettice's sitting rooms, was decorated with yellow and pink striped wallpaper, a cream, rose, and yellow Aubusson carpet, and yellow satin seating pieces. There could be no objection—even if Lord Brooke were as high a stickler as Beau Brummell—to any aspect of its decor.

It was the people, not the room, that Lord Brooke found disturbing. For one thing, there were too many of them there. A man could not read a scold to two disobedient females in such a squeeze.

Even more disconcerting, however, were the types of people present. His Lordship would wager his favorite mare that the woman in the revealing dress standing to one side of the marble chimney piece was a member of the muslin company. He'd had enough of them in his keeping to recognize the breed on sight.

Near the front windows were three bearded men in headdresses, their white robes overflowing the dainty yellow chairs that held them. It was obvious that they were from the Levant, very likely were not Christians, and might even be merchants. Whatever the case, they were not one's ordinary guests, although why that should surprise him, his Lordship could not imagine.

"I do not believe this was quite the setting I had in mind," he said dryly. "Is there not somewhere more quiet and . . . um . . . prosaic where we might go to talk?"

Jane put a slender finger to her chin as though pondering the question deeply. Her full mouth quirked at the corners with suppressed mirth. "There is the Pink Room, my lord. That is where Aunt put the four Tories. I believe they are arguing Catholic Emancipation. Would you like to go there?"

"It will have to be here, then, won't it?" His Lordship almost added "naughty minx" to his words, but that sounded somehow forbearing, even affectionate. As he had instantly reminded himself, neither adjective described his feelings about Jane Ashworth.

Lord Brooke's problems were scarcely begun. His face blanched when he saw his sister conversing with the light skirt. "Come here!" he barked. Susan reluctantly obeyed.

His Lordship, his long, well-shaped legs braced as though he expected hordes of recalcitrant females to run at him, waited until both Jane and Susan seated themselves upon one of the yellow sofas. "Listen to me," he said in a low, restrained voice, "I thought it was understood that you two were not to visit with each other anymore. Lady Jane, you gave me your word."

Jane looked up at him, a blank expression veiling her indignation. She certainly had *not* given her word. She had said merely that she would take his wishes into consideration. It was not Jane's fault that the other woman was there now. Of course, she had no intention of mentioning that fact. To do so would have been disloyal to her friend.

"*I* never promised," the less restrained Susan cried fiercely. "As I already told you, Marcus, giving up my friendship with Jane is out of the question."

Rising to her feet, her small, finely shaped head held high, she added in a ringing voice, "Do not think you can stop me, either, for I shall not listen to you."

Oh, dear, thought Jane, a worried frown creasing the smooth perfection of her forehead. Susan had thrown down the gauntlet. Being a warrior, his Lordship would be unable to resist picking it up.

Lord Brooke's expression, which had, up until now, seemed comparatively civilized, grew rigid with his rising temper. "You will or you will suffer being sent away, my girl." Turning to Jane, he said, "I'd send you off to rusticate as well if I had a say in the matter. Both of you need to be protected from yourselves."

She, protected from herself? Jane gave his Lordship a long, cold stare. What an idiotic idea. Did Lord Brooke not realize—could he not see—that she was competent to her fingertips, awake to every suit, a downy one more than capable of caring for herself? No one had ever treated Jane as though she needed to be *protected*—from herself or anyone else—since she'd been out of leading strings.

Then she realized that he must be thinking of her alleged thievery. She felt herself flush. With an effort of will, she brought her wandering thoughts under control. Turning to Susan, she said briskly, "I hope you will not quarrel with your brother for my sake. Perhaps if you obey him now, he will soften his edict later when he realizes how unnecessary it is."

How such a revelation might come about she did not know. How did one prove that one was *not* a thief? Her only hope was that by seeing that she was a model of decorum, Lord Brooke might come to realize that he was mistaken.

Jane sighed, then rose from the sofa to join the brother and sister who now stood glaring openly at each other. It was apparent that her words had done little, if any, good. She extended her hand to give Lady Susan's fingers a reassuring squeeze. Instead, however, the hand dropped limply to her side.

The cause of her distraction was the white-robed Levantine making his way toward them. She watched as his heavy-lidded, dark eyes scanned her face and Susan's, then came to rest upon Lord Brooke. "May I speak privately with you, my lord?" he said in softly accented English.

"Stay where you are," Lord Brooke ordered his sister and Jane. "I shall return in a minute." He gave them a minatory look, then followed the other man's short, bulky form from the room.

As soon as her brother was out of earshot, Susan reseated herself on the yellow sofa and pulled her friend down beside her. "I wonder what that person could have to say to Marcus. But never mind that. What I want to hear is why my brother has taken you so in dislike. You never did explain that, you know, at least not satisfactorily."

Jane was greatly tempted to reveal the truth this time, but since she would have to expose her aunt's behavior, she did not see how she could. "It is a misunderstanding," she offered, repeating her former explanation. "I cannot tell you any more than that."

Susan stared, absorbed, at the fingers of her pink gloves for a few seconds before saying, "I cannot comprehend it. Although I dislike having to admit it, I have to say that Marcus is usually fair, and even rational when we are not at daggers drawn."

Jane felt discomforted by her friend's bewilderment, and found herself delighted when a grinning Lord Brooke soon rejoined them, thereby causing his sister to cut off her importuning.

Thankfully diverted at last, Susan bombarded him with questions. "Why are you smiling? What did that man want? Did it have anything to do with Jane and me?"

Lord Brooke laughed. "If you must know, he made me an offer for you, quite a generous one, in fact."

"Do not be foolish," said Susan, scowling.

His Lordship gave Jane a sidelong glance and then looked back at his sister. "No, I mean it. That is exactly what he did. I must say that I was tempted, and not merely because of the generosity of the settlement he suggested. Just think—you would have been in Araby. Two-thirds of my problems would have been solved."

"Two-thirds?" Jane asked in a puzzled voice.

"Why, yes. One of the men who accompanied him wanted you, Lady Jane. I think he fancied your golden hair. It reminded him of sunshine warming a cool, white building. Poetic, no?" He ignored Jane's grimace. "If I could have accepted his suit in your father's stead, as well as accepted the one from Susan's admirer, all I would then have had left to worry about would have been my mother. Does your resourceful aunt have an aging emir that we could induce to take my mother?"

At Jane's gurgle of laughter, his Lordship grinned. "It was vastly tempting, I tell you."

Susan scowled.

"What is it?" asked Jane. "Surely, you do not believe that your brother would consider their suits. And since the offers were honorable ones there is no reason for us to be offended. I am not."

Susan's dark eyes shone with defiance; yet uneasy shadows were gathering strength in them. "What does it matter if the offers were honorable?" she said, unconsciously clasping her hands together. "Their women are kept close, are they not? Just the thought of what it would mean to live like that puts me up in the boughs." Turning sharply on her heel, she moved out of range of Lord Brooke's long reach. "A woman's lot here is difficult enough," she said over her shoulder. Then she disappeared through the doorway.

"Susan, come back here," Lord Brooke commanded, but if she heard him, she paid him no heed.

Lord Brooke shrugged his broad shoulders. "Again, she escapes me, and there is just you to whom to preach, Lady Jane. That is hardly fair, I know. On the other hand, you cannot deny that you deserve it." As he spoke, he bent his head toward her. Despite his words, his voice was moderate, rather than scolding, and he seemed more in charity with her than he had before.

Jane's face tilted upward, the better to take in all of his Lordship's countenance. She was so close to him that she could see the beginnings of a beard in the taut skin that covered his jaw. How might it feel if she ran her fingers over that slight abrasiveness? Except for the dark stubble, would his skin be smooth and warm?

Why was she thinking such things? What was the matter with her? If anything, she should have been echoing Susan's words instead of entertaining strange feelings about her friend's brother. She knew well from her despotic father and her dominated mother that a woman's lot could be difficult even in their enlightened country.

Blushing, Jane shifted away from him. "You are right," she said sharply, trying to break the spell. "I am unquestionably a desperate character. In fact, I mean to help myself to the crown jewels soon—at least, those which will fit into my reticule."

"You have an antic sense of humor, Lady Jane." The almost friendly light in Lord Brooke's brown eyes disappeared. "Still, I will not warn your aunt about your behavior this time. However, one more transgression and I assure you that I will."

He made her a stiff bow. "Now I must wish you a good day. Please make my excuses to your aunt. I would seek her out myself, but I would not want to interrupt her conversation with some lamplighter or denizen of Seven Dials. And stay away from my sister!" Turning gracefully, he made for the door, leaving Jane feeling exasperated and, curiously, somewhat disappointed by his departure.

Lord Brooke was somewhat exasperated as well. When he returned home to his bedroom, he sat there, elbows on muscular thighs, pondering with some irritation the problem of Jane Ashworth. He was not certain when she'd made the leap from a bad influence to a problem, but so it was. And problems had to be solved.

His Lordship rose from the brown, linen-covered armchair in which he'd been sitting and began pacing the length of his room. With its dark green wallcovering and massive mahogany furniture, its sturdy masculinity suited him. Stopping in front of a cabinet, he opened its glass doors and took out a dagger with a smooth ivory handle. He rubbed the handle absentmindedly while his mind roamed over his difficulties.

"Why so abstracted, old fellow?" The cheerful voice of Lord Freddy Manning interrupted his musings. Looking splendid in an olive-green coat and cream breeches, his brown hair artfully disordered, the youthful-looking Freddy glided into the room.

At that moment Marcus was less than overjoyed to see his unannounced friend, but he schooled his face and voice to impassivity. "I am not abstracted," he lied. "I am bored. In fact, I thought I might go to Manton's to shoot a few wafers. Not, of course, that shooting in a gallery compares to trying to take careful aim from a galloping horse."

Freddy shuddered. "Don't say another word on that subject. Wafers are the fiercest enemies I want to confront. Is that why you seemed to be hipped? Being away from the action, I mean?"

Marcus's lips tightened for a second. "That is certainly part of it. I will not deny it."

"But not all of it? Is it still your mother and sister?" Freddy's blue eyes were sympathetic. "You can tell me, you know."

It was one thing to discuss his relatives, especially when Freddy had observed for himself their want of good sense, and another to tell him about Lady Jane's transgression. A gentleman could not do that.

Still, it would help to be able to talk to someone. "You have the sex right," he informed Freddy with a disingenuous smile, "but not the relationship. It is the daughter of an old family friend about whom I am troubled. Her mother has asked me to advise her about the chit."

"Is that so? Are they in London now?"

"Yes, they are, but for reasons you will soon understand, I must keep their identity a secret. You see the girl steals."

"You don't mean it! From shops?" Freddy sounded horrified but intrigued. "That is too bad."

"No, no, you have it wrong. At least, I think you do." Marcus's broad brow creased with concern over this new possibility. "She steals from friends and acquaintances."

"Now, that *is* bad. What are you going to say to the mother?"

Marcus pretended to study the shiny tassels that swung from his beautifully polished Hoby boots. "I haven't any idea. It is very peculiar, because my impression is that the girl does not even want what she takes."

"You don't say." Freddy pulled out a handkerchief from one of his coattails pockets and enthusiastically began making knots in it. "How odd . . . although now that I think about it, I remember that I had an old uncle who stole goose feathers. He took them out of quilts and things like that. He would work a little hole in the goods and then— Oh, well, you don't want to hear about that. It did irritate his hostesses something fierce, however, when he stayed at their houses. I remember that."

Despite himself, Marcus's interest was piqued. "Really? What did he do with his booty?"

"I haven't the vaguest idea—or even why he took other people's feathers at all. He could have had all he wanted of his own, you see. He had a whole pond full of geese. Could have plucked them bare if the fancy had taken him, and no one could have said him nay."

Marcus strolled over to the chair and reseated himself. "Where is he now, in bedlam or settled in Australia?"

"Why, neither. He is nowhere. That is, he is dead. And a good thing, too, if you ask me. After awhile no one would invite him to house parties anymore, and the poor fellow had to stay home and look at the same feathers over and over again." Freddy beamed, obviously pleased with the tale.

Marcus ran his fingers through his light, wavy brown hair. "I don't think that your recollection is particularly edifying. I need to think of some way to control this girl. Perhaps I should stay close to her whenever possible and see that she does not get any more opportunities to pilfer. That might do the trick."

Freddy's artless blue eyes widened. "Are you really willing to do that? Why would you want to? I should think you'd be letting yourself in for a deal of trouble."

Actually, Marcus thought so, too. In fact, he was certain of it. As for his friend's second question, all he could think was that it was a reasonable one. Unfortunately, he did not have a reasonable answer.

"It is my duty," he improvised gruffly, unwilling to admit the truth.

"I should have guessed you'd say something like that, being a military man and all. But take my advice, Marcus: get over that sort of thing as quickly as possible. We civilians don't go about discharging duties, you know—except, perhaps, the duty to enjoy ourselves without completely beggaring our estates."

When Marcus frowned, Freddy quickly added, "Of course, it goes without saying that I admire you. What's more, I'm convinced your efforts would succeed. If you can stop the Frenchies, you can certainly stop a slip of a girl."

"You're right," Marcus said decisively, rising to his feet. "Of course I can. I can go wherever she goes, at least when I am not otherwise engaged, and every time she attempts to take something, I can stop her. After awhile she will learn that she cannot have what is not hers. It's the same principle one uses to break one's hounds of bad habits." He clapped his friend on the back, making the smaller man wince. "You are a brilliant fellow, Freddy. Don't let anyone tell you otherwise."

"What do you mean by that?" Freddy asked, but his Lordship was calling for his valet and did not answer.

After his conversation with Freddy, Marcus had sufficient time to think precisely about what he meant to do. He had three days, in fact, for he was not able to put his plan into action until the following Wednesday night.

His meeting up with Jane finally took place at Almack's. Luckily there was little to steal there, but he thought he ought to keep her within sight anyway. One never knew.

Jane was having rather similar thoughts. What was there for her aunt to take at Almack's, she wondered, as her maid, Betty, prepared her for the evening ahead. The answer, she hoped, was nothing. Maybe tonight Jane would be able to relax and just enjoy herself.

The thought sent flattering color into her cheeks and lent an extra sparkle to her large blue eyes. "Oh, my lady," said the maid, adjusting her mistress's milky pearls, "you do look a special treat tonight. I think this dress is my favorite."

Jane laughed. "You always say that, although this time I may agree with you." She gazed into the pier glass, admiring the soft white muslin gown she wore which fell open over a flower-embroidered, yellow silk slip. She gave herself a nod in the mirror and then went to join her aunt for dinner.

Two hours later, she and Lady Lettice arrived in King Street and were welcomed to Almack's by Mr. Willis, who carefully guarded the sacred gates. As they entered, they heard Neil Gow's band start up a lively Scottish reel. Jane smiled to herself. She would have a grand time tonight. She just knew it.

Glancing around she saw Susan, looking charming in a white *gros de Naples* round gown trimmed with *rouleaux* and roses in her favorite pink. Her pulse quickening, Jane wondered if Lord Brooke was there as well. She stood on tiptoe and craned her elegant pale-white neck for a better view of the men standing and strolling about.

She did not see his Lordship, though the faint nearby scent of bayberries brought him vividly to mind. She turned around quickly.

Lord Brooke was directly behind her, his impressive frame looking somewhat incongruous in the black coat, spotless white waistcoat, and knee breeches that were *de rigueur* for evening. He had his chapeau bras tucked under one arm. Its position did not hinder him from taking firm hold of Jane's dance card and putting his name down for a country dance later on.

He had not even asked her if she wanted to dance with him—which, it went without saying, she did not. Arrogant man! Jane slowly traced her finger over his name.

Soon a number of other names were added to his, for Jane was admired not only for her beauty but also for her amiable nature. She did not permit her card to be filled entirely, however, but put off several would-be partners. She enjoyed having time to stroll about the rooms with her friends as well, to chat about gowns and men and the dictatorial ways of parents and chaperons.

During more than one such occasion, she noticed that Lord Brooke was not far behind her. In fact, if it were not such an absurd idea, she would think that he was spying on her!

As the night wore on the idea seemed less outlandish. "My dear Jane," said Susan, running thin, careless fingers through her dark topknot, "have you noticed how Marcus has been lurking?"

"Surely not," said Jane, even though she considered Susan's description apt. "Why would he do that?"

Susan tapped a pink-slippered foot impatiently. "How should I know? Ever since he came back from Portugal he has been strange—or, if not strange, at least disagreeable. Lurking is disagreeable. That must be why he is doing it."

As an explanation, this hardly sufficed. "It's as though he wants to discover me at something," said Jane, supplying her own theory. She frowned. Of course. That was why he was following her. He expected her to do something dreadful, and he was waiting to pounce upon her when he did.

"Discover you doing something? Don't be ridiculous. I think it more likely that he is in love with you."

Jane flushed. "Now, *you* are being ridiculous," she said, slowly twisting the strings of her yellow reticule around her finger. "However, whatever the reason for his behavior, I do wish that he would stop."

Susan's brows arched above her dark, snapping eyes. "Then I shall go at once and tell him so. How dare he distress you!"

"You must do nothing of the sort! If he wishes to spy, or lurk, then let him. It is nothing to me," she added, apparently unaware that she was contradicting herself.

"What is this about spying?" A handsome, dark-haired man with olive skin and narrow features insinuated himself between the young women. His gloved fingers traced a pattern on Susan's arm, then dropped.

All evidence of temper gone, Susan smiled into his brooding, dark eyes. "We were talking about my brother," she said jauntily, seeming not to mind this familiarity. "We were being silly, of course. Even you are more likely to go about spying than he. Anyone is."

The gentleman's laughter seemed too hearty. In fact, everything about him struck Jane as excessive, even the scent he wore. It had a cloying smell. Musk, she thought, wrinkling her straight nose. She did not care for it.

The musk-scented man was introduced as Vincent Fleer, a nephew of that Lord Beaver who spent his days doing something secret at the Foreign Office. Jane also learned that Susan had danced earlier with Mr. Fleer and meant to be his partner again. As they waited for a set to form, Susan gave her friend a reckless smile.

A little worried, Jane glanced over at Lord Brooke to see if he'd noticed his sister's provocative behavior. What she saw made her frown. His Lordship had stopped lurking. Instead, he was smiling at a willowy redhead who gazed worshipfully into his eyes.

Now was when he should have been looking in their direction, she thought indignantly. It would serve him right if Susan did something outrageous.

At least Lady Lettice seemed to be behaving herself, she decided with a relieved sigh as she joined her aunt at the conclusion of the set. That was some consolation.

"Why do you keep turning your head, girl?" Lady Lettice tapped Jane's arm with a gaudy green fan. "Are you looking for someone?"

"No, I was just . . . turning my head. There are so many interesting people here."

Her Ladyship snorted. "I scarcely think so. There's probably not a man or woman in the lot who's more than ordinary. But, then, one can hardly expect better than that from a stuffy place like Almack's, I suppose."

Not bothering to answer, Jane turned her head again to gaze about the crowded, noisy room. Where was Lord Brooke now? Certainly, anyone that tall should be easy to find. He must nearly always stand head and shoulders above everyone else.

Her musings were interrupted by her aunt. "Look at Susan," Lady Lettice said between her long, horsey teeth. "She is fair on the way to making a spectacle of herself. I hope she does not mean to dance with that young man again."

Jane grimaced. If her unconventional aunt could not approve of Susan's behavior, what would the very proper patronesses of Almack's think? If Susan danced with Mr. Fleer a third time, she would put herself beyond the pale for certain.

Where *was* that provoking Lord Brooke? Jane half-rose from her seat. Then she saw him enter the room, another willowy redhead—where had their numbers come from all of a sudden?—clinging to his arm. Without thinking what she meant to do, Jane abruptly left her aunt and made straight for the handsome couple.

"Were you looking for me?" she asked his Lordship. She smiled cheerfully at his astonished companion. "So sorry. Not precisely a problem, but, then again . . . Of course, you understand." Without waiting for a reply, if, conceivably, one could have been given, she tugged at Lord Brooke's hand and towed him away.

"Now I can see why you do not mind living in that peculiar household," said Lord Brooke, looking both intrigued and amused. "You are a most shocking young lady. Tell me, what is not exactly a problem? Or was that just an excuse to get me to yourself?"

Jane blushed. "Certainly not. Indeed, there *is* a problem, and it concerns Susan." Quickly, she told him.

"Blast." His Lordship no longer looked amused. "Come with me." Without a word of explanation, he propelled her through the crowd. "Fleer," said he, thrusting Jane forward, "I bring you your next partner."

Shocked, Jane looked up at Lord Brooke. He was smiling at her, a warm, approving smile. "The dance following this is ours," he said in a low, intimate voice. "I look forward to it." One finger fleetingly touched her soft cheek, and then he and his unwilling sister left the room.

"Everything is going to be all right," Jane mused. Her mind was not entirely on Susan's deliverance from disaster.

CHAPTER 4

IT was obvious that Mr. Fleer was not pleased at having been so neatly outmaneuvered. Several times Jane caught him scowling in Lord Brooke's direction. Nevertheless, he did attempt a jocular, good-natured manner, especially as the set wore on. When it was over, he drew close and murmured into Jane's ear in an intimate voice, "You are an enchanting dancer. I must be certain to thank his Lordship for bringing us together."

Jane could almost have believed he meant it, not that it mattered to her whether he did or did not. Even when he returned her to Lady Lettice and lingered to chat with the two ladies for awhile, her mind was on her next partner, and sometimes adversary, Lord Brooke.

Ah, there he was, large and commanding-looking, and actually approaching them with a smile. Was it too much to hope this portended the cessation of hostilities? Very likely it was, she thought with a sigh; nothing had happened, after all, to change his conviction that she was a thief.

As his Lordship drew close, Mr. Fleer bowed to Jane and her aunt and then swiftly walked away. Lord Brooke's smile grew broader. "Thank you again for that," he said, tilting his head toward the departing Fleer. "It is no wonder, Lady Jane, that my sister counts you as her dearest friend. You come to the rescue."

He hesitated, then added too low for Lady Lettice to hear, "I wanted to assure you that although I can't, of course, appreciate a certain element of your character, you needn't fear that I'll tell anyone about it. Your secret is safe with me."

She'd, indeed, been correct: Uppermost in his Lordship's mind was the conviction that she was a thief. "The lines are already forming for the next country dance," she said between stiff lips and watched his smile disappear.

The dance in which he partnered her was the "Sabina," a longwise dance for as many as would. At its conclusion, instead of offering to promenade with her, Lord Brooke returned Jane to her aunt. She went with more relief than reluctance.

To her surprise, once they joined Lady Lettice, his Lordship seemed in no hurry to depart. Instead, he stood near Lady Lettice and engaged her in conversation.

While he did so, Jane settled herself in a chair. Turning to nod to an old friend of her mother who sat a few seats away, she noticed her Ladyship's brown satin reticule lying carelessly on the polished floor.

One glance sufficed to tell Jane that something was decidedly different about the reticule. In the interval since the two ladies had arrived, that item had grown curiously fat and lumpy.

Jane felt a constriction in her chest, and her hands became unpleasantly damp. The thing she was certain could not happen at Almack's obviously had happened. The enterprising Lady Lettice had managed to steal something. Now what was to be done?

Hardly thinking, she placed her slippered feet lightly on top of the reticule, then gave his Lordship what she hoped was a winsome smile. "Thank you for a lovely dance," she heard herself say. "Good evening." She reached out with one gloved hand and pushed him away.

Lord Brooke looked at Jane, astonished. Then he bowed rigidly over the offending hand and strode off.

As soon as he was out of earshot, Jane snatched up the reticule. "What have you got in here?" she hissed at her aunt.

Lady Lettice pursed her narrow lips, which caused her to resemble an exasperated horse. "I presume you mean what have I stolen. Isn't it just like you to mention that first thing! Not 'Lord Brooke and I had an amusing conversation,' or 'Did you observe that excessively fat woman with the canary diamond in her toque?' No, you must ask what I've put in my reticule. You've developed into a regular Paul Pry, my dear, and I don't care for it."

For a minute, her niece could not respond. The sheer audacity of her aunt left her speechless. Finally, she collected herself and said disapprovingly, "You must make haste to return what you've taken. What have you taken?"

Lady Lettice's faded brown eyes darted to the right of her, then to the left. Apparently reassured, she opened her reticule and shook out its contents. In addition to those things she had brought with her, such as a pot of rouge, out tumbled a large monogrammed lawn handkerchief, a slice of brown bread and butter, a biscuit, and a piece of obviously stale cake. These last three items, along with bohea and lemonade, made up what were euphemistically called refreshments at Almack's.

Jane looked at her aunt's booty in confusion. "I do not understand. Why did you take those things? Were you hungry?"

"Even if I were, I would not want stale cake and brown bread," Lady Lettice replied scornfully.

"Then why . . . ?"

"What choice did I have? There was nothing else to hand."

Jane stared at her relative, then dropped her eyes to pick distractedly at one of the flowers on her yellow underskirt. "I won't pretend that I understand you, Aunt. I won't even try. Just tell me one thing. Whose is the handkerchief? Never say that you took that, too?"

"Well, of course, I did." Once again her Ladyship sounded as though Jane were the veriest nodcock. "You don't think I'd set out from home with a man's handkerchief in my reticule, do you? Although it is quite nicely worked, I must say. There's nothing about it of which one need be ashamed."

Jane was not interested in discussing the handkerchief's merits. "Where did you get it, Aunt?"

Lady Lettice stroked her flat bosom happily. "I got it from that handsome Lord Brooke you seem to favor. See, his initials are in the corner. Someone has an expert hand with a needle, don't you agree?"

Although Jane's normal skin tone was pale, it now blanched to a ghastly white. "No," she cried in a tortured voice, "you cannot mean it. You didn't."

"Very well, then. If that is what you wish to hear—although, of course, I did. I saw a bit of handkerchief peeping out of his pocket and thought how lovely it would be to have it." Her Ladyship's voice quickened with excitement. "I got it loose with one little tug—that was when you two turned to go off to dance—and whipped it into my reticule. He never noticed a thing," she added with an artist's pride in her work. "It was such fun."

"No," said Jane again, this time accompanying her words with a soft moan. "Oh, dear. Put it away."

"What?" asked Lady Lettice, still holding the handkerchief in plain view. "Aren't you going to volunteer to return it, as you did the Chinese figure?"

"Certainly not," said Jane emphatically, casting morality aside without a qualm this time in the interest of self-preservation. "I haven't taken leave of my senses. You return it. You took it, after all."

"Really, Jane, you must stop asking me to do that. How many times must I tell you that I acquire things. I do not return them. If Lord Brooke wants his property back, he can just come to the house tomorrow and get it himself." She gave her niece a broad wink. "I'll have to leave you now. I need to find the necessary."

First, however, she used his Lordship's handkerchief to

sweep her cache of food under the chair. Then she handed Jane the handkerchief. "You may keep this for now, dear," she said and walked off.

As Jane sat there, looking after her aunt in stunned disapproval, Lady Lettice was replaced in her line of vision by the tall, broad-shouldered form of Lord Brooke. He was advancing once more in her direction.

"Oh, no," she murmured to herself in a distraught voice. "Why is he coming back here?"

The question, indeed, was reasonable. The answer, though she might not have agreed had she known it, was reasonable as well. Lord Brooke had just recollected his determination to save her from herself, which meant he needed to know which *ton* houses she meant to visit that week—and rob.

"Drat the man," Jane muttered. "What am I to do now?" She looked around despairingly, then settled the matter by putting the handkerchief on the chair vacated by her aunt and sitting firmly upon the piece of cloth.

Far too soon, his Lordship came up to her. With a "May I?" he took the seat beside her. "Is anything wrong?" he asked. "You seem distressed."

Jane discreetly patted perspiration from her brow. "Nothing of the sort," she said huskily. "I'm just a bit . . . um, overheated."

"Let me lend you my handkerchief."

"No! I mean . . . that is, I do not require it."

Lord Brooke looked questioningly at her but only said in a soothing voice, "Very well, then. You shall not have it. There is no need for you to become overset."

Jane gave him a weak smile. "Indeed, I am not overset."

"That is good news. Now, I suppose you are wondering why I have come back so soon." She shook her head. "No?" He sounded disappointed. "At any rate, it is because I forgot to ask you what your plans are for the remainder of the week, or even the month."

Jane shifted about in her chair and looked at him in

surprise. "My plans? Whyever would you need to know my plans?"

"Call it idle curiosity," said his Lordship, although the determined look on his attractive face belied that statement. "Do you mean to put in an appearance at Lady Irvine's rout? So do I. And how about—" His words broke off abruptly.

"Yes?" Jane prodded, intrigued by this unexpected, not to mention excessive, curiosity as to her affairs.

The look in Lord Brooke's brown eyes grew fierce as they dropped to study the border of white lawn which had revealed itself alongside her bottom. The border contained his initials. "What is that?" he asked rhetorically in a voice made unnerving by its lack of expression.

"That?" Jane's eyes followed his. Instead of answering, she went into a paroxysm of coughing.

Lord Brooke sat, his muscular arms crossed over his wide chest, and waited. He did not offer to help her. He did not so much as raise a hand to pat her back.

Hateful man! She might have been choking to death. Indeed, she rather wished she were.

"Oh, that," she said with a final cough. "I'm afraid I don't really know. It could be any of several things, I imagine: a napkin, a neck cloth, part of a shirt, or—" She peeked at his increasingly forbidding expression. "But no. It appears to be a handkerchief."

"It does, doesn't it, and it has my monogram on it. Do you suppose that means it is mine?"

"I cannot tell." Jane paused once more, this time to examine a fingernail with seeming fascination. "However, I suppose it could be. You would be the best judge of that."

A cynical smile played over his Lordship's well-cut lips. "If I may ask another question, what are you doing sitting on it? Are you incubating it, perhaps?"

"You are a fine one to ask me that," said Lady Jane. "Why did you leave it on my chair?"

A gleam, almost of respect, lit Lord Brooke's cold brown eyes, but it did not warm them. "I will say, Lady

Jane, if nothing else—and there is nothing else—one might admire you for your effrontery. You know perfectly well that I did not place my handkerchief beneath your—on your chair.''

"Well, I am pleased to hear that, at least," Jane responded regally as she arose and prepared to walk away.

"Stay!" said his Lordship forcefully. Jane froze. "Sit!"

Feeling like a puppy who'd just done something unbecoming, Jane hunched her lovely shoulders and unwillingly returned to the chair. She handed him the handkerchief, then sat down.

"Thank you. Now, I want you to admit that you stole my property. It will do you good."

"I knew you would think that I took it," Jane said bitterly. She rose once more and glared up at him. "You always do. But you're wrong. I didn't."

Lord Brooke's curt laugh was without humor. "Indeed? Who did? Your poor aunt, perhaps?"

"I did not say that," replied the horrified young woman. No matter what her aunt had done, Jane would never be the one to tell of it. "I don't know why it was there."

She was lying, had tried to conceal stolen property with her person, and, in fact, was abetting a thief. She was heartily ashamed of herself, even though she still felt that she had no choice in the matter. What was more, she quite disliked this large, imperious person for making her feel so dreadful. He had done nothing but think the worst of her since they first laid eyes upon each other. That was inexcusable—even though he'd had plenty of provocation, she grudgingly admitted to herself.

As though he recalled something he should not have forgotten, Lord Brooke's face suddenly cleared. "Of course, you do not know," he said in a tone one might have used toward an individual whose mental faculties were impaired. "That is what we need to remember."

Of all things, Jane had not expected such a response, certainly not after the severe way his Lordship had spoken to her before. "What are you saying? I do not understand you."

"I will simply need to be more vigilant," Lord Brooke continued enigmatically. "Come along." He took her arm in a firm grasp. "It is time that you went home, don't you agree? I shall help you to find your aunt."

After a search about the rooms during which Jane was his Lordship's less than willing companion, they found Lady Lettice talking to one of the waiters. Lord Brooke released his charge to her. "I suggest that you do not go out without me," he said in an aside. "Not, at least, until we've had a chance to talk over your bizarre behavior."

"I beg your pardon!"

"And so you might. In lieu of that, however, I prefer that you do as I say. I shall call upon you tomorrow so that we can finish this discussion."

All of a sudden, Jane felt tired. She had experienced too many ups and downs in her feelings this night, and her spirits, for the moment, at any rate, were low. "If you insist."

He nodded.

"I wish you a good night," she said, not meaning it one whit. Wheeling about, she took her aunt's hand, and a short while later they left Almack's together.

What was he going to do with Lady Jane, and why did he even want to try? Those were the questions Marcus Brooke asked himself as he sat alone in his mahogany-paneled study. Unfortunately, he had no good answers to either question. Her sheer audacity in stealing his handkerchief still had the power to infuriate him. Nevertheless, something inside the normally unsentimental soldier insisted that he must attempt to save her from herself. It was his duty.

He straightened his shoulders. He would have to take on this burden, in lieu of Jane's father, and deal with it, no matter how tiresome it proved.

Apropos of burdens, he knew where his sister was, but where was his mother? A quick consultation with her maid brought his Lordship the unwelcome news that Lady Rebecca had gone to Burnes's, a gaming house in Pall Mall which admitted ladies in the sequestered back half of the building. Damn and blast! He would have to go after her and bring her home.

A half hour later, he stood looking through a barely opened door at a large man with shrewd, unfriendly dark eyes. "Let me enter," his Lordship commanded, handing the man his card. "I am come to fetch my mother."

"We don't—" The man hesitated, then took a closer look at Lord Brooke's uncompromising expression and swung wide the door. "You can talk to her in the front saloon," he said in a strongly accented voice. "Polly will get her for you."

It was apparent when she joined him several minutes later that Lady Rebecca was not especially happy to see her firstborn child. "Good heavens, Marcus," she said, tugging irritably at the tucked lace collar of her ecru gown, "you didn't need to descend upon me. And just when my luck had begun to turn. Whatever is the matter with you?"

Since she held but half a rouleau of guineas in her hand, it seemed obvious that her Ladyship had been losing at the tables for quite some time. Still, Marcus bit back his retort. "The carriage is waiting below for us, Mother. We would not want to keep Tom Coachman out longer in the night air."

"I do not think he minds the air," her Ladyship said hopefully, twisting a lock of her graying brown hair. "The lower classes don't. Besides, I am certain he would not want me to leave just for that reason, especially now. I *know* my luck is returning."

Marcus's large hand went to her shoulder. "You mistake the matter, Mother." He accompanied his words with a sardonic lift of one of his straight brows. "What you feel is your luck going out of the door. We must make haste to follow it."

The hand tightened. Lady Rebecca had no choice but to accompany him. There was nothing to keep her from berating him, however, and that she did until they came to a wide landing. Its most distinguishing feature was a locked black door.

Here she halted and lifted a defiant face to his. "This door leads to the gentlemen's section," she said. "I always stop here before I leave so that I can glance through the peephole at the men playing *roulet*." Her face softened, took on a pleading look. "It's such fun to watch them without them knowing it."

Marcus's response was an indifferent smile.

Lady Rebecca chose to take this as approval. Slipping aside a barely visible circle of black metal, she applied her eye to the peephole. "Ah, there is that handsome Mr. Fleer again," she said appreciatively. "I believe he has a *tendre* for Susan. At least, he might develop one if he weren't here, or somewhere else like it, practically all of the time."

"Is that so?" Although his tone was uncaring, his Lordship's expression sharpened. "I did not realize that he had enough of a fortune, or prospects, to gamble that devotedly."

Lady Rebecca took her eye from the peephole. Her animosity apparently forgotten, she gave her son a cheerful smile. "I am certain that he does not have, Marcus. I would have heard of it if he did."

"He must often be lucky, then."

Her Ladyship giggled, then lifted her fan to give her son a coy look over the top of it. "Not at all. In fact, I believe he loses more frequently even than I, and larger sums too. I'm sure I don't know how he can afford to keep doing that. I can't."

"May I?" Marcus replaced his mother at the peephole. Yes, there was Vincent Fleer, standing at the green baize-covered *roulet* table, his eyes glittering as though touched with fever. It seemed clear that he had been bitten badly by the gambling bug.

Beside him were several men notorious for deep play. One had good reason, indeed, to think that Mr. Fleer was out of his element.

Marcus frowned. Since it was clear a spy was operating somewhere within the government, any man who had funds that could not easily be accounted for was suspect. If one added the fact that, through his uncle, Fleer had access to people in the Foreign Office, he became very interesting, indeed. He bore watching.

His Lordship cursed under his breath. Now there was another person to whom he must give his attention. He wished he could clap up the lot of them. At the least, he'd like to see them all packed off to Australia. He would stand at the dock and wave them away—unless Lady Jane had stolen his handkerchief again.

He shook his handsome head. He would not visit the larcenous lady on the morrow. Let her take care of her own fortunes, he thought. Considering that she'd managed to make off with his property so easily, she would probably do quite well.

She was *not* irritable because Lord Brooke had failed to keep his promise to visit her earlier, Jane told herself. She was also unconcerned that he was sitting next to Freddy Manning several rows in front of her and hadn't yet noticed that she and her aunt had come in. No, it was the Deerings' musicale that made her feel so cross.

For one thing, although the Music Room was quite prettily decorated in the latest mode, it was too small for the number of people it held. If the chairs had been placed any closer together, Jane thought, the guests would have been in each other's laps. For another—her head seemed to ache, she couldn't think of another reason. She frowned at her aunt, then gave that lady's sharp elbow a shove to remove it from her ribs.

"It's warm in here, isn't it?" whispered her Ladyship, unoffended. "And there are too many odors. I don't mind the roses, actually, or people's cologne, but I'm afraid not everyone washes as often as he should. One would never want to take *their* handkerchiefs."

"Thank heaven for that at least," was Jane's sulky rejoinder.

Lady Lettice ignored the remark. "Isn't that your beau?" she whispered again and pointed toward Lord Brooke.

"He's *not* my beau!" Jane said fiercely and wondered why that fact should make her feel even sulkier. "Let's not talk, Aunt. Madame D'Argent is about to sing."

For the next five minutes or so, Lady Lettice held her peace. Then she began to look about the room. Finally, she fell to examining her niece's gown, a beautiful white silk with a *corsage* of pale blue satin. "I think you should leave the room," she told Jane.

Jane stared at her. "I'll admit Madame D'Argent sings slightly off-key," she said, "but I cannot see why I must leave. Why do you not if you are bothered?"

"Because it's not *my corsage* that has a hole in it," said Lady Lettice. "It's not the wrong part of *my* bosom that's peeping out."

Jane looked down at the top of her gown. As her aunt had said, it had a hole in it, or, more accurately, a tear, and in a most inappropriate place. Quickly, she clapped her hand over it. "But how . . . ?"

Lady Lettice shook her purple-turbaned head. "I don't know. Perhaps it happened in the carriage or when you were getting out of it. I don't think that matters, child. The important thing is to cover that hole."

She looked around, her brown eyes sparkling. "Maybe I could find something that would do the job."

"No, no," Jane said hastily. "Don't find anything. In fact, do not give the matter another thought; I'll get one of the maids to make repairs." Replacing her hand with her more concealing fan, she rose and left the room.

She could have gone home, of course, but she found that she did not want to do so. As to the reason for her reluctance, she could not say. Though it was not because Lord Brooke was there, she told herself.

Thinking about that gentleman caused her to turn her head toward the Music Room. When she did so, she glimpsed a black stocking enclosing a muscular leg which ended in a shiny black pump. Someone male was about to exit the Music Room. Jane fled behind a nearby pillar.

"Whew. I'm grateful to be out of there," said Freddy Manning, stopping before the pillar. "I couldn't make out a word of what that woman was singing. She ought to take elocution lessons. Little Kitty Summers did. Do you know her? Could never understand a word she said, not that it ever mattered, except to her family. But now she speaks as clear as a bell."

Lord Brooke raised one eyebrow and grinned at his friend. "Could it be that you didn't understand what D'Argent was singing because it was in Italian?"

"Italian? Well, if that don't beat everything. Why should that female want to go and sing in a language nobody but some fool foreigners understand?"

His Lordship shook his head. "I'm afraid I can't answer that. Instead of worrying about it, however, why don't we do as we planned and go out in the garden to blow a cloud?"

"We could," Freddy said agreeably. "And then you can tell me about that girl."

Lord Brooke stared at him. "What girl?"

"You know. The chit who steals who's a friend of the family."

His Lordship put his hand on the pillar and shifted his feet uncomfortably. "Oh, that one. Well, what about her?"

"Have you broken her of her bad habit yet? Don't you remember? You said you were going to treat her like one of your hounds when it misbehaves and that would get her out of stealing. I wasn't altogether convinced when you told me that it would work, to say the truth, so I was wondering if it did."

"No," Lord Brooke said grimly. "It hasn't worked yet." There was a pause, then he added, "I was thinking about not bothering anymore, but I suppose I shall have to. I know it can be done, and I'm going to do it."

Freddy gave him an admiring look. "You certainly are determined, aren't you? I think that's grand. And I'm sure that wretched little thief will, too, when you finally get her to behave as she ought. She'll be in your debt for life."

"Oh, really?" The corners of Lord Brooke's well-shaped mouth turned up. "That might be interesting. I wonder how I'd make her repay me. Never mind. If we

A LARCENOUS AFFAIR

don't leave this room now, Madame D'Argent herself will be out here, and we'll never get to try those cigars.''

There was no doubt in Jane's mind as she watched them go that the two men had been talking about her. There couldn't possibly be more than one member of the *ton* at present who occupied herself by stealing. "Make me repay him, would he!" Jane muttered when she was certain they had left. "I could kill him."

She did an impromptu dance which consisted mainly of stamping her feet. "He said he would never tell anyone! 'Your secret is safe with me,' " she mimicked.

A little consideration made her realize that his Lordship must have concealed her identity from Lord Manning. Nevertheless, her outrage did not abate.

Her large blue eyes gleamed with angry tears. She groaned softly. "He compared me to a dog—a dog! How could I ever have been so mistaken in a person?"

There was the sound of something snapping. Jane stared down at her hand. Tightly clenched, it held the remains of her favorite fan; she had painted the white lilies on its blue vellum herself.

Now the fan was good for nothing. She looked down at the tear in her bodice. She needed that fan.

Slowly, she straightened her queenly figure. "Marcus Brooke will be the one who pays," she vowed between her clenched teeth, "for this and everything else. He will, if it's the last thing I do in my life."

CHAPTER 5

WHEN he awoke the next morning, at first Lord Brooke could not fathom why he was in such a foul mood. Then he remembered, and his handsome face broke into a scowl. "Jane Ashworth," he muttered, rubbing a thumb reflectively across the stubble on his chin. "The vixen snubbed me last night."

Indeed, she had, royally, and snubbed Freddy Manning as well. He could not comprehend why, although he'd searched for an explanation. He'd even entertained the idea that she'd overheard his discussion with Freddy in front of the pillar. But, no, she couldn't have.

"Never mind," he said aloud in an irritated voice, both confusing and alarming his valet. "I have more important matters on which I must concentrate."

In less than an hour, perfectly turned out in a tight blue coat of the valet's choosing, fawn pantaloons, and brilliantly shined boots, he was on his way to the Foreign Office to discuss his suspicions about Mr. Fleer with his superiors.

Having rather easily succeeded in convincing them that Fleer merited watching, he returned home and searched for his sister. He found her in her small sitting room. She was dressed to go out in a pink round dress of jaconet muslin and a rose spencer. Her dark hair was set off becomingly by a rose poke bonnet.

His Lordship was impervious to the pretty picture Susan made. His thoughts had reverted to the slight given him by Lady Jane. "Where are you going?" he asked brusquely. "Not to see Jane Ashworth, I hope."

"Hope in vain," Susan said airily. She picked up a pair of pink leather gloves and began to put them on. "She and I are about to go shopping."

Marcus frowned. "Shopping! She never told me that she meant to do that today."

"Why would she?" Susan sounded surprised and somewhat belligerent. "You are not her keeper. Nor shall I let you be mine, Marcus. I say that she and I shall go shopping, and so we shall—even though she doesn't know of it yet."

The martial line of Marcus's jaw became perceptibly less pugnacious. "Not know of it? Then, she could hardly have told me. I shall join you both."

After declaring his intentions, he seemed quite amazed, as amazed as Susan, who blinked rapidly several times and shook her bonneted head. "Are you sure you're feeling quite the thing, Marcus? You just told me that you mean to accompany Jane and me on our excursion."

"That's right." He swallowed painfully.

"To look at lace and ribbons and lengths of dress goods, for that is what we will do, you realize."

"I know that."

Susan's brown eyes were incredulous. "Then why would you want to go with us?"

"Why not, sister dear?" Marcus gave her an impatient push toward the door. "If we're going, then let us do it and get it over with, before I change my mind."

Certainly, if *she'd* been asked, Jane would have said she wished he had changed his mind. For one thing, he did not seem the least bit pleased to see her, making her wonder why he had accompanied his sister at all. For another, she was in no wise pleased to see him herself, being just as bruised in her feelings this day as she had been the previous evening. However, she was still eager to punish him, so she determined not to waste the unexpected opportunity.

When she finished buttoning her delft blue pelisse, she gave a jaunty tilt to the matching chip straw bonnet that covered her upswept blonde hair. Then she turned to Lord Brooke with a provocative smile. "I'm ready," she said with pretended lightheartedness.

Susan chose No. 44 Wigmore Street for their first stop. This was the site of Cavendish House, which was not one of the establishments to which Jane usually gave her custom. Nevertheless, she decided, it would do as well as any other for what she had in mind.

Their party was greeted at the door of the building by a rather stout man dressed in a dark coat and striped trousers. "May I be of assistance?" he asked, bowing deeply.

"No, thank you," Jane said with a sly smile. "I mean to assist myself."

This pronouncement caused Lord Brooke to give her a wary look. She met it with a bland expression, then whirled about on her heels and set off down one of the wide aisles with a long, determined stride.

Susan likewise went off by herself. Although one might have expected his Lordship to object to her doing so, he appeared not to notice. Very likely that was because he was grimly tracking Lady Jane.

Jane finally came to a halt at a large display table heaped with beads in a variety of sizes and all the colors of the rainbow. "Aren't these lovely?" she cooed to his Lordship as she closed her long fingers around several of the larger ones. "One can never get enough of such things, I always say."

"Do you, indeed? What *I* always say, Lady Jane, is that one should not get any unless one pays for them." Lord Brooke stared pointedly at her hand. When Jane seemed in no way cowed by his look, he pried open her fingers so that the beads dropped back onto the table. Her response was to laugh as though something vastly amusing had taken place. Then she flitted over to another table.

Lord Brooke swiftly followed her. With his eyes fixed on her in an unblinking stare, he reminded her of an eagle, sharp-visioned and ready to attack if she strayed from propriety's path. Well, why should she care how he looked, she thought with a little shrug. He was not her keeper. He was nothing to her. In fact, he was less than nothing!

"Buttons!" Jane tilted her blonde head so that he'd be certain to see the enthusiastic sparkle in her eyes. "I do so love buttons, even more than I love beads, I believe." She scooped up a fistful and dropped her glance to gaze as covetously at them as though they were diamonds and rubies.

Lord Brooke removed her reticule from her arm and put it to one side. "We wouldn't want any of those buttons to end up where they shouldn't, accidentally, of course. Would we?" he asked coolly. "That would be unacceptable."

"Really? Why do you say so? The proprietors have so many more. In fact, I don't believe they'd miss them if some were to fall into my reticule, accidentally, as you said."

His Lordship looked disgusted. "That's not the point, Lady Jane."

"Is it not?" Her tone was mock-serious. "What is, then?"

This comment received a suspicious look. She would need to be more subtle, she thought, else his Lordship might realize that she was bamming him. "Of course, it isn't," she said amiably. "I wasn't thinking."

Jane moved away from the display of buttons to a table covered with bolts of black cloth. "What lovely bombazine." She ran a beringed finger over a remnant. "It is too bad that this piece is so large."

"So large?" repeated Susan, coming back to them in time to hear her friend's remark. Then she turned her head to smile at three children who were standing near the table with their nurse.

She watched the children walk off. When they were out of sight, she looked back at Jane. "What do you mean, my dear? You can have as much or as little of the stuff as you wish. Although why you'd want any," she added, finally examining the display closely, "is more than I can imagine."

Jane gave Susan a wide, reckless smile. "I meant it is too large to fit into a reticule. It would be obvious to anyone that it was hidden there."

Susan looked up at her tall friend in puzzlement. "Why would you want to hide bombazine in your reticule? I must say, I find that exceedingly odd."

Lord Brooke squared his broad shoulders. "It's of no moment, Susan," he said severely. "You need not worry about it because it won't happen. Come along, Lady Jane." His strong fingers bit into her arm. Reluctantly she accompanied him down the aisle. Susan, after giving them a searching look, went her own way again.

At a table filled with baskets of brightly colored ribbons, Jane finally exerted her not-inconsiderable strength and put a halt to their perambulations. "Oh, la," she said archly, "you needn't have hold of me so tightly, my lord. I do not mean to run away. All I wish to do is look at these ribbons. Are they not pretty?"

"Very pretty," he said solemnly, bending his head to gaze into her large blue eyes. There was a pregnant pause before his Lordship drew away. "But, then, pretty is as pretty does, as they say. Don't you agree?"

"As concerns ribbons? No, I do not think so. Oh, look at this one." She put down her reticule, then lay a shiny length of scarlet satin across it.

With a tired sigh, Lord Brooke removed it from her reticule. "We'll just put that back."

"I beg your pardon. I may want to have it."

"I don't doubt that you do," his Lordship said, with an obvious effort to maintain his patience, "but it isn't yours." When she started to demur, he said very decisively, "If you must have it, Lady Jane, then I shall pur-

A LARCENOUS AFFAIR 65

chase it for you, but under no circumstances are you to walk away with it. Do you take my meaning?"

Jane's blue eyes taunted him. "I'd rather take the ribbon, my lord."

"Well, you can't," he snapped, the reservoir of patience having obviously dried up. "Do you hear me, Lady Jane? You can't and you won't, not ever again. I forbid it!"

Jane glared up into Lord Brooke's handsome, deceiving, lying face. *Talk to Lord Manning about her, would he?* "Oh, do you forbid it?" she challenged. "And who are you to forbid me to do anything, my lord?"

"I'll admit that one might not think I have a right." He sounded almost conciliatory now. "I'm not your father, of course, nor any sort of relative. But you are my sister's dearest friend, Lady Jane, and, besides, I care about what you do."

Jane sneered. "I'll wager that you do. About as much as you care about your dog, isn't that right?"

"My what? What are you talking about?" His Lordship put one of his large hands around her wrist. Jane tried to shake it off, but he would not let her. "Look at me," he said. "Drat that bonnet."

"Oh, certainly, curse my bonnet, too. Is there no end to your perfidy?"

"Perfidy? Me? My dear Lady Jane, what is the meaning of all this?"

Jane wanted to dig her nails into his hand, but being a lady she could do no such thing. Instead, she glowered and his Lordship at last removed it. There was a warm place where his long fingers had rested on her wrist.

"I heard you last night," she choked out. "I was behind the pillar at Lady Deering's when you talked to Freddy Manning, and I heard everything you said."

Lord Brooke's mouth tightened, and color traced his strong cheekbones. "I wondered if you might have, but, of course, I did not really . . ." His explanation dwindled away. "What can I say except that I am sorry?"

"You're sorry that I *overheard* you, you mean."

He gave her a considering look. "That is rather odd. Why were you hiding behind a pillar?"

"That's irrelevant," Jane said scornfully. She straightened her spine, her five feet, ten inches lending magnificence to her anger. "You are not a good person, Lord Brooke."

His Lordship flushed more deeply. "I believe I am, you know. If you'll just listen, I can explain everything I said to your satisfaction." He thought over his conversation in front of the pillar with Lord Freddy. "Well, maybe not everything, but enough to prove to you that I'm not quite a villain."

When he finally finished interpreting what he'd said the previous evening, including, with a great deal of embarrassment, his theory of breaking an individual of bad habits, Jane thought she just might be able to excuse him—eventually. After all, as he'd said, he did care about what became of her, just as she cared about Lady Lettice. She gave him a halfhearted smile.

"Good. May I hope that means you have forgiven me?"

Jane's smile grew a little wider. "You may hope if you wish, my lord."

"And may I hope that you will stop disliking me a little, which I believe you have done since first we met? I would be glad if you would."

Lord Brooke was behaving charmingly to her, and Jane felt herself thrown into confusion. "Indeed, I confess I have found you to be rude, arrogant, overbearing, and arbitrary," she heard herself say, "but that does not mean that I dislike you . . . precisely."

His Lordship put back his head and laughed.

"I'm sorry," Jane said.

"Do not be sorry. You were just telling the truth as you see it. There is one thing, though. I mislike bringing it up again, but I'm afraid that I must. Will you promise me that you will stop taking things from your friends? That will be much better than being sorry."

Jane sighed. So Lord Brooke wanted her to promise not to take what was not hers. *He was not hers.*

A LARCENOUS AFFAIR 67

Now why had she thought that, she wondered. Her pale white skin became tinged with pink, and she lowered her head without answering.

"Do not be embarrassed," his Lordship said gently, then spoiled the effect by giving her a brotherly pat on the back. "Besides . . ."

Besides what? Jane looked at him, a question in her eyes, but Lord Brooke no longer regarded her. He was staring past her, an expression of pained disbelief on his face.

Jane turned to see what had drawn his attention. She should have known before she turned, she thought with a sigh. He was looking at Susan, who was surrounded by a noisy, laughing crowd consisting mainly, although not entirely, of children. Among them were the three children whom Susan had smiled at earlier.

"What the devil! What is she up to now?" Lord Brooke exclaimed. "Come with me, Lady Jane." Taking her hand, he half-dragged her toward his sister and the ring of people who made up Susan's appreciative audience.

As they got closer, they saw that Lady Susan did not occupy the center of the ring alone. Her companion was a pug dog, as squat and homely as the rest of that breed. In other ways, however, the beast was not one's ordinary pet. No dog could be considered ordinary who sported a mantle of purple velvet and had a green ribbon around one ear—not to mention a pair of spectacles dangling from the ribbon. It was this vision of high fashion that was causing the group to laugh.

Irritation apparently made his Lordship forget that he was not still among soldiers. "What's that ugly, damn dog doing here, anyway?" he snapped. "The proprietors shouldn't stand for it."

Jane smiled in amusement—and relief that Lord Brooke's attention had been diverted away from her supposed sins. "If I know Susan," she said gaily, "she smuggled it in. I doubt very much that the proprietors were consulted."

Apparently, such was the case. At that very moment,

the man who had greeted them when they entered the establishment came bustling up to the revelers. "No, no, young ladies and gentlemen," he said, "we simply cannot have this. Animals are not allowed within these precincts. You, miss," he turned to Susan, "collect your charges and get that creature out of here."

"He must not remember that she came in with us," whispered Jane. "He believes that she's the children's governess—although how he could, considering the way she is gowned, is a mystery to me." She paused to reflect upon this peculiarity. "He must be too upset to think rationally."

Lord Brooke frowned. "I am not surprised. Susan has that effect upon people. I'll tell you what we should do," he added gravely, as though plotting a campaign against Napoleon. "I will carry out her rescue, and we will leave this place."

Convinced that she could handle the situation with more tact, Jane started to volunteer her services, instead. She stopped, however, and put a detaining hand on his Lordship's arm when she saw a slender, brown-haired man step forward and scoop up the dog.

The gentleman stripped it of its makeshift clothing, while it made vigorous attempts to lick him, then removed the spectacles from the entangling ribbon. "Yours?" he asked Susan with a lift of a neat, brown eyebrow.

Susan blushed—the first time Jane had ever seen her do that. "I took them from the clerk," she said, then added with painful honesty, "She didn't want to give them to me, but I convinced her to do so."

"I'm certain you are quite good at that," he said in a low, pleasant voice. "Nevertheless, she shouldn't have given in to you."

"Is that all you have to say to her?" the proprietor asked. "Sir, I must protest. Your governess had no right to conduct herself in this way."

The gentleman's expression became cool. "She's not the governess. Good lord, man, how could you think so?" Returning his attention to Susan, he pointed to the three

A LARCENOUS AFFAIR

children. "Would you mind if I asked what you've done with their nurse?"

Again, Susan blushed. "I sent her off to get a drink for Baby."

"Is that so?" Once more, the eyebrow went up. "Tell me, do you always involve yourself in the affairs of others to this extent, or am I especially blessed?"

Susan gave him a crooked smile. "You needn't be sarcastic. We just wanted a bit of fun, the children and I."

"Yes." The man's voice softened. "They could use that."

His words caused Jane, still a silent spectator beside Lord Brooke, to notice for the first time that the three children, as well as the man, wore touches of mourning. She felt an ache of pity. She was glad that Susan had been able to amuse them.

And so she told Susan in the carriage going home. "You seem to have an affinity for children," she said. "I've noticed it other times as well. They all seem to like you very much."

"It's too bad that you don't make a push to marry," Lord Brooke put in his tuppenceworth. "That might solve more problems than one."

Susan glared at him. "I have no interest in solving your problems, Marcus. Why do you not, instead, marry Jane and start a family? Then Mama would cease gambling, remember, and I could distract myself by playing aunt."

A heavy silence descended upon the carriage. Jane cast one quick, humiliated look at Lord Brooke, who sat staring rigidly out of the window.

"Please accept my apology," Susan muttered. "I should not have said that."

It was obvious that Jane, as well as his Lordship, wished that, indeed, she had not. In fact, the atmosphere in the carriage had become decidedly strained. What a morning it had been, Jane mused to herself. She hoped she never had another such.

She felt profoundly relieved when the carriage drew up

to her aunt's door. Without regret, she bade Lord Brooke and Susan good-bye.

"I hope nothing more happens," she groaned to herself upon entering the house. "I don't believe I could bear it."

"What's that, dear?" said Lady Lettice. "Did you have a good time?"

Jane's fingers plumped up her pale hair, which had been sadly flattened by her bonnet. "No, I wouldn't quite say that. But never mind me, Aunt. I need to talk to you about something of importance."

Lady Lettice followed her niece into the green saloon and sat down upon one of the pretty green and pink chintz window seats. She patted the place beside her in invitation. Instead, Jane chose a green damask wing chair, which she pulled forward the more directly to confront her aunt. "I want to discuss your appropriation of others' property," she said, wasting no time in circumlocution.

"Oh, that." Her Ladyship sounded mildly exasperated. "You do dwell on things, don't you, dear?"

Jane's hands flexed as though in preparation for strangling their victim. "Let us not wander away from the subject, Aunt," she said. "We are discussing you. I want you to swear that you will never again steal another's possessions and hide them in your reticule."

Did she sound like Lord Brooke in stating her demands? She supposed that she did, she thought rather self-consciously. But, unlike his Lordship, *she* had a real reason for saying what she did. "Are you ready to swear?" she asked.

Wrinkles like cats' whiskers fanned out around the top of Lady Lettice's narrow, pursed mouth. "How many times do I need to tell you, child. I don't steal! I must insist that you stop saying that. You will give me a bad name."

"It is not you who has the bad name, Aunt," Jane said forcefully. "It is I. Lord Brooke is convinced that I took Lady Manning's Chinese figure and his handkerchief as well. And now, though it is not your fault, he believes that I steal from shops!"

Lady Lettice's eyes began to sparkle. "Shops, is it?" she said appreciatively. "Umm. I've never done that."

"Well, don't," Jane quickly added. "And don't, please, filch objects from your friends any longer. Why do you, Aunt?"

Lady Lettice rubbed her fingers absentmindedly over the raised design on her puce day dress. "I never used to, you know. I didn't start doing it until my dear Harry died."

At Jane's sympathetic murmur, her Ladyship stopped speaking. Then she went on with a little quaver in her voice, "I realize it's not quite the thing to dote on one's husband, but I did. So life was awfully flat after that—after he was gone. I even lost interest in inviting people here.

"Then one day I read something from La Fontaine. It went, *Aide-toi, le ciel t'aidera*." With a wave of her bony hand, she translated, " 'Help yourself, and heaven will help you.' So I did. I helped myself to all my friends' things. It certainly made a difference, my dear. Just like that, life became amusing again."

She shook her finger. "Of course, you understand that I'm talking about taking things, Jane—*taking*, not stealing. Those are not the same, I assure you."

Jane sighed. "So you say, Aunt. Tell me, aren't you ever afraid that you will be apprehended?"

"Well, yes, while I'm actually doing it. That's part of the thrill and the fun, you see."

"No, I'm afraid I don't," said Jane with a shudder. "It's not the sort of experience I'd care to have. Nor must you, Aunt, any longer. I want you to promise that you'll cease your game."

"Cease my—! You don't mean it. You do?" Lady Lettice's narrow forehead creased. "I don't know why I'd want to, and, besides, I'm not sure that I could."

"I'm afraid you must, else I shall have to return to Lincolnshire." Jane's voice grew softer. "That is not a threat, dear Aunt. It's simply a fact. I cannot stay here longer if you continue to . . . uh . . . put things in your reticule, because I am getting into too much difficulty over it. Please don't ask me what sort of difficulty," she said, raising a hand to forestall her aunt's questions. "Just give me your word."

"Very well, I'll try." Her Ladyship's tone was not particularly optimistic. "I just hope the temptation doesn't come over me tonight at the Sidwells' ball."

"Heaven forfend," Jane said devoutly, and leaned over and patted her aunt's bony knee.

Her prayer seemed to have been heeded, she thought later that evening at the ball. Two hours into the ball, Lady Lettice had not taken anything she ought not have. Her brown, beaded reticule looked as innocent as if it dangled from the wrist of a nun.

Knowing that Lord Brooke had accepted the Sidwells' invitation, Jane was sorry that she hadn't prayed for his absence as well. After Susan's embarrassing remark about marriage, his Lordship was the last person she wanted to see that night. True, she was looking her best in a new trained gown of celestial blue that set off her statuesque figure and emphasized the blue of her eyes; nevertheless, she still wasn't ready to be in his company—not just yet— which made it rather odd that she continued to feel a nagging disappointment that he had not put in an appearance.

Susan was there, however, along with Lady Rebecca, the former looking as glum as Jane felt. "Is anything amiss?" Jane asked, as she and Lady Lettice stopped by Susan's chair during a stroll about the room.

"No," Susan drawled, playing lazily with one of her pearl earbobs. "Why should it be?"

"Oh, I don't know," Jane said. "You seem unhappy, rather."

Her friend's mouth quirked up at one corner. "I'm bored. It's always the same—boring people in boring, excessive numbers. How can I be expected to be happy?"

"That's certainly true, I mean what you said about the numbers," Jane agreed. "One can't find anyone in this crush. For example, I do not see your brother, although

A LARCENOUS AFFAIR 73

I'm confident he must be here. He is, isn't he?'' she asked with exaggerated casualness.

Susan yawned behind her silk fan. Then she shook her head to indicate the negative.

"I see. Has anything happened to keep him away?"

Her friend's laugh was sardonic. "Happened to Marcus? Of course, nothing has happened. It wouldn't dare. He'll be here sooner or later. I know that because he said he would, and my brother always keeps his promises." She said this last as though it were a fatal flaw in him.

Jane decided that it was time to change the subject. "That man you met today seemed nice, didn't he?"

Susan gave her a theatrically blank stare. "What man? Oh, do you mean the manager of the drygoods store? Indeed, I thought him quite dreadful."

Jane smiled good-naturedly. "I do not mean him—as you well know. I was referring to the man who was in mourning, the one who had three children and that sweet dog."

"Oh, that man. He was there so short a time, one could hardly tell. I liked the children, though."

"I know you did." Jane's smile quickly gave way to a sigh. "Oh, well."

Susan's eyebrows arched at this cryptic ejaculation, but she did not ask for an explanation.

Instead, Susan turned her attention from her friend altogether to observe Vincent Fleer, who stood a few yards away staring vacantly in their direction. Limply, Susan raised her fan and waved it at him to attract his attention.

Although he began walking toward them, reluctance showed in every step Mr. Fleer took. He smiled stiffly.

"Is something wrong?" asked Susan, not one to tiptoe around an issue.

Mr. Fleer's swarthy complexion darkened. "Not really," he replied, although the agitated movements of his fingers belied his words. "It is just that I seem to have misplaced my snuffbox. I laid it down in the library, where I'd gone to examine his Lordship's collection of travel books, and forgot to pick it back up. Then when I remembered and went to fetch it, it was gone."

He stopped speaking to take a nervous breath. "Whoever pocketed it should have realized his mistake and returned it by now, wouldn't you think? Unless he means to keep it," he said angrily.

"Is that so?" murmured Lady Lettice.

Jane cast a suspicious glance first at her aunt and then at her aunt's reticule, but Lady Lettice looked as guiltless as a babe; as for the reticule, it was no fatter than it had been. Catching her aunt's eye, Jane shrugged slightly, then turned away.

"I imagine it was quite valuable," said Susan indifferently, "and that is why you care."

"Valuable? Why, no. That is, yes, at least to me. It was my father's. I strongly hope that I shall get it back."

Susan rose languidly from her chair. "I suppose we could help you to search for it, if you wish. What does it look like?"

"White," he said, sounding as halfhearted as she, "with a milkmaid pictured on it in blue. It's nothing special." With more animation, he added, "You mustn't concern yourself about it, Lady Susan. I'm certain that I shall find it."

"Come by tomorrow," said Lady Lettice, causing the others to direct inquiring looks at her. After all, this was hardly the time to issue Mr. Fleer an invitation. He must have thought the same, for he did not deign to answer and a few minutes later made his excuses and left.

Jane was about to excuse herself and walk off as well when Susan tapped her on the arm. "Marcus has arrived," she said, pointing toward her brother. "See. Over there. The lapdogs are with him."

At her friend's announcement, Jane felt an irrational sense of pleasure. She also felt a lingering awkwardness. With some reluctance, she looked toward the door. There stood Lord Brooke, all six feet, four inches of him, splendid in a blue coat and black pantaloons that showed his lithe form to advantage.

A LARCENOUS AFFAIR 75

As for the "lapdogs," they were three young women well below the average height. In fact, they hardly came up to his chest. All had the same honey-colored hair, protuberant eyes, and small, wide noses. Jane felt sure that they were sisters.

Susan looked with scorn upon each of the trio's members' blatant efforts to gain her brother's undivided attention. "Don't they remind you of the pug dog that was in the draper's today?" she said with a contemptuous smile.

Jane tried not to laugh, so as not to encourage her friend's deplorable tongue, but she could not suppress a chuckle. Thus encouraged, Susan said, "It would not surprise me if all three of them threw themselves at his knees and barked to get his attention. Can't you just picture it?"

This time, in spite of her good intentions, Jane did laugh. Lord Brooke could not have heard her, of course, amidst all the other sounds in the noisy room. It could only have been coincidence that he glanced over at her just then. In any case, he quickly looked away again.

"He won't come to us because of what I said in the carriage today," Susan said. "He read me a rare scold after we left you, I can tell you. He tore me up one side and down the other."

When Jane didn't offer any comment on this, Susan continued stiffly, "I did tell you that I'm sorry, didn't I? Marcus always makes me angry when he plays big brother. Besides, I do think that you and he should marry. You're perfect for each other. Well, maybe not perfect. Marcus is such a Tartar. But you should not let that bother you."

"Is that so?" Jane said wryly. "How kind of you to be willing to sacrifice me to a Tartar."

Susan's grin showed her small, white teeth. "It wouldn't be much of a sacrifice, really. You'd get me for a sister—although I suppose," she added with a sigh, "after my *faux pas* today you wouldn't care for that."

Jane's laugh sounded artificial even to her own ears. "Even if I wanted your brother for a husband, which, of course, I *do not*, he wouldn't have me. He doesn't approve of me, you know."

"That doesn't matter," Susan said airily. "He doesn't approve of anyone but soldiers. Never mind," she added abruptly. "Here he comes, after all."

CHAPTER 6

ALTHOUGH Jane prided herself on her ability to cope with life's adversities, at that moment she felt like a green young girl. She was sure she wouldn't know what to say to Lord Brooke when he came up to them. *Drat Susan for her runaway tongue.*

As it turned out, she needn't have worried. Before his Lordship could do more than bow over Jane's hand, Susan commanded his attention. "Mr. Fleer has lost his snuffbox, Marcus," she said as though she really cared. "He thinks he left it in the library where he'd gone to examine the book collection. Why do you not help him to find it?"

His Lordship gave his sister a sardonic look. "Gone to examine the book collection, had he? I'd sooner think he'd gone to look for some cards or dice."

"It wouldn't surprise me," said Lady Rebecca, who'd been hiding behind her daughter until then. "He does so love to gamble, even more than I, I think." Her last words seemed to fascinate her, and she relapsed once more into silence as though to contemplate their significance.

His Lordship tapped his lower lip with a long, sun-browned finger. "Perhaps I should help him search," he said in a considering tone. He turned and looked full at Jane. "Save the supper dance for me." Without waiting for her reply, he went off and disappeared into the crowd.

"Of all the arrogant men!" Lady Susan said with disgust. "He was giving you an order, as though you were a . . . a . . . oh, I don't know what. You won't do it, will you? He needs to be taught a lesson."

"You're right," Jane agreed, although not without mixed emotions. Part of her, her head, her pride, whatever she wished to call it, craved the pleasure of refusing Marcus Brooke. How dare he take her complaisance for granted? He was not her father. Heaven forbid!

At the same time, some obviously defective aspect of her nature caused her to want very much to dance and go in to supper with him. Not that it mattered, of course; the issue was moot because she'd already accepted someone else. "In any event," she informed Susan, "I have promised myself to Lord Needing. Have you a partner yet?"

Susan frowned. "It's Vincent Fleer, although if he does not stop behaving so peculiarly, I do not believe I'll want to have supper with him. Imagine getting in the doldrums over a silly, stupid snuffbox."

Although she was as uninterested in snuffboxes as her friend, Jane was more tolerant of people's foibles than Susan—except, it seemed, when it came to Lord Brooke. "Some men do value them highly," she said mildly. "Isn't it Lord Petersham who has a different one for every day of the year?"

"In that case, I wouldn't want to have supper with him, either."

"Then you mustn't," said Jane with a smile as she rose to meet her partner for the next set of dances. "I shall see you later."

As she went down the line with the gentleman, she turned her head more than once in an effort to locate Lord Brooke. He was very likely taller than everyone else there, so he should have been easy to find. She did not see him, however.

Nor did their paths cross at any other time during the

A LARCENOUS AFFAIR

evening, not, in fact, until it was the hour for the supper dance. Then, as if conjured up by the strength of her wishes, he suddenly appeared in the ballroom.

Jane was standing with Lord Needing near an elegant baroque side table, waiting for the music to begin. Catching sight of her, Marcus strode toward her with long-legged confidence. Reaching her, he turned to her companion to say dismissively, "Hello, Needing. What are you doing here?"

"I . . . I've come to dance with Lady Jane," said the sandy-haired young man, who seemed suddenly to have developed a pronounced stutter. "She's my partner for the supper dance."

"*Your* partner?" His Lordship drew himself up to his full six feet, four inches. "She couldn't be, Needing. She is mine."

Good heaven. Did Lord Brooke mean to do battle with that nice Lord Needing over her? To her embarrassment, Jane felt thrilled to her fingertips at the thought. She quickly gained control over herself, however. "You must not mind it, Lord Brooke," she said coolly. "I was promised to Lord Needing before you asked me. If you had but lingered a moment, I would have told you so."

She looked full into his brown eyes, waiting with carefully concealed eagerness for his response. She did not get one, unless an arrogantly raised brow might be taken as such.

Filling the awkward silence, she said in a rush, "I am certain that you can find another partner, even now, if you care to try."

Would he argue with her? Truth to tell, Jane hoped that he would. Instead, he replied with a coolness equal to her own. "Indeed, I've no doubt that I can." He made them a perfunctory bow, after which she had the dubious pleasure of watching him commandeer one of the three diminutive sisters who so obviously admired him.

Jane stared at Lord Brooke and the tiny miss who stretched her neck in order to look adoringly up at him.

"How revolting," she muttered. "Couldn't he have found someone more near his size?"

Lord Needing gave her a shy smile. "I'm sorry. Did you say something?"

"No, certainly not." Jane felt herself flush. "I didn't say anything."

After that, she made certain to keep a check on her tongue, especially when she noticed that Lord Brooke appeared to be enjoying himself with his partner more than seemed necessary.

When the dance was at last over, she and Lord Needing met up with Lord Brooke and Miss Raft, Lord Brooke's tiny companion, in the beautiful, glass-domed conservatory. There they joined Susan and Mr. Fleer. The latter, if his ill-concealed agitation could be taken as a guide, was still distraught over his missing snuffbox.

The huge room seemed to Jane as though it had come out of a fairy-tale. It was filled with flowers and awash with light from huge clusters of candles and a candlelit crystal chandelier which hung from the apex of the dome. Beneath it, on a mahogany banquet table which sat upon a red Turkey carpet, a lavish supper had been set out for the guests.

"Let us sit here," said Lord Brooke, maneuvering so that Miss Raft sat between him and Mr. Fleer. Jane found herself seated on Lord Brooke's other side.

"Too bad about your snuffbox, Fleer," his Lordship said over the top of Miss Raft's honey-colored hair. "We must look for it again after supper." He then turned toward Jane and whispered, "You didn't take it, did you?"

"I . . . you . . ." Jane suddenly found she was delighted that she had not danced with him! "I'll have you know I haven't been near the Sidwells' library the entire evening."

His Lordship grinned. "Does that mean that you would have taken Mr. Fleer's snuffbox had you been near it?"

"I wish I were a man for two minutes," Jane said grimly. "I'd make you sorry for what you just said."

Lord Brooke laughed. "Only two minutes? Is that all it would take? I must say, Lady Jane, that your estimation of my pugilistic capabilities is quite lowering. I hope I could escape your retribution for longer than that—if I wanted to."

Before Jane could reply with a *truly* devastating setdown, which she was certain was about to come to her, her attention, and that of everyone else at the table, was drawn to Lady Susan. "I don't want to hear another word about the blasted snuffbox," she said loudly to Mr. Fleer. "One would think it held the crown jewels or state secrets or something like that."

Mr. Fleer paled as much as anyone with his dark coloring could. Then he said with a crooked grin, "What an absurd thing to say, Lady Susan. One would be hard put to fit anything but snuff into a snuffbox. Isn't that right, Brooke?"

Lord Brooke shrugged his large shoulders. "Don't ask me. I don't own one of the things. I only smoke cigars." He then tilted his head to look at Jane and gave her a conciliatory smile. She did not return it.

He placed a finger on her arm, then immediately drew it away. If nothing else, the gesture compelled her attention. "I've been thinking about our conversation in the draper's today," he said in a low voice. "I was wishing that we could continue it. Actually, what I mean is that you never promised me you'd desist from your . . . um . . . avocation. I suppose that's why I couldn't help but wonder if you were behind the disappearance of Fleer's snuffbox."

Jane pursed her lips and did not reply.

Lord Brooke continued, "If you had given me your word, I wouldn't have wondered. Contrary to what you might think, Lady Jane, I don't believe you would deliberately tell me an untruth." He gazed at her beautiful face, a smile warming his eyes. "I detect something steady in you, despite—certain other things."

The smile was captivating, the words approving, more or less, for once. Jane found herself wishing that the good feeling now in evidence could continue. She came to a decision: she would confess that her behavior in the dry goods store had been in jest. Then his Lordship needn't think quite so ill of her.

"There is something you should know," she said, keeping her gaze fixed on him. "I told you an untruth today, or, at least, I fear I attempted to mislead you."

She saw Lord Brooke's lean form stiffen. "Is that so? In what way, may I ask?"

Jane nibbled at her full underlip, then said, "Do you remember how I looked to be taking those beads and buttons and other things in the warehouse? Well, I wasn't really. I was only funning."

She paused to note that Lord Brooke looked less than amused. "What I mean is that I never had any intention of taking them, at least not without paying for them."

"Indeed?" His Lordship looked coldly at her over the bump in his nose. "Why would you want to do that, to pretend to take things, I mean? Let's not wrap it up in clean linen, Lady Jane. Why would you expend so much effort on trying to make a fool of me?"

"You deserved it," cried Jane, stung by his disapprobation, "for your remarks to Lord Manning."

His Lordship seemed struck by her words, although he did not look any less offended.

At last, he gave her a rueful grin. "You're right, of course. I did deserve it."

"Thank you," said Jane demurely, amusement and relief glinting in her fine eyes. "I'll accept your apology, if you will accept mine."

"Yes, let us cry peace and begin again. I'll give you my hand on it," his Lordship said, and did just that.

He felt pleased with himself after this exchange, and very much in charity with Jane. There might be hope for her yet, he thought with more enthusiasm than the subject perhaps warranted—considering that she was nothing to him.

It wasn't until quite a bit later, when he was back in his own home, in fact, that he realized that Lady Jane never had sworn to reform herself, even though he'd asked her to at least twice that he could remember. "The devil," he said, feeling once more like a fool. The lady had outwitted him. But not, he vowed, for long.

Refusing to consider his motives, Lord Brooke went off to bed, eager for the new day and a new attack upon the lovely criminal's defenses.

Nor did he forget about Mr. Fleer. He would need to do something about him, too. There was no question about reform there, of course, if Fleer was indeed a spy. Retribution would be more like it.

Coincidentally, Jane, too, thought about reform in those early hours—not applied to herself or to Mr. Fleer, but to her aunt. Her mood was congratulatory. Lady Lettice had not filched anything during the evening, not a figurine, not a handkerchief, not a button or a bow. The whole night, her Ladyship's reticule had remained deliciously flat.

Jane had started to commend Lady Lettice during their carriage ride back to Upper Grosvenor Street, but had been cut off. Now, as they entered her Ladyship's front hall, she tried once more. "You're a dear child to care, I'm sure," said her Ladyship, "but I'm too weary to talk about such things tonight." She yawned elaborately behind her narrow hand. "Why don't we wait until the morning? All I want now is my bed." With that, she grabbed a branch of candles and made her way up the stairs alone.

Jane was rather put off by her summary dismissal, and just the faintest bit suspicious. Lady Lettice was often abrupt, it was true, but not quite as abrupt as that. As for herself, Jane was nothing if not unflinching in what she perceived to be her duty. After changing into her night clothes and a robe, she went to confront her evasive aunt.

"I'm not receiving anymore tonight," her Ladyship called through her bedchamber door in response to Jane's knock. "Go away, child. See me in the morning."

Undaunted, Jane rapped upon the door once again. "Let me come in, Aunt. I want to talk to you. It will just take a minute, and I shan't go away until I do."

"Drat it, Jane. Oh, very well." Grumbling to herself,

her Ladyship slowly unlocked the door. "Come in, then, if you must. What is it?"

Jane looked about her aunt's beautifully appointed bedchamber for the abigail. "Where is Trudy?" she asked. "I thought she would be with you, to help you undress."

Lady Lettice touched the turban which still sat upon her head, even though her dress had been replaced by a gorgeous purple robe. "Once she got my gown off, I didn't need her anymore. I can remove my turban and jewelry myself, so I sent her to bed. Having answered your question, may I now be permitted to do the same?"

"Can I help you with your necklace?" Jane said, ignoring her aunt's testy remarks.

Her Ladyship fingered the heavy diamond necklace she still wore. "Oh, very well." She removed the necklace, then gave it to Jane to put away. "And now you might as well say what you want to. Otherwise, I'll never get any sleep. You want to praise me for not stealing all of the Sidwells' plate tonight, isn't that right?"

With a grin, Jane sat upon her aunt's four poster bed. "Something like that. I could not go to sleep without telling you how proud I am of your forbearance this evening. I know how difficult it must have been for you."

"Fiddle!" said Lady Lettice, playing with her fringed sash. "It was nothing. I can forbear any time I choose, *if* I choose."

"I'm delighted to hear that." Jane leaned back against her aunt's goosedown pillows. She yawned discreetly. "I'll be happy to lock up the rest of your jewels for you."

Lady Lettice removed her rings and threw them carelessly into a velvet-covered box. "Thank you, but that won't be necessary. I can take care of myself. Why don't you go to bed now, child? I have nothing left to take off."

Jane ignored the pointed invitation. "Don't forget the ruby in your turban. You'll want to put that away, too."

"Oh, that." Her Ladyship lifted a tentative hand to feel the heavy red stone. "Are you certain you're not ready to go to bed? No?" She sounded disappointed. "Well, never mind, then."

A LARCENOUS AFFAIR

Jane's suspicion that something was not right was growing stronger by the minute. "The ruby," she repeated.

"Oh, yes, the ruby. I believe I'll just leave it there. That way, the turban will be all ready to go on my head the next time I want to wear it. I like to think up little time-saving schemes like that, you know."

Jane gave her aunt a long, considering look. "I think you should remove your turban, Aunt."

"Remove my turban?" Lady Lettice twisted her robe about her skinny legs. "I thought it was the stone you wanted me to remove. You should make up your mind once and for all, you silly girl."

"I've made it up." Jane stood. "Please remove your turban, Aunt."

"Must I?" Her Ladyship sighed heavily. "Oh, very well." Slowly she raised her long, thin arms, then grasped the edges of the turban with her fingers. Her back rigid, she lifted the turban above her head.

As slowly and rigidly as before, she lowered her arms with her burden. "There. Are you satisfied now?"

Jane looked at the top of her aunt's head. Some of the gray curls had been flattened by the turban, but most were still neatly arranged.

Jane looked at the small snuffbox sitting among the curls. It was blue and white. It reminded her of a blue and white bird, a bird in a hairy, gray nest. "You took Mr. Fleer's snuffbox," she said accusingly.

Lady Lettice removed the snuffbox from her head and placed it on a table. In the accents of one who'd been cruelly maligned, she said, "I knew you'd say that."

"How could I not?" Jane cried. "Anyone would say it."

"Well, yes, I suppose so. But that's of no moment. You shouldn't snort, Jane," she advised with a frown. "It's most unbecoming."

"I agree," Jane said. Half-facetiously, she added, "I think I'll cry instead."

Lady Lettice looked as though she might cry herself.

"Oh, no, you mustn't do that. I kept my word; I didn't put the box in my reticule."

"You didn't—? And what does that have to say to anything?"

Lady Lettice appeared shocked. "What does that have to say? Well! Just that I kept my promise to you, that is all. I could have put any number of things in my reticule, you know. There were enough of them lying about. For example, I saw the most beautiful miniature of a sheep in the drawing room. I could have slipped it into my reticule without anyone being the wiser. But did I do it? I did not."

She looked at Jane proudly, head lifted, as though waiting for applause. When it became apparent that there would be none, she said, "What's more, when I was going in to supper, I saw a delightful chicken skin fan that had been left on a table. Of course," she said, with incongruous honesty, "it might not have fit into my reticule. I'm just not sure about that. The point is, however, that I didn't even attempt to find out. So there you are."

"Oh, Aunt." Despite herself, Jane found herself wanting to laugh. "What am I going to do with you?"

Lady Lettice patted her niece's lovely white hand. "You needn't do anything, dear. I did what you asked, and that is the end of it. I must say," she added, "although not easy, fighting temptation wasn't quite as difficult as I had anticipated. My dear papa was right when he said that when one does not exert himself to try something, he cannot know what he can do."

Jane shook her head. "Tomorrow, we'll think of a way to return Mr. Fleer's snuffbox without his finding out you took it."

"Indeed? Why must he be treated differently from everyone else? He can come here and get it."

Jane put her hands to her hips. "What are you talking about, Aunt?" she said in an exasperated voice. Instead of answering, Lady Lettice marched into her dressing room and closed the bedchamber door. "Good night, my dear," she shouted through it. "You really must leave. I'm too fatigued to chat any more tonight."

"I won't," Jane called, and waited several minutes for her Ladyship to give in and open the door. But she did not. There was nothing for Jane to do but return to her own room. "This isn't over, Aunt," she warned before departing. "We'll talk about it again in the morning."

True to her word, she returned to Lady Lettice's bedchamber at the shockingly early hour of nine. Her quarry, however, had already eluded her. "Her Ladyship went off to Drury Lane to talk with an orange seller with an interesting history," Lady Lettice's disapproving abigail said. "And her with that man coming to put on an exhibition in the ballroom, and all sorts of queer people coming to watch."

Jane had been discreetly searching for Mr. Fleer's snuffbox while the abigail spoke. The woman's last words brought her to a halt. "What man? Oh, blast, now I remember. The Bow Street Runner. Why didn't her Ladyship stay?"

"She said she'd be back later," the maid said sourly. "It weren't my place to stop her."

"There's nothing for it, then. I shall have to play hostess." All thoughts of misappropriated articles driven from her mind, Jane quickly left the room.

Included in the first wave of visitors was Lady Susan, attractively garbed in her usual pink. Jane welcomed her, then peered over her shoulder in search of Lord Brooke.

"Are you looking for my brother?" Susan asked, causing Jane to redden over being so obvious. "You needn't bother. He won't come, because he doesn't know I'm here, or, rather, he thinks I'm still in Bond Street with my maid."

"Why does he think that?"

"I suppose because he saw me there." She coughed, then said a bit too casually, "We saw Mr. Houghton and his children, as well. Unfortunately, they didn't have the dog with them, but I asked after him, and I sent your best wishes to all. That was when my blasted brother pointed out that Mr. Houghton hadn't met you.''

"Indeed, that's true," Jane said with a smile. "Your brother and I were mere bystanders to the drama at the draper's."

She gave her friend a searching look, but all she saw in Susan's usually expressive face was bland innocence. With equal blandness, she asked, "How do the children appear to be getting on?"

"They still seem lost," Susan answered, "especially the oldest one, whose name is Jennifer. Every time her father got at all close to me, she put herself between us. I suppose that's because not having a mother, she can't bear to be separated from him. Don't you agree?"

"Undoubtedly," said Jane, refraining from pointing out that Miss Houghton had not seemed so afflicted upon first meeting Susan.

"According to Mr. Houghton, the children do not care for London." Susan was all blandness once more. "That is why I suggested that they rent a house near Windsor. It's so pretty there, don't you think?"

"Isn't that where your brother's principal estate is?" Jane asked innocently.

"Um, yes. Yes, it is. That is how I'm able to recommend the area, you see."

Jane did see, far more than Susan would have wished her to, she thought. She put her arm about her friend and hugged her.

Susan moved out of her grasp. "Here is Miles with someone's card," she said brightly. "Let us see whom we shall have the pleasure to greet." She placed herself in front of Jane and took the card from the silver salver the butler held out. "Oh, drat. It's my brother. Deny him, Miles."

Jane looked down at Susan calmly, although, in fact, she did not feel calm. She couldn't imagine why the expectation of seeing Lord Brooke was having an escalating effect upon her sensibility, but it was, and it would have to stop.

A LARCENOUS AFFAIR

"It's no use skulking about and trying to hide from him," she said, as much to herself as to Susan. "We haven't done anything wrong—have you?—and we shall face him straight on. Admit him, Miles."

A short while later, she greeted Lord Brooke with a serene smile. His Lordship was dressed in a blue coat and pale gray pantaloons that displayed the handsomeness of his form to advantage. Jane thought him quite disturbingly attractive.

She was not sure why he had come, but if he intended private speech with her, he was doomed to disappointment. He bowed over her hand, looked disapprovingly at Susan, and then turned his attention to the other guests.

The room seemed full of people, the huge mirrored screen at the far end making the place appear twice as crowded. As could be expected at one of her Ladyship's affairs, the guests were an assorted lot, ranging from dandies and their ladies representing the highest levels of the *haut ton* to individuals whose origins it were better not to delve into too closely. Whatever their background, they were a noisy crowd, everyone seeming in the sort of holiday mood associated with a fairgrounds.

A large group surrounded a burly, balding man who gazed with dark, excited eyes at something at his feet.

"Tell me what the attraction is this time," Lord Brooke ordered Jane with a stoic smile, "or do you want me to guess?

"Ah, I know," he said with pretended gravity before she could answer. "The man is a ratcatcher who plays the . . . um . . . let me see . . . the tambourine. At his feet is a tame rat who dances. Have I guessed it?"

Jane responded with a gurgle of laughter. "You've very nearly done so," she answered. "Mr. Marker's profession is that of Bow Street Runner. One might fairly say, therefore, that his job is to catch rodents. However, he doesn't have one at his feet at the moment, not the human kind or any other. He's also an inventor, and what lies there is his most recent invention—skates."

"Skates?" Lord Brooke echoed. "There is nothing new about skates. I owned several pairs when I was a child."

"I'll wager you didn't have these," she said provocatively. With a wave of her slender hand, she beckoned him and a reluctant Susan to follow her. Politely, but firmly, moving through the knots of people, she brought her guests to stand beside Mr. Marker.

His Lordship looked down at the skates lying at Mr. Marker's feet. Lady Jane had been right. They were unlike any he had ever had. They had wheels instead of runners. "Don't tell me you mean to demonstrate these things in this ballroom," he said with disbelief.

Mr. Marker looked over his beaky nose at Lord Brooke. "Beggin' your pardon, my lord, but I wouldn't be here in her Ladyship's house, at her suggestion, with all these people, if I didn't."

Lord Brooke gave him a curt nod, then turned his head to look at Jane for confirmation. But she was looking away. If she had not been, she would have noticed that, failing to catch her eye, he turned his gaze from her face to her pale white throat and the outline of her deep bosom. *How lovely she is*, the expression on his face would have told her.

Then, as if reminding himself that she had the morality of a street urchin, his Lordship scowled. "Where is your aunt?" he asked abruptly.

His sudden change of mood disturbed Jane. She reacted by sounding as abrupt as he. "She is not here."

"I can see that, which is why I asked. Surely, she could not have meant for you to play hostess on this occasion. And I don't for a minute believe that this—this carnival—was your idea."

Jane flushed. "Do you expect me to thank you for that? In any case, my aunt will be back shortly, I'm certain." She touched her finger to her lip. "I think we shall not wait longer for her, however, because Mr. Marker must return to his work." Turning her back on Lord Brooke, she said to the Bow Street Runner, "We are all anticipation, sir. Pray, do not keep us waiting any longer."

A LARCENOUS AFFAIR

Thus bidden, Mr. Marker proceeded to sit upon the floor and put on the odd-looking skates. These consisted of dark metal plates reminiscent of the underside of a flatiron. To each of these were attached four wheels and several leather thongs for binding the skates to his boots. Finished, he stood erect, made a wobbly bow in Lord Brooke's direction, and set off to skate a short distance on the polished parquet floor.

As the wobbling continued, Jane held her breath. She did not want Mr. Marker to fail, especially with the doubting Lord Brooke looking on. But after a bit, Mr. Marker appeared to get matters under control and she began to relax.

Along with control came a discernible gain in confidence. Mr. Marker took several longer trips. He also accelerated his speed.

Jane turned toward Lord Brooke, smiling smugly. "What do you think of my aunt's protégé now?" she said.

"I think he shouldn't attempt to skate to the far wall," his Lordship answered shortly. "I'm not so sure that he could stop in time."

Jane looked at the large mirrored screen near the other end of the room. "He isn't stupid," she said, a worried frown diluting her expression of faith. "He'd never even try."

Jane, however, had misjudged the man. Buoyed by his successes, Mr. Marker apparently felt the need to conquer more distant worlds. Accelerating rapidly, he aimed himself toward the wall in question.

"Stop, Mr. Marker," Jane shouted. "Look out for the screen."

If he heard, he did not react, certainly not by slowing down. Jane said no more but thrust back her shoulders. She would have to save him. Otherwise, there was every likelihood of disaster.

"I'll do it," said his Lordship, putting out his hand to stop her. "You couldn't reach him in time."

His long, powerful legs eating up the distance, Lord Brooke sped across the floor. One might almost have thought that he, too, had donned skates. When he neared the inventor, he extended his arms and put on a final burst of speed.

It was a grand effort. No one could have faulted him for it. Alas, however, it was a few seconds too late. There was the sound of a crash. Shards of glass went flying. Both men ricocheted off the tottering screen and landed on the floor.

"Lord Brooke, Lord Brooke, are you hurt?" Jane cried. Ruthlessly pushing people out of the way, she skidded across the boards until she reached his side.

CHAPTER 7

HIS Lordship did not answer her plaintive cry, but only looked ruefully from her to his palm. Several slivers of glass, some rather large, stuck out of it, and it was bleeding quite a bit.

"Oh, you poor thing." Jane sat beside him and gently placed the injured hand in her lap. "Find Miles," she commanded Susan, who had come up behind her. "Tell him we need tweezers, water, basilicum powder, bandages, and a maid to clean up this mess. You're all right, aren't you?" she asked Mr. Marker, then without waiting for a reply turned her attention back to Lord Brooke.

His Lordship, his large hand still cradled in her lap, gave her an admiring look. "I know a regiment you might want to take over," he said with a wide grin. "I believe you could whip them into fighting shape in hardly any time at all."

"Hush," said Jane. "You're bleeding."

Lord Brooke tried to move his hand. "Yes, and on that pretty dress of yours, too. That's a crime."

"Crime" was probably the correct word, she thought, but it did not lie in his staining her dress. Rather, it was in the sensuous feelings that sluiced through her limbs from being so close to him. And he was an injured man. Had she no shame?

She didn't want to know the answer. She wanted to be rescued from herself. Where was Miles? More than Lord Brooke, it was she who needed help at this moment.

Help did come, but from an unexpected source. "Let go of my niece," shrilled Lady Lettice, advancing rapidly in their direction across the ballroom floor.

"I can hardly do that," said Lord Brooke, grinning smugly as he bent to escape the green umbrella with which her Ladyship sliced the air. "You see, she has hold of me."

Jane's face flamed with embarrassment. If Lord Brooke's hand hadn't been injured, she thought pettishly, she would have flung it from her lap.

It took her only a few seconds to realize how absurd her thought was. If his Lordship's hand hadn't been injured, it wouldn't have been in her lap. She must be losing her wits.

In any case, she couldn't fling it from her. Nor, it was more and more obvious, could she leave it where it was. Thus, she did the only thing she could think of: she settled his injured hand in her own two hands and sat there cradling it.

This new position did very little for her peace of mind, however, especially when his Lordship inched a bit closer to her and let out a contented sigh. "Where is that Miles?" she muttered.

"Yes, where is he?" Lady Lettice threw down her umbrella and began circling them. "I want him to put this young man out. I've never condoned violence in my home, and I never shall."

Mr. Marker, who up until this point had remained remarkably quiet, cleared his throat. "Violence, is it? We won't be having none of that when Edward Marker is in the vicinity. What did the violence consist of, my lady?"

"What did—?" Lady Lettice stared at him in astonishment. "Well, if you don't know, I can't imagine who would. His Lordship pushed you into that screen. I saw him do it, even if you didn't."

Jane suddenly found herself in the unusual position of wanting to defend Lord Brooke. "But, he didn't," she protested. "Or, if he did, I assure you that he didn't mean to."

"Of course, you would think that," said Lady Lettice, causing a new wave of color to wash over Jane's face. "Nevertheless, I'll not argue with you, especially since Mr. Marker does not appear to have suffered any harm. What happened here isn't of the first importance, anyway, not when compared to what happened to me."

Jane's brows drew down in an inquiring frown. "To you? Aunt, are you feeling all right?"

As soon as she said this, she realized that the answer had to be "no." Lady Lettice, who, ordinarily, was calm even when she had no right to be, was excessively agitated. She simply was not her usual self.

"Shall we?" said Lord Brooke, forestalling her Ladyship's response by rising from the floor. Before Jane could stop him, he used his uninjured hand to assist her to stand as well.

Miles finally arrived with the materials and help Jane had ordered. Moving the onlookers out of the way of the two maids with brooms and dustpans, she let Miles guide Lord Brooke to a chair and begin ministering to him.

"Now," she said, trying not to hover over his Lordship, "tell me what is amiss with you, Aunt, for it's very clear that something is."

Lady Lettice flopped into the yellow silk chair next to his Lordship's and began twisting the strings of her green bonnet. "Everything. That is what's wrong. If one can no longer go about in the premier city in England without being accosted, assaulted, and despoiled, well, why should one be here at all?"

"Accosted, assaulted, and despoiled!" Jane repeated like a dismayed parrot. "Never say so!"

Mr. Marker put his thick, wide hands to his hips and

planted his feet in a belligerent stance. "No, never say so."

"But I already did say so. And I will again and again, if I must, because every word is true." As though her fiercely delivered statement was in need of more emphasis, Lady Lettice firmly stamped one slippered foot on the floor.

"Gawd," said Mr. Marker. "Who done that to you?"

"Yes," said Jane, "and, if it wouldn't be indelicate to tell, Aunt, exactly what *was* done?"

Lady Lettice wrapped her thin arms about herself and stroked her sides as though for comfort. "It was terrible," she announced in a doom-laden voice. "I had just descended from my carriage when a young man with nasty little eyes and a scar on his cheek bumped into me. The next thing I knew he had my handkerchief and was running off with it. Of course, I called after him to stop, but he wouldn't."

"Your handkerchief?" Jane's intonation reflected her astonishment. "Is that all?"

Lady Lettice looked angrily at her niece. "That's easy for you to say. It wasn't yours."

Jane was nothing if not fair. "That is true," she agreed readily. "What I meant, however, is that I thought it might be something more serious, that he'd taken your reticule, perhaps, or knocked you to the ground, or . . . or worse."

"It was worse! That was my favorite handkerchief: eggplant satin with ecru lace. I'd had it for thirty years and meant to have it for thirty more."

Amused, Jane turned her head to look at Lord Brooke. She was surprised to see that he was not smiling. Then she remembered. His Lordship still believed she'd stolen *his* handkerchief. He probably thought her sympathies were with the thief.

Susan, however, seemed to find her Ladyship's story humorous. "What would you have done if he had stopped?" she asked with a little giggle. Lord Brooke looked disapprovingly at her.

Her Ladyship narrowed her brown eyes and looked as

stern as Jane had ever seen her. "I'd have had the coachman beat him severely, of course, before turning him over to the authorities. And I'd have given him a few licks myself with my umbrella. Anyone who steals my handkerchief deserves nothing less."

"I quite agree," said Lord Brooke. "A thief deserves to be punished." One eyebrow slanted as he looked over at Jane. "Of course, if the thief were a woman, it might not be necessary to treat her quite so harshly. I'm sure that if I tried I could think of some retribution just as telling but less . . . um . . . severe."

While Jane, who knew to whom this little speech was really directed, gave him a fulminating look, her aunt drummed her fingers on the arm of her chair. "Man, woman, what is the difference? A thief is a thief and should expect to be treated as such."

"Aunt!" Jane choked over the word.

Lady Lettice's lips pursed. "What?"

Was there any use in saying anything? If her Ladyship did not appreciate that her own behavior constituted theft just as surely as did that young man's, what more could be said? "Nothing," she mumbled.

"You'll want me to report the incident, won't you?" Mr. Marker said as he took up his skates. Lady Lettice nodded emphatically. "Then I'll take the coachman with me to provide a description, if you can spare him. Oh, and I'm sure you want to know that my invention was a raving success, even though there was that bit of a mishap at the end. Wasn't it, Lady Jane?"

"Raving," she said wearily.

"Are you tired?" Lord Brooke grinned slyly at her. "You mustn't be. I need you to bandage my hand."

Jane gave him an indignant look. She hadn't forgotten, and likely never would, that he'd been making sport of her in his talk of thieves and punishments and all that sort of thing. "Hasn't Miles done it yet? Well, I'm sure he will."

Lord Brooke sighed. "He hasn't the touch for it. I need you, Lady Jane."

She wanted to tell him that she didn't need him, but,

besides its being inappropriate to say so, Jane wasn't entirely certain that it was true.

No, that was nonsense. Except for his height, of which she deeply approved, he wasn't the sort of man to whom she could ever be attracted. He was high-handed, overbearing, domineering, and autocratic, just like her father; she could never become fond of anyone like that.

And if he wasn't domineering, exactly, he was at least *dominant*. When he was near, she couldn't seem to notice anyone else. How dare he affect her like that!

She turned to Miles. "You must summon my aunt's abigail. Her Ladyship needs to be escorted to her room so that she can rest."

"Still busy giving orders," Lord Brooke commented appreciatively. "Well, that's all right. I can wait."

"How thoughtful." Jane gave a jerk to the bandage she was unwinding.

Susan was busy buttoning her spencer. "Hurt him," she said sweetly, "but not too much. Meanwhile, I'll take my leave of you. I need to buy some new pink ribbon for the gown I mean to wear tonight."

"Tonight?" Jane queried. "Oh, yes. We're going to Vauxhall with your mama and Mr. Fleer and his friend, aren't we?"

"Are we?" his Lordship asked.

Susan's brown eyes snapped. "No, you are not, Marcus. You weren't invited, and, what's more, we do not want you."

We do not want you. Jane told herself that she needed to remember that. "Let me finish doing this bandage," she said curtly as she waved good-bye to her friend. "Be still, your Lordship."

Lord Brooke's eyes twinkled. "Yes, ma'am."

"There," she said, surveying her handiwork with some satisfaction. "Is there anything else?"

"Why, yes, so there is." His Lordship looked a challenge at her. "Though I've asked you several times, you have yet to promise that you'll desist from that unusual hobby of yours." He gazed intently into her blue eyes.

A LARCENOUS AFFAIR

"Fortunately for you, Lady Jane, I'm a patient man, as well as a determined one."

"Go to the devil," Jane said, and strode from the room.

Later that day, when she felt more in control of her temper, she went to visit her aunt. She found Lady Lettice in bed, staring vacantly up at the ceiling. "How are you, Aunt?" she asked softly.

Lady Lettice sat up slowly and propped herself against several embroidered pillows. "Dreadful," she said in a voice reeking with disillusion. "What did you expect?"

Jane sat down alongside the bed and took up her Ladyship's bony hand. "To own the truth, I didn't know what to expect. I fear I never do with you."

"I suppose you mean that you're surprised at my attitude toward the thief, don't you?" Lady Lettice pulled her hand away from her niece. "Perhaps you don't realize it, Jane, but you've insulted me. He and I are nothing alike, and to say that we are is the outside of enough."

Jane smiled gently. "I didn't say it. I know you would never wrest something from a person by force. However, I can't help feeling that taking another's property is wrong no matter how it's done—which brings me to our immediate problem. How shall we return Mr. Fleer's snuffbox?"

"Oh, that. I told him—or was it you I told? Whichever it was, he can just come and get it."

Jane sat a little straighter in her chair. "I heard you say that before, but I didn't understand you, Aunt. I must confess that I still don't. Why would he come here seeking his snuffbox when he has no reason to think that you have it?"

"That is a point, I suppose," her Ladyship said reflectively. "Then you'll simply have to tell him that I do."

Her niece looked appalled, as, indeed, she was. "I couldn't do that. Think how he'd mind."

"Why should he?" Her Ladyship patted her sunken chest. "He's not a Methodist, is he?"

Jane said tartly, "One need not be a Methodist in order to dislike having his possessions stolen."

"Who knows that better than I?" Lady Lettice replied in an aggrieved voice. "If you've forgotten already that I lost my favorite handkerchief today, I haven't."

Jane gently patted her aunt's shoulder. "No, I haven't forgotten."

"Besides, what happened to me is different, as I've told you and told you. If it weren't, then everyone whose goods I go off with would take umbrage; but they never do. They simply come to the house when they realize that something of theirs has gone missing and ask for its return—unless they don't think to, in which case I tuck it away in my special hiding place. If no one asks for it within a month, I consider the object well and truly mine."

Lady Lettice paused. "Not that I always have what they come for, of course," she added in a tired voice. "Servants can be such thieves. But if I do, I give it back, we have a nice chat and some tea and cakes or a glass of wine, and then they go home. There's never the least difficulty."

She looked at her niece expectantly, waiting for her to speak. Instead, Jane sat slumped in her chair with her mouth ajar and gazed blankly at her aunt.

"That is not an attractive expression," Lady Lettice said. "You look nearly like a fish."

Jane closed her mouth, though she continued to stare at her Ladyship. Finally, she gave herself a little shake and said in a hollow voice, "I cannot believe . . . Never did I think . . . It simply never entered my mind, Aunt, that there was such a conspiracy between you and your friends."

Now it was Lady Lettice's turn to seem bemused. "Conspiracy? Whatever are you talking about?"

"Well, I don't know what else to call it if people are aware of what you are doing and don't object. I naturally assumed that your little, um, pastime was a secret, but it's not."

Jane's eyes widened at her own words. "It's not! Oh, my goodness. That means that I can tell Lord Brooke about you."

"Why would you?" her Ladyship said huffily. "I've

never made off with one thing of his, or of his silly mother's, either. They don't own anything small."

"You don't understand, Aunt," Jane said as she stood and then began to pace about the room. "He keeps saying I— He wants to—" Unable to finish her sentence, she began to giggle. Then she threw back her lovely head and laughed.

"I do not see what's so funny, and I do wish you'd stop that pacing," her Ladyship snapped. "My nerves have had enough of a trial without your galloping about and being hysterical."

Jane paused in her perambulations. "I am never hysterical," she said with dignity. "If I were, I wouldn't have survived one day with Papa."

"You may not survive another day with me. And even if you do, what good will it be, for surely I'll be gone into my grave."

"No, no. We'll work something out." Jane leaned down and kissed Lady Lettice. "I think you're suffering from shock, Aunt. What you need is a good rest. Is there any little thing I can take care of for you?"

Her Ladyship sat up again. "As a matter of fact, there is. I'd be obliged if you would manage the details for my dinner party in two days, the one honoring the six Indian brothers I met at Somerset House."

When Jane, who had heard nothing of such a dinner party, seemed about to voice an objection, Lady Lettice said in fade-away tones, "I'm not up to it, my dear."

"Of course, I'll do it. Don't worry about a thing." She pulled the satin quilt a bit higher about her aunt's scrawny neck, then tiptoed from the room.

The rest of the day passed in a blur for Jane. All that she could think of was being able, at last, to tell Lord Brooke that she was as innocent of wrongdoing as she had always insisted.

It was too bad that she was not going to see him that evening, she thought with barely suppressed excitement. She pictured them seated next to each other in one of the painted boxes at Vauxhall. She would lean toward him. Her blonde hair would almost touch his cheek. She would discreetly inhale the scent of bayberry on his warm skin. Then she would say . . . Well, what would she say? *Pardon me, Lord Brooke, it wasn't I who made off with the Mannings' ugly Chinese figure and your handkerchief. It was my larcenous but basically moral and decent aunt.*

Jane's mouth drew down. She still couldn't tell him. All she could hope for was that someone, at some time, would mention Lady Lettice's peculiarity to him. That wasn't much of a hope.

She scowled into the pier glass, whereupon her abigail said, "Oh, my lady, you've no reason to look like that. Your gown is the most beautiful I've ever seen you wear."

Jane laughed. "You always say that, Sarah."

"But it is. The blue is perfect with your eyes, and the way the crepe clings to your figure, well! You'll have all the gentlemen admiring you."

Jane thought there was one who wouldn't if he were to see her. He'd probably think she'd obtained her gown by pilfering it. Shrugging her lovely shoulders, she accepted her gloves and went down the stairs.

When she joined the rest of their party later that evening, she was introduced to Mr. Fleer's acquaintance, an agreeable-seeming young man with a blond mustache. His name was Mr. Canning. His obvious admiration did little to assuage her dark mood.

As for Mr. Fleer himself, though he seemed at ease this evening, and did not mention his snuffbox even once, Jane still did not approve of him. Susan seemed to tolerate him well enough, however, at least as much as she did anyone else, except the bereaved man with the three children. Jane suspected that Susan was truly drawn to that man. It made her sorry to think that her friend very likely would never see him again, especially if he meant to leave London with his children.

Her musings came to an end when they arrived at Vauxhall. There they made their leisurely way down the Grand Walk until they came to their box. Mr. Fleer opened its door with a flourish. Jane started to go inside, but Susan put her hand on her friend's arm. "Oh, let's not sit down yet," the younger woman said. "I am in no mood to spend the evening staring at passersby."

"We needn't stare, Susan," said her mother helpfully. "Indeed, that would be rude."

Susan gave Lady Rebecca an impatient look. "Oh, Mama, you are too literal."

"What do you suggest that we do instead?" Mr. Canning asked with a stiff smile.

"I don't know," Susan said carelessly. "Unless . . . yes, I have it. Why don't we continue our stroll along the Cross Walk or the Hermit's? We can come back here later."

"I think we should do that after awhile," said Mr. Fleer, his dark head nearer to Susan's topknotted one than Jane thought proper. "If you do not wish to sit down just yet, then let us dance. You can work out your fidgets that way."

Susan's expression lightened. "Yes, let's dance. Jane, you and Mr. Canning must come, too. I'm sure you don't wish to waste your time being a mere spectator any more than I. You don't mind, do you, Mama?"

When Lady Rebecca readily agreed to the scheme, and even volunteered to join some card-playing friends in a nearby box to await her daughter's return, Jane said goodnaturedly, "I don't care about it if you do not, Mr. Canning." The two couples then made for the rotunda, where an orchestra played for dancing.

If Jane expected to see Lord Brooke during this time, or later, when a supper of chicken, thin slices of ham, and fiery Arrack punch was served in their booth, she was doomed to disappointment. He did not come.

The evening became sadly flat. And Lady Susan appeared to become more restless as the night wore on, refusing to accompany the others to the fireworks display.

"I saw it a few weeks ago, when I came here with the Maceys," she said with a pout. "I have no desire to see it again so soon."

"Well, I'd like to," said Mr. Canning, apparently less

agreeable than Jane had at first supposed. "That's one of the reasons I wanted to come to Vauxhall at all tonight."

Susan looked at him in a way that suggested she thought he had more hair than wit. "Then, by all means, you must go. My mama and Lady Jane will be glad to accompany you, I'm sure. I'm tired of sitting still. Mr. Fleer, you promised earlier to take me to one of the other walks. I want to go now."

"Then you shall," he said with an intimate smile that set Jane's teeth on edge. He took up Lady Susan's gloved hand. "I always keep my promises to lovely ladies."

After this speech, he leaned close to Susan and whispered in her ear. Jane could not hear what he said, but his words brought a reckless gleam to Susan's dark eyes and made her laugh.

"I really think that we should remain together," Jane said firmly.

"I don't," said Lady Rebecca with an amiable smile. "That is, I might ordinarily, but I believe I'd rather play cards again than watch fireworks. Sometimes, they blow up, you know—the fireworks, I mean, not the cards."

"I don't think we should remain together, either." Susan patted Jane's hand. "I think that you should go along with Mr. Canning, so as not to disappoint him, Mama should rejoin her friends, and I should take a walk with Mr. Fleer." Lowering her voice, she added, "I'm in one of my states, Jane. Please, won't you humor me?"

How could she refuse? Besides, there was Mr. Canning looking like a dog determined to get his teeth into a savory joint. "Let's meet here again in an hour," she said with a defeated sigh, "and not a minute more." Turning her eyes away from Susan's triumphant smile, she accepted Mr. Canning's arm and went off with him.

At any other time the fireworks almost certainly would have pleased Jane. Their colors shone brilliantly against the night sky. But on this occasion they held little appeal. She kept picturing Mr. Fleer's olive-skinned face almost touching that of her friend. In truth, she did not trust him to behave responsibly, she thought with a worried frown.

"Is anything wrong," Mr. Canning asked. "I fear that you are not enjoying yourself."

Jane pressed her long fingers to her brow. "I do have a bit of a headache from the noise." She hesitated. "I don't want to spoil your pleasure, but I believe I'd like to return to our box now. Susan and Mr. Fleer should be there shortly, I don't doubt."

"I'm not so sure of that," Mr. Canning said with an arch smile. "The Dark Walk is some distance away."

"The Dark Walk! You cannot mean it. My friend would not be so foolish as to go there." Jane reflected upon her words, then added less optimistically, "She did not say anything to me about going there."

Mr. Canning's eyes tracked the trail of light made by one of the exploding fireworks. "Fleer did," he said absently. "I heard him whisper to Lady Susan that he would take her there."

"Why didn't you tell me this before?" Jane sounded almost angry.

"I? Why would I? It is no concern of mine what your friend does. In fact, if I may say so . . ."

"Indeed, you may not. Besides, there is no time to waste." She turned her back on the fireworks. "Let us be off to apprehend them."

Mr. Canning's pale brows rose nearly to his hairline. "Surely, you are jesting. That is no place for respectable ladies."

"Then, good-bye," Jane said with a wave of a white-gloved hand. "I shall be at the Dark Walk."

Her companion gave her a look of pure dislike. "You know that I cannot let you go alone. Please take my arm." Tight-lipped, he set off with her.

The Dark Walk being the farthest of the walks from where they were, it took them longer than Jane liked to reach it. When at last they did, they searched the narrow path for quite a distance. Although they saw many couples strolling about or sitting close together on benches, they did not find Lady Susan and Mr. Fleer. "You don't think he'd have taken her into the woods here, do you?" Jane asked with a worried look.

"No, indeed. Fleer is a gentleman," Mr. Canning said without much conviction.

Jane gave him a skeptical look. "We must go amongst the trees and look for them, since they do not seem to be anywhere on the path."

Mr. Canning's response was a glare.

"Very well, then," Jane said. "Good-bye, again. I shall go in there alone."

"Lady Jane," her escort replied in a choked voice, "no, you will not. I would be failing in my duty as a gentleman if I permitted you to do any such thing. Nor do I mean to go there myself. Or stay here, for that matter. I'm sorry, but that is how it must be."

For the second time that day, Jane felt the urge to tell a man to go to the devil. Instead of so instructing him, however, she said coolly, "You must do as you please." Without a backward glance, she plunged into the woods, leaving the cow-hearted Mr. Canning to his own devices.

Even with a full moon, it was dark among the trees. If Jane hadn't been attracted to a nearby area by some sounds, she might have muddled around for ages. As it was, all she could see when she walked in the direction of the sounds were several shadowy forms. "Susan, are you there?" she called uneasily, suddenly realizing that she, herself, might be in danger.

"Oh, Jane, do hurry," said Susan in an excited voice.

Jane knew that tone. There was mischief afoot; she hadn't a doubt of it.

Drawing closer, she was able to make out Susan standing with Mr. Fleer and Lord Brooke. There was also another gentleman present whom Jane did not know. Since Lord Brooke had the fellow by the throat, it seemed unlikely that she would be introduced to him.

Events after that occurred swiftly. His Lordship released the unknown person, then immediately raised his right hand—the one with the bandage, Jane noted with horror—and hit him in the face. He hit him so hard that

A LARCENOUS AFFAIR

the man flew over a bush. From there, he got clumsily to his feet. Then he fled, in an erratic pattern, out of the woods.

"Let us go," commanded his Lordship. "You, too," he said to Jane as he ran by her.

Out from among the trees the party tumbled. Jane noted with interest that Mr. Canning was still where she had left him. The person who'd been hit and tossed, however, was another ten feet down the path, disappearing fast into the woods on the opposite side.

"Shall we go after him?" asked an obviously distressed Mr. Fleer.

"Yes, yes," Susan exclaimed. "Let's catch him so Marcus can hit him again."

Lord Brooke, looking absolutely splendid in the moonlight, Jane thought, shook his head. "There's no point going after an enemy at night. We'd never catch him."

"Hello," Jane said belatedly. "This is Mr. Canning. What were you all doing in there?"

His Lordship gave Mr. Canning a curious look. "I happened to see Susan as I was walking along, so I followed her."

Susan's admiration for her brother died aborning. "That's despicable."

Lord Brooke ignored her. "She and Fleer went into the woods."

"We were hoping to see some owls," Mr. Fleer said smoothly.

"Before I could approach, a man came up behind them. He took hold of Fleer. I arrived and told hold of him. The rest you saw." Lord Brooke rubbed his large hands together. "That's all."

Mr. Canning gazed upon the group with poorly concealed dislike. "I'd say that's enough. Tell me, Fleer, why did the man try to attack you?"

Vincent Fleer bridled. "How should I know? He must have been a bedlamite. There's a full moon, you'll notice."

Jane said, "My aunt was attacked today and robbed."

"You see," said Mr. Fleer.

"Somehow," Lord Brooke commented dryly, "I do not believe that the motives of the two attackers were the same. Come, Fleer, can't you think of some reason why a person would go after you like that? There's got to be one."

Susan laughed. "Perhaps it was someone who wanted to return his snuffbox."

"That isn't funny." Mr. Fleer turned on his heel and took a few steps. Then he turned back. "Are you coming?" he demanded of Lady Susan.

"No, she isn't." Lord Brooke's voice was curt.

"Yes, I am." Skipping a bit, Susan caught up to Vincent Fleer, and the two of them went off.

Mr. Canning offered his arm to Jane. "Just a minute," said Lord Brooke, stopping her with his uninjured hand. "I have something to say to you. Go along, Canning. We'll catch up with you later."

"Indeed, I will not," Mr. Canning said, clearly out of temper. "I brought Lady Jane to this ungodly place, against my wishes, I might add, and I mean to return her safely to our booth."

Not for anything was Jane going to give up the chance to spend a few minutes alone with Lord Brooke, even if he did mean to read her a scold, which she was certain he did. She drew herself up to her full height. The moon gilded her features and haloed her light hair, making her look more than mortal. "Go away, Mr. Canning," she said with awful majesty.

CHAPTER
8

MR. CANNING opened his mouth to protest, then took a protracted look at Jane, and closed it. Mumbling who-knew-what imprecations under his breath, he left them.

Now, alone with his Lordship, Jane felt shy. "Let me see your hand," she said, hiding her feelings in brusqueness. "No, not that one. The one that was injured today."

Lord Brooke slowly extended his bandaged hand. There was a bloodstain the size of a guinea darkening the white bandage. "Look what you've done," she said indignantly. "You've made it bleed again."

Instead of replying, his Lordship put his arms about Jane. Slowly, inexorably, he drew her close. "Don't you care about your wound?" she cried, trying, and failing, to pull away.

"Be quiet," said Lord Brooke. "I am going to kiss you."

If just smelling his bayberry scent excited her, Jane feared to think what effect his embrace might have. Desire warred in her breast with the need to preserve herself—and desire lost. "Wait!" she cried, pushing against his hard chest with an immaculately white-gloved hand.

Lord Brooke's chin set at a stubborn angle. "I don't want to wait. I want to kiss you, and I want to do it now."

With some difficulty, Jane extricated herself from his grasp. Then she stepped neatly to one side. "I thank you," she said, her expression solemn, "but you cannot. I have ever so many things I need to ask you."

His Lordship looked at her incredulously. "This minute? I have no interest whatsoever in answering questions now."

Jane knew by the warm glint in his eyes that his thoughts marched in a wholly different direction. She would have to attempt to distract him.

"But you have not told me why that dreadful man attacked you," she said, trying to sound enthusiastic about the subject. "It gave me quite a start to see you engaged with him as you were."

Somewhat to her surprise, her ploy worked. Although Lord Brooke frowned at her, he moved away a little. "No doubt it gave him quite a start, too. But you must not have been listening when I explained what took place. The fellow did not attack me. It was Fleer he was after. I just put myself in his path."

"Why would anyone want to hurt Mr. Fleer?" Jane mused. "That's the strangest thing."

His Lordship's expression became grimmer. "I do not know, but I can tell you I mean to find out. Something havey-cavey is going on involving Fleer."

Before she could question him further, Lord Brooke took firm hold of her wrist. "Enough of that subject," he said in an implacable voice. "The citadel has been breached, my beautiful girl. It is time for you to surrender."

"No," Jane protested weakly, but Marcus Brooke paid her refusal no heed. Instead, he pulled her into his arms and kissed her—for a long, sweet, passionate, and exciting time.

As he continued to kiss her, the excitement grew. Thought was replaced in Jane's brain by desire. She felt a hot ache in her throat and a hunger to get nearer to him. Although her arms were about his neck and her figure quite close to his, so that she could feel his chest, she couldn't seem to get close enough.

Or give enough. Her initial resistance changed to a languorous yearning to cede her will to him, to allow him to do to her with his mouth and his strong, gratifying hands whatever he wished. Even when his stroking fingers moved from her neck to glide over the tops of her breasts, she did not object but only pressed herself more tightly against him.

"Open your lips," Marcus whispered against her mouth, and she did. His tongue slid inside. Jane gasped in shock, but then she welcomed it and touched it with her own.

Marcus's hands slid down farther, more intimately, over her unresisting form. Then they stopped. He shook his head, and moved away from her. "I didn't expect such a—such a combustion!" he said in a husky voice. "If I had known, I wouldn't have . . ." He shrugged and left his sentence unfinished.

What was he saying? That he would not have allowed himself to behave so familiarly with a thief and all-around troublemaker? She knew how he looked down upon her. A kiss didn't change anything, except to make everything worse.

From euphoria she sank into despondency. But, of course, she would not let him know how distressed she felt, distressed enough to cry. She had pride; at the moment, it seemed to be all she had.

Jane lifted her head in a haughty gesture. "You needn't explain," she said coolly. "I understand."

"You do?"

"Yes, I do. The danger you were in stimulated your senses, you see, and so you . . . you . . . I've done the same thing myself."

"Good lord, I hope not," he said with a gravelly laugh. "Speaking of danger, may I ask why you were standing alone in the woods, or why you came to the Dark Walk at all?"

"I wasn't alone," she protested. "I came to the Dark Walk with Mr. Canning."

Lord Brooke made an inelegant sound. "That man milliner!"

"He's no such thing," she said in a cross voice, even though her own assessment of Mr. Canning was hardly more charitable.

His Lordship was not pleased by the change in Jane's mood, despite the several fluctuations he'd experienced in his. He'd liked it very much when she'd been pliant.

He gave her a cold look. "He must be effeminate, or worse. He even went away when you ordered him to. A real man wouldn't have done that."

"He acceded to my wishes because he is a gentleman," Jane snapped. "That's what a real man is."

Lord Brooke sneered. "Is that so? I beg to differ. A gentleman would have protected you. He certainly would not have permitted you to run about in the woods, where you could have come to harm."

Not for one minute would Jane have confessed that she had entertained doubts of her own as to her safety. "Pooh. I wasn't in danger. Besides, Mr. Canning couldn't have stopped me if he'd tried. In fact, he did try."

Lord Brooke's laugh was triumphant. "You prove my case."

Despicable man! She must have been suffering from a mental aberration, as well as a moral one, to have enjoyed his embrace. Abruptly, she turned on her heel and prepared to march off, alone.

"Just a minute," said his Lordship, laying restraining fingers on her arm. "You still haven't told me why you came here."

His hand felt hot on her skin, yet it sent shivery sensations up Jane's arm. Although she disliked him intensely at the moment, she longed for him to kiss her again. Without realizing what she did, she turned up her face. Her lips, stung into redness by Lord Brooke's lovemaking, shaped themselves into a lush, provocative pout.

For an instant, it seemed that his Lordship might accommodate her, but then he hesitated and backed off. Standing very straight, as though he were reviewing a company of soldiers, he said, "You haven't answered my question, Lady Jane. Why were you here with Mr. Canning? I mean, why were you in the woods?"

If she'd entertained any doubts about his feelings toward her, she didn't now. He didn't care for her. "I do not need to explain my behavior to you," she said sharply. "However, if it will cause you to stop questioning me, I'll willingly tell you that we came to fetch Susan."

His Lordship smiled unpleasantly. "I'm sure you mean that *you* did. I saw no evidence that Canning meant to look for her."

"You're correct for once," she admitted with reluctance. "Mr. Canning didn't mean to."

"So you went into the woods to rescue her yourself." Although the lines of his face softened, he said harshly, "That was foolhardy, and very typical of you. It's as I thought: You need a keeper, little one."

She . . . a keeper . . . a little one? She, who was five feet, ten inches, and competent to the bone—usually. Jane felt an unaccountable thrill beginning to override her other emotions. She quickly stifled it. The man had taken leave of his senses, she assured herself. Perhaps there was something to Vincent Fleer's assertion that the moon was affecting people's wits.

His Lordship was thinking about this same remark, but in relation to Fleer himself. Feeling certain that the attack on Fleer was not attributable to moon madness but to something more sinister, Lord Brooke knew that he must strive harder, if possible, to learn the truth about the gentleman. Although his mission was made urgent by its gravity, he couldn't deny that its importance also was enhanced by his sister's determination to continue her involvement with the man.

If he knew Susan, no order of his would stop her. In fact, it would likely drive her into Fleer's undeserving arms.

And her foolish friend, the captivating, unsettling, and

far too independent Lady Jane Ashworth, would defend her, no matter what the risks. Females! He was cursed with a superabundance of them, none of whom gave him any peace. He would welcome frequenting Mr. Fleer's haunts to learn more about that gentleman. At least there wouldn't be any women present. "Come," he said abruptly. "We will join the others."

Lord Brooke's first opportunity to carry out his new resolve concerning Vincent Fleer came two evenings later. He caught up with him, after having visited three other gaming hells in an attempt to find him, at a seedy club in Pickering Place. "I'm starting to think," said Fleer, barely taking his eyes from his cards when his Lordship greeted him, "that you shouldn't have saved my skin the other night."

Lord Brooke smiled, though the smile did not reach his eyes. "Dipped badly, are you? Then perhaps I shouldn't have. I'll tell you what—the next time I won't."

Mr. Fleer shuddered. "I pray there won't be a next time. There wouldn't have been a first if—" At his Lordship's heightened look of interest, he broke off, then said, "Ah, well, there are thugs everywhere."

"But not usually at Vauxhall," Lord Brooke said with an even cooler smile. "What do you think the fellow was after, Fleer?"

Vincent Fleer handed his cards to a man behind him and rose. "How the devil should I know?" he said, moving aside so that the man could take his place. "The only thing I've ever carried of value to me was my snuffbox, and that's gone, as you're well aware."

"What, lost your snuffbox?" inquired Lord Tutwill, an elderly gentleman decked out in an old-fashioned plum velvet coat and a bag wig. "Where did you lose it?"

"At a ball at the Sidwells' house, not that it need concern you," Mr. Fleer answered rudely.

Undeterred, Lord Tutwill said, "Did you put it down somewhere and walk off without it?" When Fleer nodded reluctantly, the other man chuckled and said, "If the usual crowd was there, I'll wager I know what happened to your snuffbox."

To the surprise of everyone following this conversation, Mr. Fleer's swarthy skin blanched, as though Lord Tutwill's words hid a shocking message. Perspiration broke out on his forehead. "Don't be absurd! How could you know?"

"Eh," said Lord Tutwill, touching his wig, "I didn't mean to distress you. There's nothing about which to get overwrought." With a bow, he rose from his chair and began to walk off.

Mr. Fleer's arm shot out. He grabbed the old man by his sleeve. "Just a minute. I want to hear what you were going to say."

"Let go of him," Lord Brooke ordered. "You forget yourself, Fleer."

For a few seconds, Vincent Fleer's face wore an ugly expression, but then he said mildly, "You're right, of course. Lord Tutwill, I apologize. And now, if you'd be so kind, won't you explain what you meant about knowing what happened to my snuffbox?"

"I'd be glad to. What I meant is that everyone—well, practically everyone—knows that if something disappears during the course of an evening's entertainment, it must have been taken by our local light-fingered ladyship."

Good God! Lord Brooke thought. He *was* going to mention Jane's name. He surged so forcefully toward the older man that the gentleman skidded backward in order to evade him. "There's no reason to bandy a lady's name about," he said in a commanding voice.

"You're too nice," said another man, coming forward. "Practically everyone in the *ton* knows about Lady Lettice, so there isn't any reason to conceal her name."

Both Lord Brooke and Mr. Fleer looked as though they'd been turned to stone by his words. His Lordship recovered first. "Who did you say?" he exclaimed, his voice cracking. "You don't mean it!"

"It does come as a shock if you don't know about her, doesn't it?" the man said genially. "She's a wonderful, batty old thing. Everyone likes her. That's why no one minds when she helps herself to some little trinket or other. Then, of course, she always gives it back when asked, so no one ever gets in a dither over it. I'll wager she's taken at least four or five ornaments from our house at one time or another. She always returns them when my wife comes for them.''

Several other men told stories about Lady Lettice's thefts after that, some quite amusing, but Marcus barely heard their accounts. Jane Ashworth wasn't a thief after all! He felt such a surge of relief, and pleasure, that it almost swamped the outrage that filled him. Almost.

He was such a damn fool. He'd been gulled and beguiled and lied to. Lady Jane had made a May game of him and not just at the draper's, although that had been the worst. It did no good to tell himself that he hadn't believed her protestations of innocence. Nor did it help to realize that she could hardly have blurted out that it was her aunt, not she, who was the guilty party. Nothing he said to himself to excuse either her actions or his own gullibility helped. He'd been an idiot. The thought did not especially endear Lady Jane to him at the moment.

He was halfway out the door before he remembered his interest in Vincent Fleer. Fleer was still standing as though frozen. Marcus did not like the man's reaction; it did not seem normal.

Indeed, his Lordship did not care for anything about the evening. With a murderous scowl on his face, he left the building, pausing only to tear his hat out of the innocent porter's fingers.

The next morning found him in no better frame of mind. He still could not forgive Jane for deceiving him. Didn't she know she could trust him? he thought, getting, at last, to the heart of his feeling of ill-usage. The answer, it seemed obvious, was *no*.

Thus, when he finally called upon Jane, he was not in the best of humors.

It did not help his mood that Lady Lettice's town house

A LARCENOUS AFFAIR

appeared to be full of red-skinned Indians, some lying on sofas, others propped up in chairs, one, even, stretched out on the Aubusson carpet. "What is this," Marcus snapped, "a rehearsal for a circus act?"

Whatever it was, it did not seem to trouble Jane, who looked lovely and regal in a day dress of cream-colored muslin trimmed in shiny blue ribbon that matched her eyes. How dare she seem so tranquil, and look so beautiful, among all this chaos, he thought, not to mention the chaos she'd created in his mind. He narrowed his eyes and glared at her, noticing as he did so that she was perhaps not quite as serene as he'd first thought.

Indeed, her pale hair was losing its pins in two places, and closer examination revealed a harried look in her fine eyes.

"Don't you care for circus acts?" he asked, putting a rein on his temper. "Then you should restrain your aunt. This is her doing, isn't it?"

Jane sighed. "It is and, then again, it isn't."

One of his Lordship's straight brows elevated. "What is that supposed to mean?"

"It means that after my aunt's handkerchief was stolen, she took to her bed. She's *still* in her bed."

"I'm sorry to hear that," said his Lordship, not sounding the least bit sorry. "But I do not see what her collapse has to do with these . . . these . . ."

"People?" Jane interrupted.

"Yes, these people. In what way are they responsible for keeping your aunt in her bed?"

Jane looked surprised. "Did I say that? Of course they aren't responsible. What I meant is that she was the one who invited them to the dinner party we held last night. Because she has continued to be out-of-sorts, she asked me to be in charge of it."

Lord Brooke tilted his handsome head to one side as though that angle made thinking easier. "Yes," he said. "I can understand all of that. And, knowing you, I am sure that you made a splendid job of it."

Jane looked at him doubtfully, searching for some hidden irony or sarcasm in his words. "Unfortunately," she said in accents of melancholy, "I didn't do a splendid job. When Aunt said she'd invited Indians, I assumed she meant East Indians. That's why I ordered Cook to make all those vegetable curries filled with hot peppers and all manner of unusual spices."

His Lordship's thin nostrils flared. "Now that you mention it, I do detect a hint of exotic spices hereabout: ginger, I think; yes, definitely ginger. And there's another one that's distinctive—cumin or coriander or one of those things that East Indians use in their cooking."

Jane flushed. "You must have an acute sense of smell! We've had the windows open all night, and today, too."

"Really? I don't see why. The aroma is actually rather pleasant."

The flush receded. It was replaced by a definite look of irritation. "It's not my doing. These people can't bear to be anywhere very long that doesn't have open windows and quantities of air coming in. The servants all swear they'll catch their deaths, but what can I do?"

His Lordship cast another look at the sprawling American natives before returning his attention to Jane. "Ask them to leave. I do not see why they needed to come back today anyway. Surely, last night was enough."

"But that's just it," Jane cried. "They didn't come back. They never went away."

Lord Brooke looked startled. "Are you saying that Lady Lettice invited this lot to be her houseguests? That's a bit much, even for her, I should think."

"Oh, no," Jane said quickly. "That was my fault, too, because of my mistake about where they came from." She wrung her hands in an uncharacteristically helpless gesture. "I never thought that the food would make them unwell, because they seemed to like it so much and ate every last bit, but, apparently, it didn't agree with them.

"And now they won't leave. They say that they must stay here until they are strong again. It's not that I mind caring for them," she added, "but I don't know where I'm going to get some of the ingredients they say they must have for their medicines. You don't happen to know where I might obtain erect knotweed, do you?"

Lord Brooke laughed despite his ill-humor. "I do not even know what it is."

"Nor do I," said Jane gloomily. "However, I have several of the footmen out looking for it. Surely, with all of the exotic specimens to be found in orangeries nowadays, someone must have it."

"I'm convinced you'll find it, if anyone can."

Again Jane looked closely at his Lordship to ascertain if he were being sincere. It certainly seemed as though he were. She felt a bubbling excitement. Could it be that he had come to accept her, and even admire her a little, at last?

His next words robbed her of that thought. "I seem to have strayed from my purpose in being here, which has nothing to do with Indians. Could you leave this tribe for awhile and adjourn with me to some place more private?"

At her look of surprise, he said, "It is nothing illicit, Lady Jane, I assure you. You need not fear because you are unchaperoned."

Feeling disappointed as well as apprehensive—the memory of his lovemaking still sparked in her mind—Jane, nevertheless, did as she'd been bid and took Lord Brooke to the Blue Room, a small parlor decorated, not unexpectedly, in shades of blue.

As they walked, she cast surreptitious glances at his firm, tall figure, clothed with elegant simplicity in a double-breasted riding coat, tight-fitting breeches that clung to his rippling thigh muscles, and highly polished Hessians. He looked wonderful as usual, she thought, not that his appearance was germane at the moment. She wondered what he would have to say to her.

Once inside the Blue Room, he began to speak almost before they seated themselves. "I heard something last night that really surprised me, Lady Jane. I heard that your aunt is famous—or, rather, infamous—as a—" Here he paused, obviously embarrassed. Then he shrugged. "I heard that your aunt takes other people's possessions."

"Who said that?" Jane demanded indignantly.

"Does it matter? The point is, Lady Jane, that it's never been *you* who have helped yourself to Chinese figures and the like. It's been your aunt. If I read your character aright, your role in her larcenous affairs has been to cover up her misdeeds." Thinking how Jane had tried *literally* to cover up the evidence of her Ladyship's theft of his handkerchief, Lord Brooke could not help but smile.

"I do not see what is so humorous," she said peevishly, thinking about all the trouble she'd been put to in attempting to make right her aunt's wrongs, not to mention the censure she'd incurred from his Lordship because of them. It seemed less than fitting to her that he talked about her Ladyship's lapses from grace with a smile, as though they did not matter very much.

In fact, Jane had another reason for her prickly response, but it was one she did not care to think about if she could avoid it. The truth was that she felt vastly unsure of their relationship now. They'd been adversaries for so long, she could not imagine what it would be like if they weren't. If his Lordship need not concern himself about her morals, perhaps he would not concern himself about her at all.

His next words answered that fear. "I think you ought to marry me," he said.

"What?" Jane looked shocked, almost as shocked as Lord Brooke, who had no idea until he uttered the words that he meant to say them. Recovering quickly, she said softly, "Why should I do that, my lord?"

As she spoke, she gazed up at him, her blue eyes luminous, waiting for him to say that he'd discovered that he loved her.

"Because you need to be rescued from this lunatic asylum, that is why," he said stiffly. "Since your father isn't here to save you, it appears that I'll have to be the one to do it."

Jane told herself that some men found it hard to reveal their feelings. She'd try again. "I still don't see why you feel responsible for me. Why is it up to you to 'save' me?"

"I can't answer that," he said, digging his heels into the carpet as though to brace himself against the winds of ill-fortune. "Oh, well, for my sister's sake, I suppose. You are her dearest friend."

Jane stared at her hands, which were twisted into a knot, then carefully raised her head. "But I am not yours, Lord Brooke. Therefore, thank you, but no thank you."

His Lordship looked as though Jane had struck him sharply between the eyes. "What? Do you mean that you are denying my suit? You can't do that."

"Oh, can't I?" She stood up and glowered at him. "Why can't I?"

Lord Brooke rose as well. "Because you can't, that's all. You—you need me."

Jane laughed. It was a sound devoid of humor. "In case you haven't noticed, Lord Brooke, I *don't* need you. I am perfectly capable of managing my own life."

"Oh, certainly. Anyone can see that. You've cast your lot with a woman who steals, a woman who collects monkeys, ballroom skaters, and Indians around her, not to mention females who are no better than they should be—and you tell me that you can manage your life. Hah!"

"You forgot to mention that I let men to whom I'm not betrothed kiss me in the moonlight. You mustn't omit that evidence of my foolishness and incompetence."

"That was different," he said tensely.

"Why, no, it wasn't so different."

His Lordship took a quick step toward her, and Jane hastily stepped back. "In any event, I don't require your assistance, my lord. So . . . so why don't you go home and . . . and look after your mother? Nothing is called for from you here."

She looked fully into his eyes now, wondering what his reaction to her words would be. Underneath the anger, he looked pained, she thought, as though she had slapped him.

Well, she was pained, too. *Marry her because she needed saving, indeed!*

At least she'd shown him what she thought of that notion—which made it excessively odd that she felt so blue-deviled. "Was that all you wanted to say? If so, I'll bid you farewell and get back to my guests."

"Yes, do so," his Lordship said brusquely. "No, wait. First, you must take care of something for me. I need to see Vincent Fleer's snuffbox. I assume Lady Lettice did take it?"

Jane nodded reluctantly.

His Lordship continued, "You must give it to me. I have reason to believe that it may contain something of importance."

"A snuffbox?" She gave him a disbelieving look.

Lord Brooke put his hand around her wrist and said in his best aide-de-camp voice, "Do not question or argue with me, Jane. I must have that snuffbox."

She'd been absolutely right to refuse his suit, she thought without pleasure. Lord Brooke was a dictator, just like her father. "I don't know where it is," she informed him with a touch of spite. "I'll need to ask my aunt where she puts her . . . her . . . the things she means to give back to her friends. But I can't do it now; she's still too distressed. You'll need to come back tomorrow."

His Lordship hesitated. "For her sake, I will wait until tomorrow. However, you must promise me that if Fleer comes for his snuffbox, which I feel certain he will, you'll tell him the same thing and put him off. Remember, it's possible that the contents of that box may be very important. Trust me."

Jane gave him such a despairing look at these final words that if he hadn't felt so discouraged about their whole relationship, he might have pulled her into his arms and kissed her, kissed her into submission, kissed her until she said yes to his suit. As it was, he was only too glad to leave her.

"Send those Indians away," he told her before accepting his hat and cane from the butler. "If they're still here tomorrow, I'll do it for you." With a chilly bow, he took his leave.

Jane stared after his departing Lordship. Why had she developed tender feelings for a man who was used to giving orders? Someone, moreover, who didn't have any sensibilities. Why couldn't she have felt affection for a man like Mr. Canning?

CHAPTER 9

IN the middle of the night, Jane came awake with a jolt. "Is something wrong?" she cried, hearing strange whoops and the sounds of bodies in motion. She descended the stairs and entered the Yellow Room, holding a branch of candles before her. A gust of air from the open windows put them out. "Oh, dear. Is everyone all right?" she called into the darkness.

No one answered. "What is happening?" she called more sharply to the several dark shapes she sensed more than saw there. Cautiously, she advanced farther into the room.

Again, there was no reply, but someone, or something, jostled her arm. Jane jerked away.

Feeling the wall, she located the door once more. She quickly walked through the opening, and left. She returned a few minutes later, however, still holding the branch of candles, now relit. Shielding it from the drafts with her free hand, she looked about the room.

The scene that met her eyes was mesmerizing, involving as it did the sight of four of their Indian guests, dignified despite being nearly mother naked, strolling about the very large, formal Yellow Room. But even they could not compare to the vision of the tall, copper-colored individual from whose bare shoulders descended a glorious red satin quilt. He looked like a king. For all she knew, he *was* a king.

"Is something amiss?" she asked in an unusually timid voice.

The man she thought of as the king smiled at her. "We thank you for sending good medicine. Now we are strong again and can leave this house in the morning."

"I do not understand," Jane said. "I did not send you any medicine. Even if I'd had some, I wouldn't have had it brought to you in the middle of the night."

The king raised his hand. "I say you cause of our healing. A good battle, even not so very good, makes us all better."

Jane was aghast. "I assure you, I had nothing to do with a battle—if there was one, though I don't see how there could have been. Was there one?"

The king smiled sagely. "Just one little, so not so good. When the man come in the window, we let him. What is one man? But when the others come in, we think it not safe for the house. Is this mistake? Your aunt not invite them to visit her that way, is that so?"

Even Lady Lettice was not as bizarre as that. "No, I am certain she did not. I fear they were breaking in, or climbing in, uninvited. You did say they entered by the open windows, didn't you?"

One of the other "braves"—Jane supposed that was the right term—nodded. "They are war party, I think," he said. "They dress in black, and their faces are black. We do same thing when we not want enemy to see us." He looked around. "This is important room. They must want take some things from it."

Well, what other explanation could there be? Jane dismissed a nagging feeling that the illicit entry was connected with Mr. Fleer and his snuffbox. The idea was ridiculous, of course. If Fleer wanted his snuffbox, all he need do was come to the house and ask for it. Surely, whoever informed him and Lord Brooke that Lady Lettice filched things must also have explained that she returned them upon request.

In any case, she had to get the blasted snuffbox from her aunt and give it to its owner, after first letting Marcus Brooke examine it, naturally. She'd do that much for him.

"What happened to the interlopers?" she asked sternly. "I hope you showed them that entering people's homes uninvited is not at all the thing."

All of the Indians, the ones still strolling about the room and the ones who had returned to the floor, began to laugh. Raising his hand again, their spokesman said with a grin, "Finding us in room make them very, very . . . um . . . how you say?" He stopped speaking to let his mouth fall open as might a person deeply shocked. "Like that," he said. "When we throw them from window, I think they happy to leave."

Even though Jane did not usually find burglary amusing, she could not help but join in their laughter.

After the mirth died down, the Indians resettled themselves for the night, or what was left of it, and Jane returned to her bed. This time, she did not rest quite as soundly, her dreams being a mix of warriors, burglars, and Marcus Brooke, whose handsome image presented itself to her in elusive, frustrating snatches.

A few hours later it was morning, and she went to bid farewell to her guests. They were already gone, however. Indeed, all traces of them had been removed from the Yellow Room.

Jane ensconced herself there. It was as good a place as any other to await the arrival of Mr. Fleer or Lord Brooke, or both.

It was Vincent Fleer whom Miles ushered in.

Repressing a feeling of disappointment, Jane watched him pause in the doorway to look carefully around, his olive-skinned face cautious, even, perhaps, a touch apprehensive. Then he walked toward her. She noted that he appeared very neat in a double-breasted riding coat and light-colored breeches. In his hand he carried a thick rid-

A LARCENOUS AFFAIR 127

ing crop. She could not imagine why he had brought it into the house or failed to relinquish it to Miles.

When he reached her, he struck one of his top boots with the crop before saying, "Isn't your aunt here? It was she I asked to speak with."

"How do you do?" Jane replied. "My aunt is indisposed. May I substitute for her instead?"

Vincent Fleer's brows were black slashes against his olive skin. He arched one of them and gave her an appraising look. "I don't know. That remains to be seen. But tell me, is there anyone else here, any other visitors to your charming home, I mean?"

As soon as he asked, Jane was convinced that he was inquiring about the Indians rather than Susan or some of their other mutual acquaintances. Despite his seeming insouciance, something about him suggested he was not at ease. He wouldn't have been like that if he expected to see other members of the *ton*. In fact, Jane wondered if he'd brought the crop into the room as a ready, if meager, defense against the men.

Yet, he shouldn't have even known of their existence. Between Lord Brooke's insistence that he see Fleer's snuffbox first and Mr. Fleer's strange behavior, she felt convinced that something unsavory must be going on. She'd need to be very careful about what she said.

"No other visitors are here at present," she told him. "However, I am expecting Lord Brooke at any moment."

"In that case," Vincent Fleer said rapidly, "I beg you to allow me to see your aunt at once. I have something particular to ask her."

"I'm afraid that's not possible." Jane gave a decisive tug to the sash of her green muslin dress as though to underline her denial. "Why don't you ask me instead?"

"Very well, I will. I have reason to believe that my missing snuffbox is here."

"Here, in this house?" Pretending surprise, Jane widened her eyes. "But how could that be? I thought you misplaced it at the Sidwells' ball."

"No, I don't think so. I mean, I don't think I misplaced

it. Why don't you ask your aunt if she knows where my box is?"

Jane had a mental image of Lady Lettice sitting with her turban off, Mr. Fleer's blue and white snuffbox set like some strange little bird among her gray curls. "I can't imagine why you'd want me to ask her," she said mendaciously, "but, in any case, she isn't nearby. Indeed, she is still in her room. She has been feeling poorly lately."

"Is that so?" Vincent Fleer sounded less than sympathetic. "Then, perhaps you can help me. May I?" He seated himself near her and leaned forward so that Jane caught the smell of the heavy, cloying scent he habitually wore. She did not like it. She did not like him, although he was good-looking enough to appeal to most women, she imagined.

No, her taste ran, unfortunately, to very tall men with strong, masculine features and an air of command tempered by . . . "What did you say?" she asked, flushing.

Despite the slight smile on his lips, Mr. Fleer's brown eyes were hard and assessing. "I said, I was told by a reputable source that your aunt likes to borrow things from her friends, things like my snuffbox. Not a jot of harm in it, naturally, but, still, one would like to have one's property returned."

Jane rose, forcing him to do the same. She said coldly, "I'm convinced this is nonsense. However, since you request it, I shall ask my aunt what, if anything, she knows of your snuffbox. Blue and white, wasn't it? Then I shall advise you of her answer, although I already know what it must be."

"When?"

"When shall I advise you? I don't know. Tomorrow, I suppose. Or the next day." Surely, within two days Lord Brooke should have finished examining the snuffbox, she thought.

Vincent Fleer moved a little closer. His face no longer bore even a pretense of a smile. "I'll expect to hear about my property no later than this afternoon. In fact, I'll come back myself then to find out what you've learned. Please don't disappoint me."

He was threatening her. For a moment, she was taken aback. Then she thought about her father. She never allowed him to intimidate her, and she wouldn't allow this jackanapes to do so, either.

Besides, she had given Lord Brooke her word that she would put Mr. Fleer off. It would have taken a far more terrifying person than Vincent Fleer to make her break a promise, even to his Lordship.

A combative smile touched the corners of her lips. Lord Brooke would learn, if he didn't yet realize it, that she could, indeed, be relied upon to manage any situation—without his help, thank you!

The smile vanished. "Surely, you don't suppose that I would want my aunt to keep your property, do you?" she asked frostily.

"No, no. I'm not accusing *you* of anything. I'm not accusing anyone. It's just that I can't help but be concerned. The box had been my maternal grandfather's, you know; it is very dear to me."

Jane looked at him inquiringly. "Really? I was sure you'd said it had been your father's."

"First, my grandfather's, then my father's. What is the difference?" He raised his crop. "I have a right to my property."

"Don't we all?" said Lord Brooke, entering the room from a nearby side door and walking over to stand beside the shorter man. His Lordship put one of his big hands on Mr. Fleer's arm. "What's this, Fleer? A crop in a drawing room? That's nearly as bad as bringing in your horse." He pretended to look about. "You didn't bring in your horse, did you?"

Jane did not hear Vincent Fleer's reply. She was too intent upon studying Marcus Brooke, her blue eyes unconsciously admiring. Like Fleer, his Lordship was dressed in riding clothes. There, in her estimation, the similarities ended. Lord Brooke not only was taller and sturdier of frame than Mr. Fleer. He seemed more manly, too. Oh, so much more. Having him there made her feel safe.

But she didn't want him to keep her safe. Instead, she wanted . . . She wasn't sure what she wanted. For a perilous few seconds, Jane felt like crying. Then she gulped and got herself under control.

"Mr. Fleer came to ask about his snuffbox," she said in what she hoped was a calm-sounding voice. "He seems to think that my aunt has it."

Lord Brooke gave her an unfriendly smile before saying, "Is that so? Why do you think she has it, Fleer?"

"Why shouldn't I think it? You heard what old Tutwill said, the same as I."

"But I wouldn't have gone off half-cocked to confront her Ladyship, or Lady Jane either, if I were in your shoes. I would have handled things differently."

"Who the devil cares!" Frustration and anger showing plainly now, Vincent Fleer started toward the door. Before he got very far, however, he whirled about toward Jane. "I hope you'll remember what I told you." Then he completed his exit.

Lord Brooke waved his hand at Jane to precede him to a sofa, then followed her. "What did he tell you?" he asked as they seated themselves. "It sounds to me as though he was threatening you."

She nodded. "He was, in a way. But that doesn't trouble me."

"It does me," his Lordship said. "I may have to do something about him."

"Do something? Why, what do you mean?"

Lord Brooke's voice was dispassionate, as though he were talking about the weather or the availability of fresh fish. "I mean, I may have to hurt him, or worse."

"Good heavens," Jane said, horrified, "don't do that. Don't do either of those."

Lord Brooke shrugged his shoulders. "Why not? He deserves it."

Jane gave him an exasperated look. "Isn't that just like

A LARCENOUS AFFAIR

a man, to think about harming someone just because his speech might be considered threatening!''

His Lordship began to look irritated. ''But I am a man. It seems perfectly natural to me to want to protect you, no matter what you seem to think.''

''Indeed?'' she asked softly. ''And why is that?''

Perhaps this time he would say something more loverlike than when he'd offered for her.

Lord Brooke had already been rebuffed once. He was not about to show a softer side of himself. One did not point out the weak spots in one's defenses to others. Every male, not just military men, knew that. ''Why?'' he repeated. ''Because one must always protect women—and children and the elderly, as well. That is a gentleman's responsibility.''

''How touching,'' Jane said dryly. ''Thank you for your concern.''

Lord Brooke scrutinized her. ''I seem to have offended you again. What is it that you want me to say?''

''I? Why, nothing! Indeed, I'm not offended. It's your imagination. That is, I don't care for violence, even to such a one as Vincent Fleer.''

''Ah, yes, Fleer. I'll need to see that snuffbox. Why don't you be a good girl and get it for me now?''

Despite her dislike of violence, Jane had a strong urge to hit Lord Brooke. Better yet, she'd show him how very little she needed him. Lump her with children and the elderly, would he! She would get the snuffbox, but she wouldn't give it to him until she'd winkled out its secret.

''It might take a little while,'' she said. ''I'll need to ask my aunt, then get the box from its hiding place—all that sort of thing.''

''I'll wait.'' He leaned back in his place, looking as solid and inflexible as a rock, and stretched his long, long legs before him. ''You'd better run along,'' he said coolly, ''or your nemesis will have returned by the time you bring it to me.''

If Jane did not run, she at least went quickly up the stairs to her aunt's room. It was dark. She went over to the windows and pulled back the mauve silk curtains. "Good morning," she said loudly to the thin, nightcapped figure lying listlessly in bed.

"Close those curtains, Jane," her aunt responded weakly. "I cannot bear the light."

Jane ignored the order. "I need to talk to you," she said. "Certain things have happened."

Her Ladyship propped herself up on one bony elbow. "What sorts of things?"

"The house was broken into, for one," Jane said, then added with a reassuring smile, "but nothing was taken and no harm was done."

If she expected this news to galvanize Lady Lettice into a show of her old spirit, she was only partially correct. "I knew it!" her Ladyship cried, sitting upright. Then she slumped against her embroidered bed pillows. "First it was my handkerchief. Now it's my home. Someone is attempting to do ill to me. Where's my valerian?"

"Aunt, it's no such thing." Jane's voice was carefully calm. "Many people's houses are broken into."

Her Ladyship responded with a disbelieving snort.

"Well, perhaps not so many people's are," Jane modified her statement. "Nevertheless, it does happen. Don't you remember when thieves broke into the Duchess of Mercer's house and stole all the plate?"

"Oh, her."

Jane's chuckle caused Lady Lettice to scowl. "I do not find this humorous. Someone hates me, and if not, the reason is insanity brought on by a peculiar juxtaposition of the heavenly bodies."

"That there's a certain amount of insanity about, I don't doubt," Jane agreed, thinking more of being kissed in the moonlight by Marcus Brooke and unexpectedly proposed to than of sick Indians, robberies, and threats, though she thought of them, too. "In any case, nothing was taken, our house guests have departed, and the servants have put things to rights. Everything will be peaceful from now on, I promise you."

This optimistic remark elicited only a groan.

"Why don't you get out of bed and join me in the Yellow Room? It would do you ever so much good to be up and about. Besides, Lord Brooke is there."

Lady Lettice clutched the ivory wrapper about her skinny shoulders as though it was all that protected her from a ravening world. "He is? Oh, no, I couldn't, not yet. Maybe tomorrow . . . or the next day."

Jane looked worried. "I'll say no more about today, Aunt, but tomorrow I think you really must get up. It isn't good to keep to your bed like this." She started to walk toward the door, then recalled her purpose in being there. "There is one thing. I need to know where you keep the trinkets people haven't yet asked you to return."

Lady Lettice sat bolt upright again, this time with all evidence of malaise gone. "And why do you need to know that, missy? I haven't taken anything of yours."

"Oh, Aunt, I'm aware of that. It's not for me; it's for Mr. Fleer. He came for his snuffbox, and means to come back for it again very shortly." No use telling her about Lord Brooke's part in this, she thought.

Lady Lettice did not appear to think there was anything odd about Mr. Fleer suddenly appearing to ask for the return of his property. "Tell him to come again next week," she said decisively. "I'll get it for him then."

Jane ran a hand distractedly through her blonde hair and said, "Please, Aunt, I don't have a great deal of time. I told you that Lord Brooke is waiting for me."

"And what does your beloved have to do with this?"

Jane sighed. Lord Brooke was not her beloved. At least, she knew she was not his, which was far more important, and very depressing. "Indeed, he isn't, and you haven't answered my question. I need to get that snuffbox."

"Oh, very well. It's in the cupboard, in the pink silk hatbox under my bible."

"Under your bible?" Jane was scandalized. "How can you keep it there?"

"What a strange thing to ask," said Lady Lettice. "Why shouldn't it be there?"

What was the use? Jane would never understand her

aunt. "I cannot imagine," she said, then retrieved the blue and white snuffbox and took it to her room.

Once there, she quickly opened the box. To her disappointment, it contained nothing more than snuff, a very ordinary type, at that, if she wasn't mistaken. Jane carefully emptied it out onto a paper, then began pressing and pushing at the receptacle in an attempt to discover its secrets. She was unable to find any.

She finally gave it up. If this box was a storage place for anything more interesting than second-rate snuff, it would surprise her, she thought. Hurriedly, she poured the contents back into the box and brought it down to Lord Brooke.

"What took you so long?" he demanded. "By my reckoning, you've been away a quarter of an hour at least."

Why was she so interested in this rude man? If she had any sense, she wouldn't think about him at all.

It appeared, however, that she didn't have any sense. "I was trying to find the secret to the snuffbox," she explained. "There isn't one."

"I thought you smelled of snuff," his Lordship replied, taking the box from her. "I prefer the scent of that lime-and-honey perfume you sometimes wear."

She was wearing it now. Jane found herself moving a little closer to give him the benefit of whatever of its aroma still lingered on her skin. "What are you going to do with that snuffbox?" she asked. "I've already tried everything possible on it."

"Just a minute," his Lordship said, his big fingers working with surprising deftness at the fastening of the box. "There. I thought there might be a secret place."

Jane's chagrin lasted only a second or two. She stared in fascination at the narrow space revealed underneath the snuff compartment. "Is there anything inside?" she asked avidly.

Lord Brooke gave the box a shake and a piece of paper fell out.

"What is it?" In her eagerness, she crowded so close that her full bosom pressed against his arm.

A LARCENOUS AFFAIR 135

His Lordship caught his breath, then moved away. "Not now," he muttered.

"What did you say?" she asked. When he shook his head, she said, "Quickly, let me see the paper."

Instead of sharing it with her, Lord Brooke scooped it up and read it, then put it in his pocket. "I can't do that," he said gruffly.

Jane's face took on a look her father would have recognized without any difficulty. "But, of course you can. I have every right to see it."

His Lordship's tense expression softened into a grin. "Is that so, you termagant? I don't think that at all."

"But I do. This is my house, isn't it?"

"No, it's your aunt's."

"Yes, and it was she who stole the snuffbox," she retorted triumphantly, before lapsing into blushes at what she'd said.

His Lordship cocked an eyebrow at her. "My dear Jane, you don't want to know what this contains. It isn't very nice."

"Yes, I do. Don't you trust me?"

Marcus put his two big hands either side her face and tilted it toward his. By the look in his eyes, he was no longer angry with her. "More than any other female in England," he murmured against her mouth, and kissed her.

"Umm," Jane said dreamily. This is the way it should be. Putting her cheek against his, she whispered, "May I see the paper now?"

"You jade!" His Lordship didn't seem to know whether to laugh or berate her. His white teeth flashed in a grin. Then he enunciated very slowly, "No, you cannot."

"But why not?"

There was no hint of passion or indulgence about Marcus Brooke now. "Because, although this paper is in some sort of code, I think it will prove that Vincent Fleer is spying for the French."

Jane was shocked. Although she'd never liked Mr. Fleer, she'd thought no worse of him than that he was too coming. Now here was Marcus Brooke saying that Fleer was likely a traitor. "I'm sorry to hear that. I never thought this business would be so serious."

At his grim nod, she added, "I could help you entrap him, you know. I'm sure I could think of some way to do it."

Lord Brooke's long fingers went securely about her arm. "Thank you, but no. Attempting anything like that would be far too dangerous. Therefore—although I know you resent my desire to take care of you—I advise you to stay in the house and see to your aunt's numerous, peculiar guests."

It was lovely to have him touch her, especially when his hand relaxed and slid along her skin; but it wasn't pleasing at all to be told, even obliquely, to tend to one's embroidery and leave the business of solving things to a man. Jane's generous mouth tucked in until it formed a narrow, stubborn line.

"On second thought, I think you should leave London this afternoon," said his Lordship, observing her expression. "That doesn't give you much time, but I'm sure you could get ready if you tried."

"What, leave my aunt? I wouldn't do any such thing."

"Of course not. You must take her with you, and my sister, too. Fleer is an unscrupulous man, Jane. You don't seem to realize it, but it's possible that you're in danger, you and your aunt both."

"And Susan?"

His Lordship laughed. "Probably not. But any time I can get her away from London to the comparative anonymity of the countryside, I'll do it."

"I don't think the countryside provides anonymity at all," Jane said doubtfully, then added, "But what does it matter? I have no intention of going."

Lord Brooke gave her an annoyed look. "You should listen to me, you know. All right, then; at the least, deny yourself to Vincent Fleer when he returns. I don't want him in this house with you. As insurance, I'll take the snuffbox." He scooped it up and placed it in his pocket.

"If you think it best," Jane said meekly.

His Lordship stared at her suspiciously, but since she didn't offer any other arguments, he took his leave.

Jane spent the rest of the daylight hours awaiting Mr. Fleer, with whom she had every intention of speaking, despite Lord Brooke's admonition and the fact that she no longer had the snuffbox. While she waited, she entertained herself with several brilliant schemes by which she might trap Vincent Fleer into incriminating himself as well as the person or persons for whom the snuffbox message was meant. She was certain that it must have been someone at the Sidwells' ball, someone who would have taken the message and replaced the box, perhaps with another set of instructions in it, if her aunt had not stolen it first.

She wished she could convince Marcus of what she'd deduced. Surely, then, he would be quite impressed with her. He might even kiss her again, or even ask once more for her hand.

Not that she'd accept him, she told herself hastily. He wasn't at all the sort of mate of whom she dreamed. Her ideal husband was gentle, kind, and agreeable. He wasn't a former military man who expected unthinking obedience from the females in his family—but never got it.

Jane started to laugh. Maybe there was hope for them yet. Meanwhile, she would have to be patient.

Patience, it turned out, was what she needed, for Mr. Fleer did not return, not that afternoon nor during the evening, either. Finally, Jane gave up her vigil and went to bed.

She awakened some time during the middle of the night. "Not again," she groaned, hearing a noise from the floor below where all should have been quiet. On this occasion, however, there were no guests in the house.

Suddenly, her door flew open, nearly causing her to have a heart spasm. "Who is it?" she asked, trying to sound brave.

"It's I, Jane, your aunt," a wavering voice responded. "I think the burglars are back. I heard them. At least, I heard something I shouldn't have. I came to get in bed with you."

Jane lit the globed candle that was on her nightstand and held it up. "In bed?" she said to her white-faced relative. "Surely, you don't expect me to stay here. I must go downstairs and see what is happening."

"No, no, don't do it. You'll be killed, or ravished, and then what shall I tell your father? You know what a fuss he'll make."

Jane was in no mood to discuss her absent parent. "It will be all right," she said soothingly.

Lady Lettice's skinny fingers clutched at Jane's arm. "But, it won't. If I lose you, after having lost my darling Harry, I'll have to put twice as many of my friends' possessions into my reticule. I know you wouldn't want to be the cause of that."

Despite the possible gravity of the situation, Jane had to smile. Taking both of her aunt's hands into her free one, she said, "You have nothing to fret yourself about, dear Aunt Lettice. All I mean to do is to sneak downstairs and see who has broken into our home."

Ignoring her aunt's moans, which were steadily escalating, she thought about what she'd just said. Despite being tall and knowing herself to be able, even she could see that just walking into a group of thieves was not the best idea. Lord Brooke certainly wouldn't have approved. "I expect I should take a gun with me," she said. "Do we have one?"

Lady Lettice stopped moaning. "There's that little pearl-handled one I got from the Durnings' house. They never did come by and ask for it. Do you think that would do?"

"I don't know. Is it loaded?"

"Yes, yes, it is. I especially remember that."

"Then that's the one I'll use. Is it also in the hatbox under your bible?" Lady Lettice nodded. "Then I suppose I'd best go fetch it."

"I'll get it," said her Ladyship, surprising Jane. Off she went and came gliding back a short while later, holding the small pistol. She had another surprise for Jane after that. "I'll accompany you downstairs," she said. "I cannot let you go alone." By way of explanation, she added, "Your father, you know."

Jane tried to dissuade her, but Lady Lettice would not hear of it. Unable to do anything else, Jane straightened her aunt's crazily skewed nightcap and let her join the expedition.

Softly, the two women made their way down the freestanding staircase to the floor below. Jane, holding the light in one hand and the pistol in the other, led the way. In lieu of a weapon, her Ladyship produced a small, carved animal horn with a sharp point. "It came from the Roswells' country house," she explained in a whisper. "They never stopped by for it, either. I think Mrs. Roswell was happy to see it go."

"You'd better stay well behind me," Jane whispered back. "I don't think that's much of a weapon."

"I disagree. It would be perfect for sticking in a burglar's eye."

Goodness gracious, thought Jane, she was surrounded by bloodthirsty people. At least, if Lord Brooke had been there, she would have been surrounded. At that moment, she wished she were.

"In here, in the Yellow Room," she whispered into her aunt's ear. "I think that's where the noise came from."

She shielded her candle with the hand holding the gun, then slid into the room. Lady Lettice was close upon her heels. Almost at once, Jane felt a draft. It was good that she hadn't left the candle exposed. Even being globed, it might have gone out, just as it had done the night before.

"I think we should leave." Lady Lettice stood on tiptoe to whisper this sage advice in the direction of her niece's ear. "I'm not dressed properly for the temperature in this room. Besides, I haven't seen anyone."

Still, someone was there, or had been. Otherwise, the sash wouldn't have been raised.

CHAPTER 10

"IS anyone here?" Jane called sharply.

No one answered.

"They must have left," her aunt said, relieved. "Let us do so, too. What I mean is, let us return to our beds. We can examine the room in the morning."

"Why don't I close the window first?" Jane suggested, temporarily putting the gun in the pocket of her robe. "You can hold the candle. Then I think we might walk about a bit to see if we notice anything out of place. If nothing else, that should make you warmer."

Lady Lettice sighed. "Are you certain that you want us to do those things?" At Jane's affirmative reply, her Ladyship sighed more deeply, then said in a resigned voice, "Very well. Let's get on with it."

Since the Yellow Room was well supplied with sofas, chairs, chests, and all manner of other furnishings, Jane had a great many places to peer around or under or into after she closed the window. Lady Lettice trotted loyally, if unwillingly, beside her, lighting the way.

Thus far, they had seen nothing to suggest that an intruder had been there. If it had not been for the open window and the fact that both she and her aunt had heard the strange noise, Jane would have thought that she'd been imagining things.

Then she saw the broken vase lying on the floor. Here was something that could not be dismissed as a figment of the imagination. She directed her aunt's attention to it. "That's probably what caused the noise we heard," she whispered.

"I don't think so," her Ladyship whispered back. "I've been going over it in my mind, and I believe what we heard was the sound of the window being opened."

Vase or window—what was the difference? What mattered was discovering their thief. If they did, they could tie him up—that is, after they found some rope. Then, if he was Mr. Fleer or one of his henchmen, Jane could turn him over to Marcus Brooke in triumph. The thought of how humbly grateful his Lordship would be was very satisfying. Jane took the gun from her pocket and rubbed it with affection.

Unfortunately, Lady Lettice did not have the same motivation. "That was my favorite vase," she complained, so far forgetting herself as to raise her voice. "It's a Portland vase. One doesn't find many of those about."

Jane tapped a finger to her lips in a bid for quiet. "Never mind the vase, Aunt. Let us find the person who broke it."

"I don't think he's here," said Lady Lettice. "He's either in another room or already out the window and gone. Wake the servants to look for him, if you must, and let us leave this place."

No sooner had she finished saying this then there was the sound of a sneeze from behind a yellow bergere chair to the right of them. "Oh, my goodness," said Lady Lettice, and dropped the light, which quickly extinguished itself.

The darkness startled Jane, so much so that she jumped back, squeezing her hands together as she did. This latter action made the gun go off. For such a small gun, it made a great deal of noise.

"Oh, my God," said a voice which Jane immediately recognized as belonging to Marcus Brooke. "Put that gun away, you fool."

"It's Lord Brooke," Jane said, starting to sob. "Your Lordship, never say I shot you."

"Be still," replied her dearest one. "I am going to light some candles."

What happened then took place so quickly that it was forever after a blur in Jane's mind. "No, you shan't," said a low, intense, male voice, and a chair went crashing over. It was followed by the discharge of a pistol which sounded far more deadly than the one Jane had fired.

"Your Lordship, are you hurt?" she cried. Throwing caution to the winds, she rushed toward the place from where she thought Lord Brooke's voice had emanated.

After take a few swift steps, she ran into someone. "You long-legged bitch," said an angry voice. "I'll make you sorry you ever interfered."

There was the sound of a fist hitting soft flesh. Then a body dropped to the floor.

"Jane?" Lady Lettice called. "Are you all right?"

Jane did not answer. By the dim light of the candles, which his Lordship had finally lit, her Ladyship found her way to where her niece lay on the floor. "You've hurt Jane," Lady Lettice screamed at Jane's masked assailant. "Prepare to die."

So saying, she raised the animal horn in the direction of the intruder's face. There was a loud yelp, then a series of crashes as the person ran to the window. He quickly raised the sash, jumped from the window, and disappeared.

As for Jane, she regained consciousness after awhile, only to wish she hadn't. She had a most dreadful headache, she discovered, and the light hurt her eyes. She shut them tightly. "Close the curtains, please," she whispered weakly. "I don't mean to get up for awhile."

"Oh, my dearest, you aren't in your bed," said a voice she recognized as belonging to her aunt. "You were most

A LARCENOUS AFFAIR

foully assaulted and are lying on the floor of the Yellow Room."

Jane wanted to shake her head in disagreement over this statement, but she was sure that the movement would hurt too much. No matter; she knew that her aunt was wrong. She was not lying on the floor, at least not all of her was. She was lying across a man's thighs, which, although ridged their whole length with muscle, felt warm and peculiarly comforting. "Am I all right?" she asked almost indifferently.

The owner of the male thighs said gravely, "Your aunt wasn't entirely certain for awhile that you would be, but I had no doubts. I would not permit you to slip away and leave us."

So she was resting on Lord Brooke. That was nice. But what was he talking about?

"Leave you?" she asked. "I don't mean to leave at all."

"We'll discuss that later," said his Lordship, sounding his usual, definite self once more. "Now, I'm going to have your aunt take a pillow from that sofa and put it under your head so that I can get up."

Jane opened her blue eyes a crack. Mostly what she saw was Lord Brooke's nose, thin, crooked, and imperious. "Must you?" she addressed it peevishly. "I'm perfectly fine as I am. I mean, I'm not certain that I should be moved even a little."

His Lordship smiled down at her. "A little won't hurt. Besides, as much as I've enjoyed holding you, I can't stay on the floor indefinitely. There are things that I must do."

"Can't you have the servants do them?"

Lord Brooke's smile faded. "I'd rather not have them involved in this matter, Jane. We don't want talk. The fewer people who know what's going on, the better. That is why I decided to guard your house myself tonight, just in case Fleer determined to pay an early call."

"An early call? Don't be absurd," Lady Lettice said peevishly. "Early doesn't mean in the middle of the night.

And what *is* going on, that is, besides insanity, attempted robbery, and assaults on innocent people in their homes?''

"That reminds me of something," Jane said as eagerly as the pain in her head would permit. "When I was thinking about the snuffbox before, it came to me that Mr. Fleer must have left it where he did because he expected another one of the guests to pick it up. Don't you agree?"

"What are you talking about?" Lady Lettice asked. "I picked it up. I don't know why he'd imagine anyone else would." She half-closed her eyes as she pondered the matter. "And why are we discussing Vincent Fleer anyway? You don't really think he had anything to do with what happened here tonight, do you?"

Neither Jane nor Lord Brooke answered. For her part, Jane was occupied in looking up at his Lordship again. She was awaiting his response to her brilliant insight. When it came, it was not nearly as enthusiastic as she'd hoped. "About your theory," he said, "it could be right. Or it could be that one of the Sidwells' servants was in Fleer's employ and was expected to collect the snuffbox and deliver it somewhere else. There are any number of possibilities, but, at the moment, I'm afraid that is all they are."

"Of course," said Jane, her disappointment palpable.

"However, your guess is a good one," he added kindly.

To Jane, whatever the intent, Lord Brooke's remark patronized her. He was treating her as a child, like one of the children he'd said it was his duty to defend. But she didn't want to be his child. She wanted to be his helpmeet and lover and all of those other things cherished women were to men. At least, sometimes she thought she might want to be, if she could manage to overlook his commanding ways and unromantic attitude.

Her voice took on a sharp edge. "And how did you get in here, may I ask? Did you come through the window along with the thief? Or did you come through the window, and he through the door?"

"I cannot speak for the thief," said his Lordship, "but I am not so undignified. I came in through the door."

"Really?" She raised her head a little but quickly put it down. "How could you have done that?"

"I had a bit of help," he said, taking hold of one of her hands and patting it.

"Well, I never . . ." Lady Lettice's narrow frame swelled visibly with indignation. "Who let you in? If you don't tell me, I'll discharge every one of the servants, I vow I will. Except Miles, of course."

His Lordship chuckled. "As a matter of fact, it *was* Miles. I enlisted his help."

"My butler? How dare he?"

"You mustn't blame him. I explained the seriousness of the situation to him, and he agreed to cooperate."

Her Ladyship shook her head. "That's more than you've done for me. What is the situation?"

Lord Brooke hesitated. Then he said, "I suppose I'll have to tell you—right after you get Jane that pillow I asked for." He waited patiently until she'd done so, then rose to his feet as her Ladyship adjusted the pillow under her niece's head.

"May I?" He seated himself and leaned forward so that Jane needn't look up too far. "The situation I mentioned has to do with Mr. Fleer's snuffbox. There was a message in it."

"And what is so wrong about that?" said the champion of the odd and unconventional. "A man has a right to leave a message in his own snuffbox if he chooses."

"Yes, Aunt, but it was the *sort* of message it was."

Her Ladyship cocked her head, making her look, in Jane's opinion, like a poorly fed bird. "What sort was that?" she asked.

Jane and his Lordship exchanged questioning glances. Then he said, "I'm not altogether sure yet, but I believe it was giving away some information that shouldn't have been given away."

"To the opposition, I suppose? Fleer's a Tory, isn't he? Or is he?" Without waiting for an answer, her Ladyship said, "I don't have the interest in politics that I used to have. All I can say is that I think it's foolish for grown men to go about making a fuss over snuffboxes, and criminal for someone to be hitting my poor Jane over the head. How is your head, dear?"

Jane's color was starting to come back nicely, and when she spoke her voice seemed much strengthened. "Better, Aunt. I really do believe I could get up if I had some help."

"Don't move," Lord Brooke ordered. "Not yet."

Jane's lips twitched. "Yes, sahib."

"I am only thinking of your welfare," said his Lordship, looking testy. "If you have a concussion, it would be very bad for you to get up precipitously. But, of course, if you resent my telling you what to do, then, by all means, do get up."

It was Jane's turn to flush. "I don't resent it—in this case."

His Lordship laughed. "Good, but I wish you hadn't put on that addendum—especially since I have one more order to give you."

"Oh? What is that?"

"I want you and Lady Lettice to stay at my estate outside Windsor for awhile. You'll be safe there, I think, safer than you would be here."

Instead of answering him immediately, Jane slowly raised herself from the floor until she sat upright. The movement made her dizzy and rather sick to her stomach, but she forced herself to ignore her physical symptoms. "You'd already suggested something of the sort yesterday, and I refused. Don't you remember?"

His Lordship nodded his head.

"Then why are you asking me again?"

He laughed. "I'm not asking you. This time I'm telling you. Jane, go to Brookefield."

"I don't believe we should do that," she said slowly and stubbornly. "We'd miss part of the season, people would talk, and . . . well, I just don't think it would serve."

"It has to serve. For one thing, I need time to work on

our problem without the distraction of worrying about you."

Jane gave him a fulminating look. "But you don't need to worry about me. I can take care of myself."

Lord Brooke leaned closer to her and stroked her silky cheek with the pad of his thumb. "I can't seem to help it. Besides, I think that after tonight, even you'll agree that you're in some danger. If our thief got in once, he can do so again."

"He'll want to think about it before he tries," said Lady Lettice triumphantly. "I stabbed his face, you know. Next time, I'll do worse." She smiled at Jane. "Next time, I'll take the pistol, Jane. I don't think your aim is any good."

"I didn't aim," Jane corrected her.

"Yes, that's what I mean."

His Lordship said firmly, "There won't be a next time, if I can help it. That is why you must leave for the country, and take my mother and sister with you."

"Your mother, too? You didn't mention her before."

"I know that. It was a sudden, brilliant inspiration." Before she could voice any further objection, he said, "I'll tell them not to let anyone know where they are going."

"But it's all so odd," she persisted, "leaving like that in the middle of the season. No matter what you say, I know that people will talk."

Lord Brooke shrugged his broad shoulders. "Perhaps they will, for awhile. However, they'll stop when they hear that you accepted my mother's hospitality because you hoped it would improve your aunt's health. That's an excellent excuse, don't you agree?"

"I do," said Lady Lettice.

Jane was outflanked, and she knew it. She spread her hands in a gesture of resignation. "Will you go there, too?" she asked almost shyly.

Lord Brooke smiled ruefully. "I'm afraid not, at least not for awhile. As I said, I need time to deal with the problem on which I'm working."

Jane was vastly disappointed. She'd thought—*she'd hoped*—that if she had to leave London, at least his Lordship would soon follow. Visions of her riding out on horseback with him, of their taking long, unchaperoned walks together, of her being kissed in sun-dappled woods and on moonlit paths had flitted through her mind.

Something of her disappointment must have shown in her face. "You'll have an enjoyable time," his Lordship said bracingly. "All of you will. You'll see; it will do you much good.

"I expect I'll miss you," he added, pressing a finger against the tip of her nose. "But we can talk about that, and other things, when we meet up again." Then he was gone.

"Well, well," said Lady Lettice.

"And what is that supposed to mean?"

"Oh, nothing."

Jane looked at her aunt disapprovingly. "I see that you've made a miraculous recovery. You don't seem to be in the doldrums at all anymore."

"You're right," said her Ladyship blithely. "I feel fine, or at least I will after I get some sleep. Now, let's go to bed. We'll need our strength in the morning to plan for our lovely excursion to the country."

But it wouldn't be a lovely excursion, not for Jane, at any rate. It would be more like banishment, with no chance of seeing Marcus Brooke for who knew how long.

And what had he meant by saying that they would talk when they were together again? She knew she wouldn't be able to stop trying to decipher the hidden meaning of that.

How neatly he'd cut up her peace. It would serve him right, she thought spitefully, if Lady Lettice filled up the reticules she took with her with every small thing in his house—which, more than likely, she would.

It took two days for everyone to get ready for the trip to Brookefield. During that time, to Jane's surprise, Mr. Fleer failed to appear at Upper Grosvenor Street to ask for the return of his snuffbox.

It was another surprise that Susan and her mother agreed willingly to accompany Jane and her aunt—although on

A LARCENOUS AFFAIR

second thought, Jane wondered if Susan's decision had been based on her desire to see Mr. Houghton again. She *had* said he meant to look for a place to rent in the neighborhood.

"I'm on a repairing lease," Susan's mother announced gaily when Jane questioned her concerning her feelings about leaving London during the season. "It's quite a relief, actually, to go away."

Susan agreed with her. "I want to get away from all the noise and nonsense of London, too."

Now that they were at Brookefield, however, Susan was not so sure that she hadn't made a mistake. She brushed her fingers against her pink muslin gown as though she were rubbing off cobwebs or something equally repulsive. "Everything here is in the most disgusting condition," she said.

It was true that the property looked as though no one had cared for it in a long time. Jane had thought that very thing as they had been driven up the long, lime-bordered avenue. The grass on either side of the drive was dreadfully in need of cutting and was full of wild onions and other unacceptable growing things. As for the house, at the very least it could have used a new coat of varnish at the windows and on the massive front doors, not to mention that the bricks needed repointing.

The inside of the four-story dwelling was impressive due to its sheer size and fine old furnishings, many dating from the time of Queen Anne and even earlier. However, it appeared equally neglected. Jane wondered if his Lordship had bothered to visit his estate since returning from Portugal.

"Things can soon be put to rights," she told Lady Rebecca and Susan. "Indeed, there's no reason why you can't begin giving the servants your orders now."

When they responded by staring blankly at her, Jane said briskly, "Well, then, I can tell them what to do, if you like." Her offer accepted, she set about directing the staff and soon had them hard at work taking down curtains, washing windows, and polishing fireplace fenders.

"You should have been a general," Susan said not at all admiringly. "No wonder you and Marcus seem so right for each other."

"Do you truly think so?" Then Jane blushed and added stiffly, "I would have expected you to say that we have little in common."

Susan shook her head and grinned.

"Unlike you and that nice Mr. Houghton."

Her friend's grin vanished and was replaced by an expression of feigned indifference.

"Who?" asked Lady Rebecca.

When Susan did not reply, Jane frowned thoughtfully, then said, "I do not think you've met him. Indeed, I, myself, have never been introduced to him. He is a widower with three children whom we first saw at a drygoods store." She turned to Susan and asked innocently, "Didn't you tell me once that he planned to settle nearby?"

Susan's suddenly shy expression would have answered Jane even if her friend hadn't mumbled, ". . . marches with ours."

"What does, dear?" her mother asked.

"I said that I heard Mr. Houghton has taken the property next to ours."

"How lovely," Jane exclaimed sincerely, all thought of roasting her friend forgotten. "I would like to see him and the children again, and that adorably ugly pug dog, too."

"By all means, do so if you wish." Susan sounded bored to flinders. "As for me, I mean to spend my time with Vincent Fleer."

Her words had the effect of wiping the pleased look from Jane's face. "What are you talking about, Susan? Mr. Fleer isn't here."

"No, but he will be," said Susan, looking at her beautifully buffed fingernails. "I know for certain that he'll be here tomorrow."

"But how could he be?" Jane protested. "He has no idea where we are."

"Of course he does. Just before we left, I told him our location and invited him to visit us."

"Oh, Susan, how could you? Didn't your brother ask you not to let anyone know where we were going? He told me that he meant to do so."

Susan's expression combined mischievousness and perversity. "What is that to me? Surely, you don't expect me to start obeying Marcus at this date, Jane."

Perhaps she did not, but, of a certainty, her brother did. "You must not see Mr. Fleer when he comes," Jane counseled. "I'm afraid I can't explain why just yet, but please accept my word for it."

Susan patted Jane's hand. "You're even beginning to talk like Marcus. Don't fret yourself, though. I know what I'm doing."

The problem was, of course, that she did not know. Even Jane could not fathom why Vincent Fleer would want to be at Brookefield while they were there. She wondered if he might think that she and her aunt had brought the snuffbox with them.

If so, would he attempt to wrest it from them, that is, if he truly were the person who'd broken into Lady Lettice's home? Jane sighed. There were too many things left unanswered, which meant that there were too many uninformed decisions to be made. The most pressing was whether to tell Susan her suspicions concerning Vincent Fleer.

Jane considered the matter, then decided not to do so. One never could predict how her friend would react to anything.

"At least promise that you won't go anywhere with him without me," Jane said. "You can do that, can't you?"

Susan gave her a considering look. Then she slowly nodded her head in agreement.

"Good," Jane said. "And thank you."

Susan's dark brows went up. "For what?"

"For trusting me."

Susan laughed. "You're going to be my sister. It will be an uneasy alliance if I don't trust you."

"You must stop talking as though a marriage between

Marcus and me is a *fait accompli*, or even a possibility," Jane scolded. "It's no such thing."

"Isn't it?" Susan laughed again. "I know Marcus better than you do, better than he knows himself. Believe me when I say he cares a great deal for you, Jane."

Susan was wrong, of course, Jane told herself, despite Lord Brooke's proposal of marriage. His interest in her was simply to rescue her from a morally untidy life. "Have you thought that I might not want him?" she asked, pride choosing her words for her.

Susan gave her a pert grin before walking to the door. "I can hardly fault you for that."

A note came for Susan the next morning as she sat in the sunny south dining room with Jane and Lady Lettice. Susan read it, then raised her eyes to Jane, who watched her with thinly veiled anxiety. "It's from Vincent," she said with a grin. "He wants to meet me at the gatehouse at two and tells me not to bring anyone with me."

"I've never heard of such a ramshackle thing," exclaimed Lady Lettice. "No gentleman would ever make such a request. Why can he not come to the house?"

When Susan pretended not to hear, her Ladyship set her coffee cup down hard, ignoring the dark liquid that slopped over the rim. "Are you going to inform your mother about this invitation? Where is she, anyway?"

"In bed," said Susan airily. "Well, Jane, do you want to accompany me?"

"I shall do so as well," Lady Lettice declared before Jane could do more than nod. "I mean to give that young man a piece of my mind. Spying for the Tories is one thing, but attempting to arrange assignations with well-brought-up young women is quite another."

"What did you mean about the Tories?" Susan asked with a little laugh. "Vincent doesn't have any interest in politics."

Jane said, "Never mind about that. I wish you wouldn't go to meet him."

Predictably, her request was refused.

A LARCENOUS AFFAIR 153

Trying not to look distressed, Jane folded her napkin and put it beside her plate. Then she rose from the table. "I must beg to be excused. I promised the housekeeper I'd meet her in the stillroom, to help her make some lavender water. I shall see you shortly before two."

"Never fear. I'll wait for you," Susan called cheerfully after her.

Jane, herself, was waiting for Lord Brooke. She had dispatched a note to him via a groom the previous day informing him that Vincent Fleer might be expected some time soon in the neighborhood. She hoped his Lordship would respond to it quickly. Indeed, she hoped that he would come to Brookefield himself. She looked up eagerly every time the door opened.

By two o'clock he still had not come, so she had no choice but to locate Susan and Lady Lettice so that they could set out upon their excursion to the gatehouse. Suppose Fleer had been the man who'd struck her, she thought, unconsciously balling her fists. It would not be easy to be civil to him.

She found the two women, along with Lady Rebecca, in the first floor grand saloon. Instead of being prepared to go out, they were seated near a tea table, partaking of refreshments with Mr. Houghton and his three children.

Mr. Fleer was not among the company. Indeed, from the bemused look on Susan's face, Jane would venture that she had totally forgotten about him.

"How do you do?" said Jane, smiling broadly, as much with relief at not having to meet Vincent Fleer as with genuine pleasure at the Houghton family's visit. Never having been introduced to Mr. Houghton, she had that honor bestowed upon her by Susan. She extended her hand to him, then grinned at his daughters and bent to give his tow-headed small son a pat.

The party resettled themselves on various faded, shabby sofas and chairs, the two girls either side of Mr. Houghton. The little boy leaned against him, one small foot resting on his father's shiny boot.

Jane noticed that Mr. Houghton had his gaze fixed on

Susan. Wouldn't it be grand, she thought, if Susan were to make a match at last? Mr. Houghton appeared to be such a nice person. As for the children, they might be just the thing to keep her friend busy and out of mischief.

"Well," Lady Lettice said brightly, "this is certainly much better than having to spend time with that shifty-eyed weasel, Fleer. I never did trust him."

"Do you really have a weasel?" asked the boy, big-eyed. "May I see it?"

Lady Lettice looked nonplussed.

"We don't actually have a weasel here," Jane said, trying not to laugh. "However, in London, we do have a monkey who comes to see us. Perhaps you can visit us there someday and get to meet him."

"Yes, please," he said, then looked to his father with eager blue eyes.

"We already were in London," said Jennifer, the elder of Mr. Houghton's two daughters. She accompanied her words with a cool little smile.

The younger girl, introduced as Miss Anne, leaned over just then and whispered in her father's ear.

"I'd forgotten," he said with a pleasant smile. "Anne has brought something to show you all, especially you, Lady Susan, since you are very familiar with the subject. Anne, why don't you bring it to Lady Susan?"

Suddenly shy, Anne shrank against the cushions.

"Never mind," said Susan. "I shall come to you." She rose and walked to the sofa where the Houghton family sat. "You may take my place, if you like," said Mr. Houghton, rising.

"Why don't you sit in that blue chair?" said Jennifer, rising as well and insinuating herself between Susan and her father. "You'll be able to see much better from there, not that there's anything special for you to see."

Susan gave Jennifer a too-bright grin.

On second thought, Jane decided, perhaps the children weren't just the thing to keep Susan out of mischief. More to the point, perhaps it was not a good idea for Susan to spend a great deal of time in Mr. Houghton's company.

She liked him well enough already; that was obvious. If she developed a real *tendre* for him, Jane guessed the older girl would resent it bitterly.

"Sit down, Jennifer," Mr. Houghton said firmly. "Anne, let us see what you have made."

The object to be viewed was revealed as a miniature, done in oils, of the Houghtons' dog. Except for Jennifer, they all crowded around Susan, who sat with one arm about Anne and the other about the little boy, to view it.

Thus occupied, none of them noticed Vincent Fleer as he walked into the room. In fact, he remained unobserved until he cleared his throat.

Everyone looked up then and stared at him. Mr. Fleer's darkly handsome face, with its bit of white court plaster on the cheek, assumed a social smile.

"Aha," said Lady Lettice, wide-eyed, suddenly rising and pointing an accusatory finger at him. Her brown eyes fixed on the court plaster. "It was you I stabbed in the dark! I knew it all the time."

CHAPTER
11

GALVANIZED by Lady Lettice's words, Jane grabbed a china figurine and leaped to her feet. "How dare you come here!" she cried, brandishing the piece of porcelain as though it were a heavy wooden club.

Mr. Fleer's normally rather sly expression transformed itself into an approximation of innocence. "I don't understand," he said, sounding meek. "Have I offended you and your aunt in some way?"

Not for a minute did Jane think she or Lady Lettice had made a mistake about his character and actions. She had no doubt that he had broken into their house and hit her on the jaw.

Upon consideration, however, she decided not to press the issue. It would have been rude, to say the least, to involve Mr. Houghton and his children in the scene that must ensue if she did. As it was, Mr. Houghton and his daughters stared at the three of them as though they might possibly be mad.

"Indeed, no, you haven't offended us," she replied as pleasantly as she could manage. She turned to her aunt. "We were mistaken, Aunt Lettice."

"Maybe you were," said her Ladyship, a scornful expression on her narrow, horsey face. "I, on the other hand, know what I know about Fleer."

At these words, Mr. Houghton's young son jerked up his head and moved a tentative few steps from his father in the direction of Vincent Fleer. "You're not a weasel," he said in an accusing voice. "They were only funning."

Susan began to laugh, in her usual care-for-nothing way. His lips twitching, Mr. Houghton quietly called his son to his side and told him to sit down.

As for Mr. Fleer, for a moment he appeared nonplussed. Then, with a smile, he walked over to Mr. Houghton and thrust out his hand. "How do you do?" he said. "I'm Vincent Fleer. You must forgive me for not staying to chat, but I'm in a great hurry. I stopped by, for just a moment only, in order to give Lady Susan a message."

"What sort of message?" asked Lady Lettice fiercely.

"I'm afraid I can't discuss it. It's a personal, private message."

"Young ladies don't get personal, private messages, particularly not from your sort," said her Ladyship.

As though to prove her wrong, Lady Susan got up from the blue chair she'd been sitting in and said with a provoking grin, "Come into the hall, Mr. Fleer. You may give me your message there." She walked past Mr. Houghton, moving her slender hips in a provocative manner. Then she crooked her finger at Vincent Fleer and left the room.

She returned alone a short while later, in time to hear Mr. Houghton announce that he and the children had to take their leave. Her mouth turned down in disappointment, but almost immediately she seemed to recover. As though she were barely interested, she wished the Houghtons farewell.

A short while later, she accompanied Jane to the latter's green and white bedroom. Although furnished with a charming old four poster and a few fine paintings, it needed refurbishment as badly as the other rooms. However, at the moment, neither of the young women appeared to have any interest in the subject of its inadequacies.

"Mr. Houghton's older daughter hates me," Susan said as soon as she seated herself across from her friend. She accompanied her words with a gay smile ill-suited to their meaning.

Although Jane agreed with her assessment, she merely asked, "How old is she?"

"I believe she's twelve."

"That's a difficult age, and she undoubtedly misses her mama."

"Yes, and she wants to make certain that I'm not her next mama."

Jane stared at her friend, her blue eyes appraising. "Do you wish to be?"

"I? Of course not. Would you like to hear what Vincent said to me?"

The Houghtons were forgotten. "Tell me," Jane replied urgently.

Susan made an elaborate show of smoothing her pink muslin skirt over her knees before saying, "He still wants to meet me, so I agreed to join him in an hour, at an empty cottage on our property. It's probably in terrible condition because it's been tenantless since the old midwife who lived there died; however, I couldn't think of any other place."

Jane dismissed these last bits of information for the irrelevancies they were. "Why would he want to do that?" she asked, her tone suspicious.

Susan shrugged.

"You cannot meet him, Susan," Jane said forcefully. "It's not just that such a meeting is highly improper, although, as you must know, it is. I don't trust him, and—and he is a dangerous man."

"I see you've taken your aunt's nonsense to heart," Susan said flippantly. "I am loath to say it, but I think she has lost her wits."

"Indeed, she has not. Mr. Fleer *is* a dangerous man,

A LARCENOUS AFFAIR 159

and a bad one. I did not mean to tell you this, but it appears that I must: he is a spy for the enemy."

Susan looked at Jane as though the latter had suddenly sprouted whiskers and a thick tail. "Don't you think you're being a bit extreme? I'd hardly called the Tories the enemy."

"They're not. I'm talking about France."

Susan leaned over to Jane and patted her hand. "You're overwrought," she said with unusual gentleness.

Before Jane could protest this assessment, there was a knock at the door. "It's I," called Lady Lettice. "May I come in?"

Not waiting for an answer, she entered the room and with short but determined steps walked over to the two young women. "I suppose you're talking about that dreadful Vincent Fleer," she said without roundaboutation.

Susan looked up at her. "Are you referring to Jane's assertion that he is a spy?" When her Ladyship nodded, Susan said, "Is that why you dislike him so? Until this, I had thought you found him rather amusing."

"Amusing?" Lady Lettice was all indignation. "Is a snake amusing? He hit Jane in the face, you know."

"Did he really? I don't see how he could. She's bigger than he."

Jane flushed and said defensively, "I wasn't standing straight. However, that doesn't matter. What does is that Mr. Fleer truly is a spy. The evidence for what I say was found in his snuffbox."

"So that's why everyone was interested in that stupid box," Susan said. She stared unseeingly before her for a few seconds, then added in an offhanded manner, "Well, even if he is a spy, he can't be a very good one. Nothing he attempts seems to go right for him. I know for a certainty that he's deeply in debt due to his incessant gaming."

Jane couldn't help asking, "They why do you persist in befriending him?"

"That's easy. It's because he is like me. He's incautious and easily bored, and he craves excitement."

"I don't think those are good reasons for you to keep this assignation."

"Assignation?" Susan laughed. "It's hardly that. Indeed, since you are convinced that he is a spy, I believe it's my duty to meet him, so that I can persuade him to admit to what he's done and give himself up to the authorities. That would be the best thing for everyone, don't you agree?"

Lady Lettice said, "Child, don't do it."

"You needn't worry," Susan replied gaily. "I'll be careful about what I do." She turned to Jane. "You may help me if you like."

"Help you? Your brother would never forgive me," Jane said with conviction.

"Really? Doesn't Marcus wish Vincent to be taken prisoner?"

"Not by us, I am sure."

Susan walked to Jane's dressing table and began toying with one of the silver-backed brushes that her friend had brought with her. "That's just like him, isn't it? He's the most selfish beast in nature."

But he wasn't selfish. Hadn't he offered to marry Jane simply in order to save her? What could be more self-sacrificing than that, especially since it was obvious that he did not love her; if he did, he would have said so. The thought was like spirits poured into an open wound.

Susan's words interrupted her musings. "Of course, we needn't obey him. Oh, Jane, it would be such an adventure. And if Vincent is a spy, and we get him to confess it, Marcus will be proud of us."

That was a tempting thought—but not tempting enough. Jane shook her head.

Lady Lettice gave her niece a disapproving look, then said, "I could assist you in your endeavor, Susan."

"Truly? Why would you want to do that? Just a few minutes ago, you told me Mr. Fleer is a snake and dangerous."

Lady Lettice stroked her flat bosom thoughtfully, then replied, "I've volunteered because you might want to avail

A LARCENOUS AFFAIR

yourself of my special . . . um . . . abilities. Just suppose Mr. Fleer decides not to turn himself over to the authorities but to lock us in the cottage instead, in order to escape. I could secure his key and hide it before he gets out the door. There is a key, isn't there?''

"I'm not certain," Susan said, then apparently taking note of Lady Lettice's look of disappointment, added cheerfully, "Surely, there must be."

Jane knew that if she had even a modicum of sense, she would not go anywhere with those two. On the other hand, as anyone could see, they needed her. "I would be willing to work out a way to capture him," she advised. "The first thing, of course, is to decide how many menservants we should take with us."

"Not a single one," Susan said emphatically. "We'll do it ourselves. Here's my plan; see what you think. We'll go to the cottage. We'll take some rope with us—oh, and a loaded pistol, of course. I'll trick Mr. Fleer into confessing and then explain that he must surrender. If he won't, I'll shoot him."

Lady Lettice frowned at her. "Then what's the rope for?"

"In case I miss."

Looking rather pale, Jane made one last effort to stop them. "I sent Marcus a note yesterday informing him that Mr. Fleer might come. Surely, your brother will be here momentarily, and with other people to help him. We do not need to see to Vincent Fleer, because they will."

But Susan did not want her brother and his allies to see to him. She had made up her mind to do it herself, with some help from Lady Lettice, if not Jane. Nothing that was said to her—and Jane said quite a bit—dissuaded her.

What else could a true friend and devoted niece do? Jane had no choice but to go with them.

Her mouth set disapprovingly, she went off to write another note to his Lordship, telling him to follow them to the cottage. Then she obtained a length of rope from the butler and with reluctance went to join her companions.

They were waiting for her in a basket chaise, of which

Susan held the reins. It began to move as soon as Jane stepped into it.

The three women traveled some distance down the sweeping drive that went from the house to the main road. Then Susan veered off onto a rutted lane. "This is the way to the cottage," she said, speaking for the first time since they'd set off.

When they drew close, Susan stopped the carriage. "There it is," she advised in a near-whisper. "I'll tie the horse up here."

The cottage, which stood in a clearing by itself, was an old, two-storied building with a steep thatched roof. It looked as though it might have been well-cared-for once, but now part of its white fence lay on the ground and thick weeds grew among the remaining flowers.

There was no other carriage around, and the house appeared deserted. "Blast," Susan said loudly. "Where is Vincent? I'm not in a mood to be kept waiting."

Although Jane, and even Lady Lettice, protested, they were swept incautiously into the cottage by their impatient hostess. It was dark inside and smelled of dirt, stale air, and sweat. In addition to these deficiencies, it apparently contained not a few cobwebs. Wishing she were somewhere else, Jane brushed one from her face. Then she put down the rope she'd been carrying and set about opening the shutters.

The flood of light enabled them to discover suddenly that Vincent Fleer was sitting upon one of the steps which led to the upper story. Behind him were two other men, ruffians if Jane had ever seen any. All three had large pistols in their hands.

Jane started to back toward the door, but Fleer's words stopped her. "I'll shoot you through the heart if you attempt it, Long Meg. Doing so would give me the greatest pleasure, you must know."

"How dare you speak to my friend so," Susan said vehemently. She started to put her hand to her reticule, wherein lay the pistol. However, Jane shook her head, and Susan, for once, took heed.

Mr. Fleer laughed. "I like you, Susan, as much as I've ever liked anyone. Unfortunately for you, however, that isn't very much, so try to mind your tongue, my dear. I'm in the position of power here."

"Pooh. I'm not afraid of you, Vincent."

Fleer rose from his perch and dusted off his buckskin breeches with his free hand. "Nor should you be, for awhile at any rate," he said, descending the rest of the steps to the worn wooden floor. "I have no intention of harming you. I need you."

"Indeed?" Susan tilted up her head in its pink bonnet. "For what do you need me?"

"Why, to be my hostage, of course. I suspect that big, bad brother of yours means to capture me. I shall use you to dissuade him from attempting it. I'm going to leave these shores for France, my sweet. You shall go with me, as my insurance."

"So you *are* a spy! You were right after all, Jane." As Mr. Fleer cast a look of dislike at Jane, Susan continued, "Now that you've confessed, so to speak, I think you should give yourself up rather than leave England for a foreign country. I don't believe you'd like living in France for very long."

"I'd like it a lot better than swinging from a gibbet. No, it's France for me, and for you as well. But do not fear; I'll make your stay with me enjoyable. After all, we're two of a kind, my dear. We don't care for anyone or anything, least of all for what Society thinks."

Indignant, Jane wanted to tell him that his words weren't true. Susan cared for Mr. Houghton; she was convinced of it. And if there was anything she could do for Susan to make that relationship prosper, she meant to try.

First, however, she had to manage to keep herself and Lady Lettice alive. Even if Vincent Fleer had some fondness for her, which it was patently obvious he did not, it was unlikely that he meant to take *three* hostages.

As though he'd read her mind, he said, "Naturally, we'll need to get rid of the beautiful Amazon and her dotty aunt."

Like a puppet whose strings had been loosed, Susan collapsed upon the dirty floor. "Kill me now," she said.

"What? Get up, you little idiot. I told you I have no intention of killing you."

"You'll have to, Vincent. I shall not budge an inch unless you take my friends as hostages, too."

"Now, just a minute . . ." said Lady Lettice, but no one paid her any heed.

Mr. Fleer's dark, brooding eyes swept over Jane and her aunt. Then he said, "Oh, very well, I'll do it."

Susan rose at once, smiling, but Jane was not reassured. She was certain that as soon as he could, Fleer would dispose of them. All of a sudden, she felt afraid.

Mingled with her fear was sadness. There were so many occasions she wished she could have shared with Marcus Brooke, not as adversaries but as friends: going to balls, riding in the park, taking a boat out upon the Thames; Brookefield was very close to the Thames. Now, she would never do any of those things with him.

Memories came to her, of the way Marcus looked when something amused him, and when he was in a temper; of the scent that was unique to him, a heady, masculine mix of bayberry, clean, starched linen, and cigar smoke; of the feel of his mouth on hers when he'd kissed her at Vauxhall Gardens. How she wished he'd continued to touch her that night. Now, very likely, he'd never have an opportunity even to kiss her again.

She jerked herself back to her present situation to hear Fleer say, "We'll have to leave you three for a little while. Since I hadn't expected to take the lot of you, we'll need to obtain a larger conveyance."

"Very well," Susan said casually. "We'll make ourselves comfortable here and wait for you."

Mr. Fleer's cohorts apparently found her words amusing. They laughed and slapped their thighs. Jane could not say that she blamed them. One would have to be a very trusting person to accept such a remark.

Since she had no reason to assume that Vincent Fleer was trusting, she was surprised when he said, "I think that's an excellent idea." He paused, then added with malicious enjoyment, "Of course, we'll need to make certain you don't change your minds. Isn't it lucky that there's some rope here to ensure that you don't."

He bent to pick it up, grinning smugly the whole while. Jane wished she could wipe the grin from his face almost as much as she wished she hadn't supplied him with the rope.

"You won't object to this, will you?" he asked her facetiously.

"Not at all," Lady Lettice replied in her stead. "Just get on with it."

"These gentry morts ain't natural," one of Fleer's accomplices commented with a grin, but he was ordered to shut his mouth and proceed with his task.

Soon the men had bound the hands and feet of the three women and then departed. "What have you been up to, Aunt?" Jane asked when she was certain they had gone. "I know you've done something. You aren't wearing a turban. Is there some little surprise for us in your reticule?"

"I told you that you'd need me," her Ladyship said with a wide smile that caused the wrinkles to spread over her thin cheeks. "However, what I took from Fleer isn't in my reticule. Don't you remember that you made me promise not to put other people's possessions there anymore? It's under my skirt."

Jane said excitedly, "What is, Aunt?"

"Mr. Fleer's knife, of course. I borrowed it when he bent down to get the rope."

"Oh, Lady Lettice, you're wonderful!" Susan said exuberantly. She quickly sobered, however. "Do you think it will do us any good?"

"Of course it will," said Jane. "Now here's what we'll do. The first thing, Aunt Lettice, is for you to roll over, so that we can get hold of the knife."

When this command was obeyed, a small, shiny knife with a black handle was revealed.

"I can reach it," said Susan. With great care she took

the knife between her hands, straining against her bonds in order to do so. "Hold still, Jane. I mean to free you."

Fortunately, the rope was neither very thick nor tight about Jane's limbs, so that Susan finally managed to cut it. A short while later, the ropes which bound Susan and Lady Lettice were severed as well.

"You're bleeding," her Ladyship said to Jane. "Let us return to the house at once to bandage your poor wounds."

"They're hardly that," said Susan. "I'd say they're scratches more like." She gave Jane an encouraging pat. "Use our handkerchiefs to stop the bleeding, Jane. We need to go after Vincent."

"I don't want to go after him, not anymore," Lady Lettice said. "He's a nasty man and best left alone."

Susan gave her a cheerful smile. "Consider yourself excused, then. As for me, I still have my gun, and I mean to shoot him in the legs as soon as we find him."

"What good will that do?" said the ever-practical Jane as she wrapped her handkerchief about her left wrist. "There are three of them. While you shoot Vincent, the other two will shoot us."

Susan acknowledged that they did seem to have a problem. "If only Mr. Houghton were with us," she said with a sigh. "He seems such a sensible person. I'm convinced he would know what to do."

The three women cautiously stuck their heads out the door. "Mr. Houghton isn't here," said Lady Lettice, as though his absence were unexpected. "No one is except us. I say we should return to the house at once, while we have the chance."

Jane hesitated, then straightened her tall figure and thrust out her chin. "Susan is right," she said. "You should go back to the house, Aunt, for assistance if nothing else. We will remain to capture Fleer in case he comes back before those you send to help us get here." She turned to Susan. "Have the pistol ready. We're going to lie in wait for them outside."

"But I thought you said you'd be shot," Lady Lettice screeched.

"We won't think about that," Jane said resolutely. "Our duty is clear."

Jane would have been less confident if she'd known that Marcus did not receive her note informing him of Fleer's arrival in the neighborhood until very much later than he should have. He was away from home when it was delivered, helping a friend, a dedicated mathematician, decipher Fleer's code. It took them all day and part of the night to finish solving the problem.

What the deciphered code contained was information about British troop movements, damning proof of Fleer's involvement with the French. That the man was a traitor no one could doubt any longer.

Still, Marcus did not go back to Grosvenor Square. Accompanied by his friend Freddy Manning, whom he'd taken into his confidence, he made the rounds of Fleer's various haunts. He hoped to capture Fleer at once, and certainly before his family and their guests returned from Brookefield. Marcus had no desire to provide grist to the scandalmongers' mill by having Fleer taken into custody—or killed—when he was in their company. Think how bad that would be for Jane's reputation, he thought with a frown. Oh, yes, and Susan's too, if she still had one.

Always, Fleer seemed to be just one or two steps ahead of them. The doorman at the last club they looked in said he'd overheard Mr. Fleer say he was going away directly he left there, to "Brooke" something or other.

"The devil!" Marcus said with a frightening scowl. "He means to go to Brookefield. I'll wager anything my sister put him up to it."

It would have been just like Susan to do that, despite his having insisted that she not tell anyone where she was going. Now, perhaps, she'd put herself in jeopardy, and Jane as well.

Yes, definitely, Jane would be in danger. If he knew her—and he should because he thought about her often enough—she'd be organizing her ragtag troupe of ladies and leading the charge against Fleer, who'd already struck her once.

Marcus's lips thinned. It would be intolerable if anything happened to Jane. He had made himself responsible for her welfare.

No, he thought, that wasn't precisely right. Indeed, it wasn't right at all. The truth was that he loved her, loved all five feet, ten inches of her, loved her to distraction! What was the use of denying it, at least to himself?

"What is it?" Freddy's voice intruded into his thoughts. "You look as though you've been hit by a lightning bolt."

"I think I have," Marcus murmured.

He shook his head as though to clear it. "There's nothing else for it," he announced in a hard voice. "I shall have to pursue him there, today, now."

"You don't mean to go after him alone, do you?" Freddy said, looking at his friend's grim face with considerable alarm.

"I don't have time to arrange an escort."

With a sickly grin, Freddy said, "I'm not much for violence, as you well know, but I could accompany you."

"Let us go, then."

After several grueling hours on horseback, Marcus and Freddy arrived at Brookefield. Once there, Marcus did not waste any time. "Has a Mr. Fleer been here?" he asked the butler as soon as the door opened.

"Yes, my lord, but he left awhile ago. And I have a note for you from Lady Susan's friend, Lady Jane," he added in a complaining voice, as though he were in danger of being worked to death.

Frowning, Lord Brooke read Jane's note, then turned to Freddy Manning and said curtly, "We must go to them at once."

They changed horses, then set off along the road Jane and her companions had followed not so long before. Along the way, they came across Lady Lettice.

"Hurry," she said, "oh, hurry. Vincent Fleer . . ."

Marcus was in motion before she finished her sentence, leaving Freddy to catch up as best he could. Marcus dismounted close by the cottage and proceeded the rest of the way on foot. His neglected friend hurried behind him, stopping only once to curse when he stepped into a rabbit hole and wrenched his ankle.

Marcus held up his hand. "There it is," he whispered, pointing to the dilapidated-looking cottage.

"It appears to be empty," said Freddy, trying not to sound pleased. "Your sister and Lady Jane have probably returned to the house by a different route and are awaiting us in the saloon."

Marcus ignored these blatant efforts to get them to depart. "What say you we examine the inside of the cottage and then, if it's indeed empty, separate and reconnoiter a bit? Follow me."

His tanned face was taut with excitement as he preceded Freddy to the front of the cottage. Then he cocked his gun and kicked open the door.

There seemed to be nothing to see. "I told you," said Freddy, obviously relieved; "no one is here."

Marcus bent his tall frame and scooped something from a corner of the dirty floor. "Someone was here," he said, holding up a white silk handkerchief embroidered with the initial "J." "This is Jane's; I'm certain of it."

He pointed to a few dark spots on the handkerchief, his expression grim. "And this is blood. If he's done harm to Jane or my sister, there is nothing I won't do to find him and punish him. Let us go outside now and see if we can discover some clues there."

The men left the building and began to examine the ground around it. "Over here," Marcus called in a low voice. "I think I've found something."

He pointed to an area of trampled grass. "There were horses here a short while ago. They went that way and appear to have been pulling a heavy object, a carriage, very likely. Come, we'll follow their trail."

"I wouldn't," Freddy said, shaking his head.

Marcus gave him an impatient look. "And why is that?"

"Because I think the women are in that ditch over

there," he said, pointing some yards away. "If not, Vincent Fleer has on a pink bonnet."

Marcus started to turn to where Freddy pointed, but quickly threw himself flat upon the ground. Freddy followed, just in time to avoid a bullet, which went whistling over their heads.

"Damn it, Susan," Marcus Brooke called angrily. "Stop shooting at us."

As though in reply, another bullet whizzed by. The men hared off and took cover together in a stand of trees.

"I don't think that one was from your sister," Freddy said. "I believe it came from some other place nearer here."

Cautiously, Marcus raised his head. He was in time to see Vincent Fleer and two other armed men leap from a large, old carriage and hide behind a cattle shelter of thickly leaved bushes. Marcus raised his pistol and took careful aim. There was a cry, and one of Fleer's henchmen fell over in the dirt.

"Two to go," Marcus called loudly enough for Fleer to hear him. "Likely it will be your turn next, Vincent."

There was a laugh. "I'm not that easy to kill," Fleer called back. "However, you might be more vulnerable."

He raised his gun; but before he could take aim, Marcus snatched Freddy's loaded pistol and shot again. This time, Fleer's other companion fell. They could see his breeches-clad legs and brown boots, one of which had a hole in the bottom.

"Now there's only you, Fleer," said Marcus. "Are you ready to surrender—or to die?"

Vincent's answer was lost as he crouched to avoid a bullet fired from the ditch. His next remarks, however, were clear enough for all of them to hear. "Bloody hell. I see pink. Did you escape from the cottage, Susan?"

"Of course, I did," she said, recklessly standing to glare at his hiding place, "but that's neither here nor there. I am quite annoyed with you, Vincent. You must give yourself up like a man and stop causing all of this trouble."

A LARCENOUS AFFAIR

Probably to everyone's surprise but Susan's, Fleer stepped over his fallen companions and came out from behind the bushes. "You have the right of it, sweetheart," he said with a jaunty lilt in his voice, "so I'll fight no more. I surrender to you and your good sense."

"Throw down your pistol, Fleer," Marcus said in a commanding voice, unimpressed by his rhetoric.

Vincent's lips parted in a slow, spiteful smile. "Oh, dear, I meant to, but I'm afraid I've changed my mind. I believe I'll keep it—and use it on your sister."

He took careful aim, then pulled the trigger. Susan screamed and fell back, clutching at her right arm. A thin, red line appeared on the pink sleeve of her spencer.

"Is she badly hurt? I'm coming," Marcus called out in a voice filled with dread. He seemed to have forgotten about Fleer.

Vincent made use of the subsequent noise and confusion to effect his escape. Still holding his gun, he sped off across the wide, green field. His booted feet seemed barely to touch the ground as he ran.

Jane looked up at Marcus, a tender smile lighting her lovely face. "It's all right," she said. "Truly. The bullet only grazed her."

Although his brown eyes blazed with deadly anger, Marcus said quietly, "I leave her in your capable hands, then. Besides, the servants your aunt will dispatch should arrive shortly. I'm going after Fleer. This time he won't be in any condition to escape."

Freddy looked at his friend's set face. "I'll go with you, but promise not to tear his head off or anything nasty, Marcus. I couldn't bear to watch."

"You must avert your eyes when the time comes—and save your breath for our pursuit."

It would have taken too long to fetch the horses, so they set off running after Vincent. The sky was serenely blue and cloudless and birds sang in the scattered trees. The day would have been perfection had their errand not been so grave.

"There he is," said Marcus, pointing some yards ahead

to a high hedgerow that separated the field from the highway. "He means to go through that break there."

A short time later, they availed themselves of the same exit and came out a short distance from where Fleer stood. He was shifting his legs, waiting impatiently for a rapidly approaching carriage to go by. It was clear he meant to cross to the other side of the road as soon as he could and disappear into the thick woods there.

"Fleer," Marcus called sternly, "throw down your pistol and surrender. Your race is run."

A devilish grin spread over Vincent's face. "Would you like to wager on that?" he said before darting into the road.

His pursuers watched as the horrified coachman pulled back desperately on the reins, with almost no result. The carriage horses struck Vincent with enormous force and knocked him to the ground. Their heavy hooves pounded and cut him. Then a large wheel rolled over him, its great weight crushing and pulverizing his bones.

Vincent lay like a broken, discarded doll in the road, his limbs obscenely askew. The skin of his hands and face was covered with blood and deep bruises, and a thin stream of blood trickled from a corner of his mouth.

Marcus and Freddy ran to where he was and bent over him. Vincent looked up at them with a faint, self-mocking smile. "I gambled and lost," he whispered almost inaudibly—"but, then, I always did."

He sighed deeply, and closed his eyes.

CHAPTER 12

"HE'S dead," Freddy said as he ran his shaking fingers through his brown hair.

Marcus straightened. "Yes, and now we'll probably never know who his contact was."

Freddy seemed shocked by Marcus's lack of sentiment. "Is that all you have to say? The fellow is dead."

"I'm not a hypocrite, Freddy. He was a traitor, and he shot my sister. Besides, I've seen too much of death for it to affect me as it does you. Forget about all this. Let's get back to life."

To Jane, a voice inside him said. To Jane, if she would have him.

Marcus waved a hand toward Fleer's crumpled body. "We'll take him back to the house in the carriage. We'll have to be careful how we manage this. I don't want to upset Jane and the others with having to see him in this condition."

"Um . . . you seem to concern yourself about Lady Jane's sensibilities quite a bit," Freddy replied, a tentative smile on his face. "Am I mistaken, or is that evidence of the way you feel about her, my friend?"

Marcus was not about to declare his intentions toward Jane without first talking with her. It was true she'd given him an encouraging smile before releasing him to pursue Fleer. However, she had also previously rejected a perfectly well-meant proposal from him, the heartless wretch. Although he loathed admitting it even to himself, he was less than confident of her feelings for him.

"I don't respond to nonsensical questions," he said brusquely, accompanying his words with a dampening look. "Are you coming with me, or must I leave you behind?"

Freddy walked quickly to where the carriage had come to a halt at one side of the highway. "I'm coming with you, of course, but how are you going to convince the coachman to cease his lamentations?"

In fact, it took a generous bribe and repeated promises that he would not be brought up before a magistrate before they could get the man to cooperate. Finally, however, he left them and their burden at the Brookefield estate office, where Marcus saw to it that arrangements were made for Fleer's burial. Then Freddy accompanied him to the stables, where Marcus directed several grooms to collect the horses that had been left behind as well as the bodies of Fleer's two associates.

At last, they went into the house. Freddy looked at Marcus a bit helplessly. "I don't mind confessing that I'm exhausted," he said, finishing with a yawn as though to prove the accuracy of his words. "Is there anything else we must do?"

Marcus was tired, too. First, however, he needed to see to his sister; then he would try to find some time to be alone with Jane before he had to return to London in the morning. His pulse accelerated as he thought of the tall, lovely woman he hoped to make his bride. She was perfect in every way—except, that is, for putting her friends above him and for her habit of wanting to take care of everyone and everything. He would need to redirect her enthusiasms.

He could not keep back the thought that she might not

A LARCENOUS AFFAIR 175

wish to have her enthusiasms redirected. Would *he* want to be made to change? But that was ridiculous; he was a man and a lord. It was his nature and his role in life to take care of others, especially the woman who would be his wife.

"There's nothing else," he said gruffly. Squaring his shoulders, he opened the wide door into the grand saloon. As he'd supposed, Susan was ensconced there, holding court on a faded green brocade sofa. In a semicircle around her were her mother, Lady Lettice, Jane, and Mr. Houghton, all seated upon equally faded pieces of furniture.

Had the place always been so shabby? he thought with sudden embarrassment, glancing at the rain-spotted gold draperies and chair upholstery so worn that threads hung down like fringe from the seats. For very certain, he needed to put his life in order.

Resisting an impulse to do more than glance at Jane, he walked over to the recumbent Susan. Her face was pale against the dark brown of her untidy, topknotted hair. A makeshift bandage covered her slender arm above her elbow.

"Well?" Susan asked, sitting quickly upright. "What have you to tell us?"

Just for a minute he thought that she referred to his decision concerning Jane, but then he realized that she was asking for news of Vincent Fleer. "Fleer is dead," he said bluntly. Turning his head to where Jane sat, he saw her blanch.

Susan asked indignantly, "Did you kill him, Marcus? I thought Freddy told you not to."

Marcus's brown eyes narrowed in annoyance. "No, I did not kill him. Indeed, he killed himself, by running in front of a speeding carriage. I would have killed him, however, if that was the only way I could have stopped him. He was a traitor to England, besides having deliberately shot you."

"It's likely for the best," Jane said soothingly. "Will you tell his uncle the truth?"

"I must." Marcus smiled. *Trust Jane to get to the heart*

of things. "He'll want to know, and we'll have to decide how much, if anything, should be revealed to other members of the government. First, though, I need to learn from the doctor the condition of my ungrateful sister's arm." He walked briskly over to a bell pull. "I shall send for him at once."

"I don't want a doctor," Susan said with a pout. "My arm is fine."

Mr. Houghton rose to his feet, a pleasant but firm smile on his face. "I think your brother will want Dr. Byrd to decide that," he said. Still with the same smile, he turned to address Marcus. "I hope you don't mind. I took the liberty of sending for him, against Lady Jane's wishes, I'm afraid, as well as those of your sister. Lady Jane wanted to care for Lady Susan herself, and, in fact, had already given orders for certain medicants and a supply of linens to make up into bandages."

For the first time since coming into the room, Marcus looked fully at Jane. She must have changed her gown, he thought, because the blue muslin she wore looked fresh and unwrinkled, not to mention exceedingly attractive. Her beautiful face was rosy with blushes. "I know firsthand what a good physician she is," he said, his words causing her cheeks to turn even rosier. "She took care of me once when I skated into a—well, never mind about that."

"Perhaps some day you'll tell me the story," Mr. Houghton said. "I couldn't stay to hear it now, in any case. I promised the children I'd visit the nursery while they were having their supper." He bowed, then looked at Susan. "With your permission, I'll come back this evening to hear what Dr. Byrd had to say."

To Marcus's surprise, his hoydenish sister gave Mr. Houghton a shy smile and nodded her head, causing Marcus to wonder if the two of them were, in fact, becoming enamored of each other. Susan was such a rash, intemperate creature that if she liked the man, he was probably an ax murderer—or a spy.

At the moment, however, she looked less rash than drained. As though something vital had gone out of her,

A LARCENOUS AFFAIR

she watched dully as Mr. Houghton left the room. Then she sank limply against the cushions.

"I'll be glad when the doctor comes," Marcus said in a worried voice.

"I told you that I don't need him." Like a spoiled child, Susan stuck out her lower lip and frowned at her brother.

Before he could argue with her, as he appeared about to do, Jane whisked him from the saloon. "I'll make certain that her wound is tended to and give you a full report," she said as they stood together in the hall. "You needn't worry about a thing."

As he started to thank her, she added with an uncertain smile, "I hope you don't mind, but I ordered hot water to be made ready for you and Lord Manning. I thought you both might enjoy a bath after what . . . after all your exertions."

A bath would be good. A kiss on her soft, ripe lips would be better. What he wanted most was to take Jane in his arms and make love to her until her head spun. Maybe then she'd forget about solving his, and everyone else's, problems and respond to him with the passion he was convinced she possessed. After that, after he had her clinging, dizzy, and helpless, he'd propose to her.

Unfortunately, before he could so much as take her hand in his, she excused herself and returned to the saloon to attend to Susan. He'd have to bide his time, at least until after the doctor left.

Since Dr. Byrd arrived approximately twenty minutes later, Marcus did not have long to wait. The doctor was rushed upstairs to Susan's rather gloomy bedroom, where she had gone after Mr. Houghton departed. She sat upright in bed, a feather pillow propping up her injured arm. Her mother and Lady Jane were with her to lend their emotional support.

"Let us see what we have here," Dr. Byrd said cheerfully, unwinding the bandage Jane had applied. "It looks to me as though your arm was grazed by a bullet, young lady. Is that possible?"

Susan ignored his question. "Will I be incapacitated for a long time?" she asked eagerly.

Dr. Byrd gave her a reassuring smile. "No, no. Three or four days of rest should do it, I think. As injuries go, this one is next to nothing."

If he intended his diagnosis to please, he was much mistaken. A black scowl spread over his patient's small, piquant face. "That can't be so," she said in an emphatic voice that belied her next words. "I am weak and faint. I don't believe two weeks would be long enough for me to recuperate."

"Weak and faint?" he repeated doubtfully. "Well, yes, I suppose you could be, from the shock of the accident, if nothing else." When she started to brighten, he said, "That must be the explanation."

"Naturally, you'll want to tell my brother what you think. Isn't that right?" she asked, smiling smugly.

Jane gave her friend a suspicious look as the still nodding doctor was ushered out. "What are you planning, Susan?"

"I?"

"Yes, you. Whatever it is, I won't be a part of it. I mean to leave Brookefield in a few days, just as soon as you are well."

"As shall I," said Lady Rebecca. "I've had enough excitement here to last a lifetime. All I want to do is return to London and take up my usual pursuits. They don't give me palpitations, not even when I lose at cards—which is a good thing," she added brightly, "considering that I do that so very often."

Susan stared off into space, apparently forgetting that Jane and her mother were there. Since Jane had become caught up in her own thoughts, which dealt with spending mornings, afternoons, and evenings in Marcus's company in London, she barely noticed.

At last, Susan looked up. "No matter what you do, Jane, I mean to stay here for several more weeks."

"By yourself? Even you cannot be excused for that, Susan."

A LARCENOUS AFFAIR

"Of course not. I shall be here with my mother."

Lady Rebecca swiveled her head as though in search of the sad creature who had given birth to this unnatural child. There being no other candidate but herself, she said in a horrified voice, "Here with me?"

Instead of answering, Susan bestowed a beatific smile on her. She followed that with an exaggerated yawn and blinked her dark eyes several times in succession. "You'll have to excuse me," she said after the display. "I find I am weary and need to sleep."

Ignoring her mother's still vehement protests and Jane's condemnatory looks, she turned her back on her companions and closed her eyes. There was nothing for them but to walk from the room.

Jane parted from Lady Rebecca outside the distraught woman's door, then went in search of Lord Brooke, to warn him to gird for trouble with Susan. She found him in the library.

This well-proportioned room seemed in a much better state than most of the others. Still-beautiful Turkey carpets covered the parquet floor, and the walls were lined with mahogany bookcases filled with handsome leatherbound volumes and classical sculptures. His Lordship looked much at home in the rich, masculine ambience created by these furnishings, Jane thought.

When Marcus saw her, he jumped to his feet. Though she could not have known it, he had been thinking about her.

"I was wondering when you would keep your promise to discuss the doctor's report with me," he said with a lazy grin. "I knew you would keep your word."

She took the seat he offered before returning his grin with a strained smile.

"What is it?" he asked, narrowing his eyes. "I thought there was nothing to worry about. The doctor told me that Susan's wound is minor. Do you know something that I do not?"

Jane hesitated. Although she had come to tell him her fears about Susan, she found that she could not be disloyal to her friend, not even when this involved the man she loved. "Did Dr. Byrd tell you that Susan might be suffering from shock?" she asked instead.

"Shock? Certainly not. Is she?"

"She thinks she is," said Jane in an equivocating voice.

"And what do you think?"

"I . . . I don't know."

Oh, dear. Why did he have to look at her like that, as though he had discovered that she was in Napoleon's employ—or the Devil's? All he said, however, was "Naturally, she's up to no good. What do you believe she means to do?"

Jane spread her shapely hands in an uncharacteristically indecisive gesture. "She might mean to stay at Brookefield for awhile, perhaps for several weeks. Of course, Lady Rebecca would stay with her."

"Here? Why would they want to do that?" Marcus stared coldly over the bump in his nose at her as though *she* were Susan. "They have always said they loathe the country. In fact, it still puzzles me why Susan agreed so readily to come here."

Jane gave him a look. Obtuse man. It was perfectly obvious that Susan wanted to be near Mr. Houghton. Why couldn't Marcus see that?

Apparently, he was not as obtuse as she'd thought. "It's that Houghton fellow, isn't it?" he said accusingly. "She's fallen in love with him."

"I'm not certain that I would put it that strongly," Jane said hastily. "She hardly knows him. It would be absurd in her to fancy that."

"Of course, it would, but that's never held her back before. That reminds me of something," he added. "Am I correct in thinking that it was Susan who advised Fleer she meant to come to Brookefield, and that you and Lady Lettice would be here as well?"

Jane rose abruptly from her chair and went to stand behind it, as though to shield herself from his questions. "I don't know," she mumbled, not looking at him.

Marcus drew close to her. He put his hand to her chin

and tilted her face toward his. "I do not believe you, Jane. I think you have turned craven on me."

"Are you calling me a coward?" she said fiercely, using indignation to cover her confusion. "I am never a coward."

"Are you not? I think you must prove that."

"But how can I? Shall I go out looking for highwaymen to engage with, or challenge someone to a duel?"

Marcus's smile was thin. "It would not surprise me if you were to do either of those—in order to save a friend. That is one of your failings. You are loyal to a fault—to everyone but me, I'm afraid."

Jane glowered at him. "*One* of my failings? Pray tell me, what are the others? No, never mind. It is enough to know you think that."

Matters were not going as Marcus had planned. His beloved's face wore an intense look of dislike. He could hardly press his suit when she wore such an expression. "I didn't mean that the way it sounded."

Jane's expression softened slightly. Marcus knew he should stop there and keep the ground he had regained. There was too much on his mind, however, and he had been under too much of a strain to take his own good advice. "What I meant was that your loyalty seems never to be to me," he informed her in an aggrieved voice. "I see how kind—how good!—you are to everyone but me. What have I done to you to be treated differently?"

Jane, of course, had been under a good deal of strain herself. Perhaps that was why all of the grievances she had ever held toward him now came out, first in a trickle of words, then in a stream, and finally in a torrent. "What have you done? You snubbed me the first moment you set eyes on me."

Marcus had the grace to redden.

"Then you accused me of riding in the park with Susan in a cart pulled by ugly dogs."

Although the flush on Marcus's face deepened, he opened his mouth to protest.

"Don't interrupt," Jane said imperiously, too upset

to be diplomatic. "Then, *then*, you accused me of stealing, and never did believe me even when I told you that I didn't."

When she paused to take a breath, he said hastily, "But what else was I to think? I saw you with your booty, and, besides, you told me that you liked to steal. That was in the draper's. Don't you remember?"

"Oh, fiddle." Jane dismissed this evidence as though it had never happened. "You should have known I wouldn't do those things."

"I did know. That is, I couldn't believe . . ."

"Yes, you could."

"Very well then, I could. But I never stopped trying to reform you. I could have done that . . . stopped trying, that is. You weren't my responsibility, not really."

"Then, why didn't you?"

She was so angry with him that he was reluctant to say what he really felt. "Why do you think?" he temporized.

"I don't know. I think perhaps it's because you're so domineering that you want to direct everyone's life, even someone like me who is not related to you."

Marcus had not expected such an assault. He drew himself up to his full, overpowering height and looked down his aggressive nose at her. "I, domineering? I am nothing of the sort."

"But you are," she said emphatically, trying not to be intimidated. "You are just like my father."

"Don't be ridiculous. I am nothing like him."

"How would you know?" Jane said, thrusting out her chin pugnaciously. "You've never even met him."

"You see! That proves my point."

"You're absurd."

Marcus banged his fist on a nearby table. "You always fight me, Jane, always resist me. You want to manage everything and never depend upon me. I cannot understand that. Do you truly dislike me so much?"

"I? I do not dislike anyone—although I like some people far more than I do others." Her blue eyes pierced him.

"What did you mean when you said I want to manage everything? Do you consider me a managing female?"

Instead of answering, he put his hands on her arms. "Jane," he said huskily as he slid his fingers over her silky skin, "why must we quarrel?"

Resolutely, she pulled away from him. "The answer to that is simple, my lord. You are an ill-tempered, dictatorial man. Now, if you will excuse me, I must go upstairs to oversee the packing. It is time my aunt and I left for London. Perhaps I will see you later. Perhaps I will not."

"Is that all? Have you no other word for me?"

"What would you have me say?"

Their quarrel had escalated past all redemption. "I suppose there is nothing more for either of us to say," he replied stiffly. "I did not realize that you held me in such low esteem. Very well, then. I see that it's hopeless. You have my word that I shall not propose to you a third time. And, now, I bid you good-bye."

"What? Wait!"

If he heard her, he did not acknowledge it. She stared at his retreating back, at the proud carriage, and the wide, muscled shoulders held stiffly, unyieldingly. Then he was gone.

Jane gazed unseeingly at the wall, her mind on what Marcus had said. Why would he have mentioned a third proposal to her when he hadn't made a second? Had he? Indeed, no; there hadn't been anything loverlike about their mutual exchange of words, let alone his conversation.

Well, there was one thing she knew: whether for the second or third time, he had no intention of suing for her hand again; he had said so quite plainly.

Not knowing what else to do, she walked slowly up the stairs to Susan's chamber. "Are you still sleepy?" she asked.

Susan put down the romance she was reading. "Not if you don't mean to scold me. What have you been up to? Your face is red."

Jane opened her mouth to answer, but instead of saying anything, she sobbed once, loudly, and then began to cry.

"Jane, what are you doing?" Susan was plainly astonished. "I've never seen you behave this way before."

"Don't think I'm crying," said Jane, swiping at the tears which ran down her face. "I never cry. I'm too sensible to do such a thing."

Susan looked at her and said nothing.

"Oh, Susan, I'm not sensible at all. I've fallen in love with a wonderful, beautiful man—who doesn't want me."

"Oh, really? I thought you were in love with my brother."

Jane choked on another sob, then abruptly stopped crying. "I *am* in love with your brother. I'm speaking about him, of course."

Susan grinned. "Did you quarrel with the monster?" she asked sympathetically.

"He's not a . . . Indeed, we quarreled a little." There was no need to tell Susan just how bitter their quarrel had been.

"Was it because of me?" her friend asked, in no way abashed.

"Yes, well, I suppose it was, in part. At least, I think so." Jane sighed, then added forlornly, "Actually, I'm not certain why we quarreled."

Susan said cheerfully, "That is the most fun, I think. However, if your argument was about me, you shouldn't have bothered. I shall stay here for a while, and Marcus will not try to stop me. He knows that such tactics won't work. If he did succeed in making me return to town against my will, I'd be sure to do something so dreadful he'd wish he had left me at Brookefield."

Jane took a lacy handkerchief from her sleeve and discreetly blew her nose. "Is it because of Mr. Houghton you wish to stay?"

"No . . . well, yes," Susan admitted defiantly. "I have a feeling about him, Jane, about him and me. I like him, more than I've ever liked any other man. I like his children, too, even his older daughter, who hates me. They're a challenge. I mean to stay and face it. Besides," she added with a sly grin, "my abigail overheard in the village that Mr. Houghton will be out of mourning very soon. I couldn't possibly leave now, when things could get a deal more interesting."

She licked her lips, making her look to Jane like a cat who anticipated feasting on cream. Her brown eyes sparkled. She had finally found something—someone—worth striving for, Jane thought.

Her own eyes filled with tears again. She wished Susan good luck. If only she, herself, had been so blessed.

The next morning Marcus and Freddy Manning left for London. They went without Susan, just as she had predicted. Jane stood at her bedroom window and watched the two men ride away. Though Marcus looked back once, she did not wave.

What would have been the point? He had not attempted to speak to her again after their quarrel. She told herself that she was glad.

Meanwhile, Susan continued to mend at a remarkable rate, her recovery plainly aided by the visits of Mr. Houghton and two, at least, of his three children. The oldest's ongoing unfriendliness, however, was more than made up for by the approval of the others.

Because of the delightful way matters were going for Susan, Jane felt sure she'd never convince her to leave Brookefield anytime soon. She was correct. Lying in her great bed, her slender form covered by a sheer pink robe, Susan flung her arms wide and yawned. "I think I'll stay here forever," she said, "or at least for another month."

"A month . . . ?" Jane choked over the words. She didn't want to remain there even one more day. She wanted to return to London, where she might, at least, have a chance to see Marcus, even if he didn't mean to propose to her again.

She missed him. She missed the smell of his bayberry cologne. She missed his roughly handsome face. Most of all, she missed his caring nature that he kept hidden beneath a brusque soldier's exterior. "I shall return to London tomorrow," she said. "Lady Lettice will accompany me."

And so they did, despite her friend's pleas to her to stay on. Fortunately, Lady Lettice was nothing loath to go with her. She adored London, as her ecstatic response to it plainly showed as they drew near to Mayfair.

"I'm certainly glad to be back here," she said, opening the window on her side of the carriage to inhale with pleasure the smells of coal fires, horse droppings, and nasty, unidentifiable objects moldering in the kennels by the pavements. "There's nothing to compare with London. Don't you agree? My heavens, I never want to leave again."

Jane *would* have agreed if Lord Brooke had been at her aunt's house to greet them. But he was not there. Nor did he visit another day, though she stayed at home morning after morning in the faint hope that he'd forgiven her and would come to see her.

In the afternoons, when she went driving in the park with one gentleman or another, she looked for him, but he was never about. It was the same at the balls, routs, and breakfasts she attended. Either he had been there briefly and gone, or he had declined his hostess's invitation. Yet he must have known she had come back to town. All she could suppose was that absence had not made him change his mind about her.

Her spirits sank lower and lower. Finally, she gave herself a shake, metaphorically speaking, and came to a decision. "I'm going back to Lincolnshire, Aunt," she addressed Lady Lettice one rainy afternoon, after first cornering the elusive lady in the green saloon.

"Don't say that to me, Jane," her Ladyship replied, "at least not until we've drunk some tea."

After taking several sips of the dark beverage in her saucer, Lady Lettice looked into her niece's troubled blue eyes. "Well, what *is* the matter?"

Jane put down her cup, its contents untasted. "As I said, I've decided to go home."

"But you can't. Your father hasn't yet come back to England. You'd be there alone, except for the servants."

Jane gave her a lopsided grin. "Can you think of a better time to be at home?"

"It's because of me, isn't it?" her Ladyship said, twisting her narrow hands together. "You're so unforgiving."

Her niece gave her an uncomprehending look. "Because of you? Why, how could you think that?"

"Because I know how you are about things. I promise you, however, it was just a small slip, easily forgiven by the average Christian. Besides, I've never pretended to you that I'm a saint."

Jane stared at her. "What are you saying, Aunt? I don't understand."

"Don't try to shame me, Jane," Lady Lettice said with a touch of defiance. "I tell you, I couldn't help it."

The light broke. "Aunt Lettice, are you trying to tell me that . . . ? Don't tell me you . . ." Despite herself, Jane started to laugh.

"Well, I certainly didn't expect *that* reaction," Lady Lettice said hopefully. "Does that mean you don't mind that I helped myself to a small remembrance?"

"A small remembrance? Oh, Aunt, never say you took something from Brookefield!"

"Very well, then, I won't."

"You'll have to return it," Jane said firmly.

"If I do, will you promise to stay here and not leave for your home?"

Jane sighed. "No, I'm afraid I can't do that."

"But you can't go home by yourself. Even Lord Brooke's wild sister doesn't stay at Brookefield alone."

Jane flinched at the mention of Marcus's name. She said, "I shall hire a woman to go with me as my companion. No one can object to that. And I don't care if anyone does," she added stubbornly. "I won't stay here any longer."

Lady Lettice cocked her head to one side, making her look like a knowing horse. "If you're not leaving because of something I've done, then it must be because of your beloved. Don't think I haven't been aware that he's not been dancing attendance on you since we got back."

"You've got to stop calling Lord Brooke my beloved, Aunt." Jane laughed bitterly. "It should be apparent even to you that he isn't."

Lady Lettice shook her head. "The man loves you, Jane. I can always recognize the signs. Tell me everything that's transpired between you. Everything! I shall soon sort out what's gone awry."

CHAPTER 13

JANE looked doubtfully at her aunt.

Lady Lettice returned the look, her brown eyes shrewd. "I know you believe I have one or two peculiarities," she said, almost causing Jane to laugh despite her low feelings. "Nevertheless, you mustn't underestimate me. I'm very wise in the ways of men and women, not to mention other aspects of life. Now, tell me everything!"

And so Jane did, from the first meeting between her and Lord Brooke to his unromantic proposal to his final unproposal. Lady Lettice sat quietly throughout the recital. Only her thin hands, toying with a painted vellum fan, moved in her lap.

With a catch in her voice, Jane finished her story and looked down at her aunt. Lady Lettice nodded as though satisfied with what she'd heard. "It's as I said. The man is head over ears in love with you."

"He has an odd way of showing it," Jane said with a touch of her usual spirit. "I suppose if he thought himself totally obsessed with me, he'd feel obliged to leave the country so there'd be no chance I'd ever see him again."

Lady Lettice ignored these bitter expressions of a

wounded heart. "He loves you," she said blithely. "The problem is that you and he are too similar—only in different ways."

Jane could make nothing of this assessment and for response raised her pale eyebrows and stared sharply at her aunt.

Lady Lettice appeared not a bit discomfited by Jane's look. "What I mean," she continued, "is that both of you care deeply about others. That is the similarity. The difference is that the others about whom his Lordship cares are his family, a few close friends like Lord Manning, and you. He makes no room in his life for the general run of humanity. You, on the other hand, can't seem to help but care about anyone who is in need. You're not discriminating."

"Oh, well," said Jane, not certain whether or not to feel offended by her aunt's assessment of her, "that's the way I am. I cannot see why it should matter much to Marcus."

"Well, of course, it does. He's jealous."

"Jealous?" Jane laughed mirthlessly. "How could he be? I don't have another suitor, not anyone I'd consider as a possible husband, at any rate. I should think that would be obvious to everyone, even Marcus."

Her Ladyship took a sip of her now-cold tea, then cleared her throat noisily. "But that's just it. It's not only other suitors of whom men are jealous. No, indeed. Men in love are apt to be jealous of anything and anyone that diverts their beloved's complete attention from them—even their own babies."

Why was her aunt speaking of babies? If Jane kept on as she was, she'd never have a life's companion, let alone a baby. "I fail to see . . ." she said before her Ladyship interrupted her.

"Take Lord Victor, not that you'd want to, of course. He's that large, overbearing fellow we met at the Pierskalls' last night, the one who tried to push Lord Needing out of the way at the punch bowl." Reluctantly, Jane nodded.

"Where was I? Oh, yes, Lord Victor could hardly wait to marry in order to get an heir. I vow, his wife started increasing as soon as she took her first step out the church door. So, was Victor happy when she presented him with a huge, fat son nine months and four days later?"

"Well," Jane breathed. "Was he?"

"No, he was not. He was jealous of his wife's attentions to the child he'd wanted above all else."

"But that's absurd," Jane said, frowning at her aunt. "How could a man be jealous of a baby, especially one that's his longed-for heir?"

"That's what I'm trying to tell you. Men can be jealous of anything, even a baby. It's the way they are. I suppose we should be grateful that they're not like male bears and devour their young if given the opportunity.

"But never mind that," she said quickly when Jane seemed about to protest this digression to the animal kingdom. "The point is that you have the same problem with Lord Brooke as Lord Victor's wife did with him—but worse. Lord Victor was only jealous of his baby. Marcus Brooke, on the other hand, is jealous of your attentions to everyone: me, those Indians you made sick, and, in particular, I believe, Lady Susan."

"Oh, no. His own sister? How could he be?"

Her Ladyship drew in her lips, so that she looked more like a wise, if emaciated, horse than ever. "Whether he admits it to himself or not, he wants your undivided attention, undivided love, undivided loyalty; and that's because he's the type to give you those things in full measure himself now that he's admitted you into his heart."

"Really? What am I to do, then?"

"As to that, you must convince him that your devotion will always be to him *first*. I think that he will come to be satisfied with that. It is better than nothing. Besides, after he accepts that you won't disappear into the air one day and leave him loveless, he probably won't care how many people you take care of—as long as you continue to put him first, of course. That is the most important thing."

Lady Lettice concluded her little speech by looking very

pleased with herself. Jane, however, appeared not to share her aunt's emotion. "That's all very well," she said, wrinkling her lovely pale white brow once more, "but what am I to do about my situation? I can't force my way into Marcus's house and demand that he listen to my explanation and then marry me."

"Certainly, you cannot. What you must do is wait until the Randolphs' masquerade ball, which is in two weeks. Mrs. Randolph is Lord Brooke's cousin on his mother's side. He'll be sure to accept her invitation, so you'll have your opportunity to talk with him then. Now, as what personage do you plan to go?"

Since Jane had not known of the masquerade until her aunt mentioned it, she'd naturally given no thought to her costume. For several days afterward, however, she could hardly concentrate on anything else.

She knew this might well be her last chance to make a favorable impression upon his Lordship, or even to have the chance to converse with him. Thus, she was determined to present herself in the best light possible.

At first, she considered going to the ball got up as Boadicea; surely a warrior-queen must find favor with a military man like Marcus. However, after thinking about that lady's ignoble end, Jane decided that Boadicea might not be the best choice after all.

She pondered several other possibilities after that, and finally settled on Good Queen Bess because that monarch had never gone down to defeat. Of course, she'd never married, either, but Jane didn't think that lack in her heroine should signify.

Lady Lettice lost no time in vetoing this selection. "Wear one of those great, ugly gowns and an odd red wig?" she asked Jane incredulously. "Where are your brains, child? You must make full use of all the beguilements at your disposal, and dressing like an old, long-dead queen, no matter how distinguished, isn't the way to do it."

She looked Jane up and down critically. "I think you should go as Juno. As well as being most attractive, she was the patroness of well-being and marriage. Since it's your well-being *through marriage* that we're trying to ensure, there's no more appropriate character you could choose to portray."

"But—"

Lady Lettice, caught up in a gorgeous fantasy of her own making, ignored Jane's attempt to demur. "We'll dress you in gold, in a sort of clinging toga-tunic affair, leaving one shoulder bare. You do have good shoulders, don't you? I can't recall."

What was the use of pretending to maidenly modesty with such as her aunt? Jane nodded.

"Wonderful. We'll leave your hair up as it is and place a diadem on it. A gold diadem on your yellow hair," she said dreamily. "It will be splendid."

Jane asked uncertainly, "Do we have one?"

Her Ladyship put a finger to her lip and thought. "I'm afraid we don't," she said after a minute, "but I know just the place to get one. Lady—"

"Aunt, if you steal a diadem from one of your friends, I won't go to the masquerade at all."

"Oh, very well. We'll buy one if you're going to be that way." She stroked her flat bosom approvingly. "As for me, I shall go as Aphrodite, goddess of love and beauty. I can hardly wait."

In fact, the days until the masquerade went amazingly quickly even for Jane, what with fittings and rummaging in warehouses for the proper accoutrements for their costumes. Almost before they knew it, it was the night of the Randolphs' ball.

From the line of carriages leading to the Curzon Street address and the time it took for Lady Lettice's conveyance to move to the head of that line, it was obvious that the affair would be a huge success. Apparently, everyone who was anyone had been invited and had accepted.

For Jane, of course, there was only one guest whose presence mattered. Behind her gold demi-mask, her blue eyes searched discreetly but ceaselessly for Marcus

Brooke. Surely, as tall as he was, he should have been easy to distinguish if he were indeed there.

At last, she saw him, towering over the other gentlemen in the room, impeccably dressed not in a costume but in proper evening attire. In a concession to the fact that he was at a masquerade, he, too, wore a half-mask.

She stared intently at him, but he did not look over at her. His attention was directed to a slender, dark-haired young woman. Head bent, he seemed to be listening raptly to her. Jane felt an intense pain in the upper portion of her toga.

It was quickly followed by another pain, near her ribs. This one was occasioned, however, not by heartache, but by her aunt's sharp elbow. "There he is," Lady Lettice hissed, "talking to some hussy."

As though he'd heard her Ladyship's words, Marcus raised his head and half-turned toward them. His glance caught and locked with Jane's. She felt as though there was no one in the room but the two of them. The sounds made by the orchestra, by people's laughter, and by conversations loud and murmured went unregistered. Mindlessly, she started toward him.

"Not yet," Lady Lettice whispered, grabbing Jane's arm. "At least give him the opportunity to approach you first."

So Jane waited—and waited. Refusing invitations to dance, she watched as Marcus joined the lines with the dark-haired young woman. When the set ended, she saw him offer his partner his arm so that they might promenade about the room.

Jane continued to watch as the couple moved closer to her and her aunt and then came abreast of them. Marcus nodded politely to them both, but it was obvious that he did not mean to stop. Indeed, from his cool expression, it seemed safe to assume that he did not intend to request a dance from her that evening, or even to engage in conversation with her. A hopeless sigh from Lady Lettice indicated to Jane that her aunt agreed with her.

A LARCENOUS AFFAIR 195

Jane's shoulders slumped, but then she straightened her spine. She was Lady Jane Ashworth, five feet, ten inches tall, and very able. What's more, she was a golden goddess, at least for the night.

She would not permit Marcus Brooke—and love—to pass her by. If strong measures were called for, she was capable of them. Now she needed to decide what those strong measures should be.

A passing waiter juggling a tray full of glasses gave Jane her answer. She snatched a glass of champagne from the waiter, then turned toward Marcus and his partner with a wide smile. They paused, giving Jane the opportunity to pour the glass's contents down the front of the young lady's shepherdess costume.

The poor creature shrieked once before Jane commandeered Marcus's attention by waving her arms feebly and saying in a loud, but wavering voice, "One of my spells, I'm afraid." She looked at him beseechingly. "Please, my lord, won't you help me to get some air."

"That's not exactly what I'd like to help you get," Marcus said grimly as he abandoned his companion to take Jane's wrist. He dragged her to the back of the room to a door that led to a stairs. "Let us go to my aunt's sitting room," he said without any evidence of enjoyment at being in her company. "You can get air there."

When they entered the sitting room and he'd closed the door, he lit some candles. Then he went over to a window and threw up the sash. The sounds of carriages and other street noises drifted in.

Jane seated herself cautiously upon a green sofa as though she were made of something fragile. She looked about. The sitting room was papered and painted in several shades of green and filled with plants. It made Jane think of a forest or a jungle. She liked being in such a setting with Marcus. It seemed so . . . so fertile.

At least, she would have liked it, she amended, if he hadn't glared at her as he was doing.

She shut her eyes. "Stop that," Marcus said irritably. "You're not faint. For whatever reason, you threw that drink at Miss Linley on purpose. You are just like my sister," he added, as though that was the worst thing he could say about Jane.

"Really?" she asked brightly, opening her eyes. "How is Susan? I have not heard from her since I left Brookefield, though I've written to her twice."

Marcus looked at her indignantly. "Is that all you have to say? Aren't you going to explain why you behaved like a savage to an innocent girl?"

Jane pressed a languid hand to her head. "I did explain; don't you remember? But, of course, I shall beg Miss Linley's pardon again as soon as I regain my strength. Now, won't you tell me about Susan?"

Marcus spread his palms in a gesture of defeat. "If a scribbled note saying that she doesn't know when she'll be ready to leave Brookefield is something of value, you are welcome to that information."

He scowled fiercely, seeming for a minute to forget Jane's sins. "I don't know what I'm going to do with that chit. I told her in no uncertain terms to come back here, but she won't. I think she gets more rebellious every day."

"I wouldn't trouble myself about her as long as she's content to stay at Brookefield," Jane said gently. "I have a good feeling about her, about her and Mr. Houghton. She does, too."

"Have you both, indeed?" Marcus asked coldly. "I cannot fathom why. A widowed gentleman such as Houghton couldn't possibly want to attach himself to a scapegrace like Susan. Besides, she's not at all in the style of his first wife. Someone told me that Mrs. Houghton was quite a lady.

"Yes, I know," he continued, "you have a good feeling. Well, put your crystal ball away and face facts. If she isn't careful, she's going to ruin herself. And you, too, for associating with her."

Jane rose and put a hand on his arm. "Would you care, Marcus?" she asked earnestly.

"About you? Certainly not. Why would I?" He moved slightly, so that her hand fell away. "Are you feeling well enough to return to that stupid masquerade in the ballroom? Who are you supposed to be, anyway?''

"I'm Juno."

"Indeed? I thought you were the sun, or something equally garish and blinding."

Jane's large blue eyes filled with tears. "Oh, Marcus, don't be mean to me. I cannot bear it."

"All right, I won't," he said hastily. "For God's sake, Jane, don't cry. Please don't cry."

"I shan't," she said as a plump tear brimmed over and coursed down her face. "I never cry . . . except lately."

Marcus's arms seemed to reach out of their own accord to pull her close to him. "My poor girl," he crooned, "why do you do it lately?"

It was now or never. "I think it's because I love you, but you won't ask me ever again to marry you."

"You love me?" He tilted her head back so that he could see her expression clearly. "Do you really?"

"Of course I do. And I want you to know that if you were to relent and marry me, I'd always take care of you first, because you *are* first—always."

Although Marcus seemed somewhat confused by this information, he merely nodded.

"Does that mean yes, you will marry me? I am so glad." As he bent her head forward again so that he could kiss her, she added, "However, I suppose I must point out that we might have a few problems."

"Umm," he said, his mind still on lovemaking, "what makes you think that?"

"For one thing, you did say that I am a managing female."

Marcus relaxed his grip a trifle. "No, I didn't. When you asked me, I just didn't say that you weren't one. However, you are, of course."

"If that is what I am," she said seriously, "I might not change. Can you bear it?"

"People can change," Marcus answered readily. "I mean to."

"Do you really?"

"Of course. I intend to be everything you want me to be."

Jane moved out of his arms entirely and fixed her eyes on his. "I'm glad to hear that, because I've been thinking about that, about what you should be, I mean."

"You do mean to take matters into your own hands, don't you?"

Jane looked closely at her dearest to see if he was criticizing her. His face was grave, but his brown eyes held laughter.

"I'm afraid I must be incorrigible," she said with a deprecating grin.

"That's all right. I don't mind as long as the one you're trying to manage is me."

"I'm afraid I'll do my best. Now, let me tell you what I've been thinking. First, though, I must point out that we are much alike. Even my aunt thinks so."

Marcus's eyes roamed over her beautiful face, down to her full breasts and round, womanly hips, so fetchingly revealed in the tunic, and he started to laugh.

Jane put up her hand. "No, I mean it. Perhaps you did not realize it, but you, too, want to manage things."

"It should not have taken you more than a minute to come to that conclusion," he said agreeably. "Naturally, I want to—and do—manage things. I am a man."

"That is the problem," Jane said, frowning as he laughed again. "No, listen, Marcus. The difficulty is that you don't have anything worthwhile to manage, especially now that your mission concerning Vincent Fleer is at an end."

Marcus shrugged his large shoulders. "What am I to do about that?"

"The answer is simple," she said earnestly. "You must manage your estates. The first thing for you to do is to return to Brookefield and put it in good order."

"Be a country squire, do you mean?" Marcus sounded displeased. "That's a fine occupation, indeed, for a soldier—an ex-soldier!"

"But it is. You could provide food for our people and

the men fighting the war. You could provide a better life for your tenants." Here she hesitated, then said with a blush, "And a beautiful home for your children."

"Our children, for *you* to manage."

"Yes, ours."

"I'll have to take your idea under advisement," he said good-naturedly. "It may have some merit. Now, give over arranging my life, termagant, and kiss me."

After all, one needn't resist all orders. The mature person did not let prejudice blind her to the possible merits of a suggestion, especially if it was for her own good. "Yes, my lord," Jane said sweetly and went back into his arms.

The noise of the door being pushed open made them draw apart. "Oh, you were kissing," said Lady Lettice as she walked into the room. "Good. At least I think it's good. You are going to marry, aren't you?"

Jane nodded her head.

"How delightful. I thought you would. In fact, I already have the perfect present picked out for you."

Jane gave her a suspicious look. "You didn't tell me that."

"Didn't I? Well, I do. It's a bronze statue of Eros, about this high." She spread her hands five inches or so. "He's wearing a strap with a quiver of arrows attached, and not much else. Doesn't it sound lovely?"

Marcus frowned down at her. "It sounds familiar. In fact, it sounds like a sculpture we have at Brookefield. It's in my library, I believe—or, at least, it was. What you have in mind wouldn't *be* mine by any chance, would it?"

"Of course. Do you think you'll like to have it?"

Marcus laughed and said, "Absolutely."

"I was sure you would," Lady Lettice said with a happy grin. "I shall leave you now. Go back to doing whatever it was you were doing before I entered."

Marcus and Jane hardly waited until the door closed again to take her advice. After all, Lady Lettice was a very wise woman.

From the *New York Times* bestselling author
of <u>Forgiving</u> and <u>Bitter Sweet</u>

LaVyrle Spencer

One of today's best-loved authors of bittersweet
human drama and captivating romance.

___THE ENDEARMENT	0-515-10396-9/$5.99
___SPRING FANCY	0-515-10122-2/$5.95
___YEARS	0-515-08489-1/$5.95
___SEPARATE BEDS	0-515-09037-9/$5.99
___HUMMINGBIRD	0-515-09160-X/$5.50
___A HEART SPEAKS	0-515-09039-5/$5.99
___THE GAMBLE	0-515-08901-X/$5.99
___VOWS	0-515-09477-3/$5.99
___THE HELLION	0-515-09951-1/$5.99
___TWICE LOVED	0-515-09065-4/$5.99
___MORNING GLORY	0-515-10263-6/$5.99
___BITTER SWEET	0-515-10521-X/$5.95

For Visa, MasterCard and American Express
orders ($10 minimum) call: 1-800-631-8571

Check book(s). Fill out coupon. Send to:
BERKLEY PUBLISHING GROUP
390 Murray Hill Pkwy., Dept. B
East Rutherford, NJ 07073

NAME_____

ADDRESS_____

CITY_____

STATE_____ ZIP _____

PLEASE ALLOW 6 WEEKS FOR DELIVERY.
PRICES ARE SUBJECT TO CHANGE
WITHOUT NOTICE.

POSTAGE AND HANDLING:
$1.50 for one book, 50¢ for each additional. Do not exceed $4.50.

BOOK TOTAL $ ____

POSTAGE & HANDLING $ ____

APPLICABLE SALES TAX $ ____
(CA, NJ, NY, PA)

TOTAL AMOUNT DUE $ ____

PAYABLE IN US FUNDS.
(No cash orders accepted.)

209C

JILL MARIE LANDIS
The nationally bestselling author of Rose and Sunflower

___ **JADE** 0-515-10591-0/$4.95
A determined young woman of exotic beauty returned to San Francisco to unveil the secrets behind her father's death. But her bold venture would lead her to recover a family fortune—and discover a perilous love....

___ **ROSE** 0-515-10346-2/$4.50
"A gentle romance that will warm your soul."—Heartland Critiques
When Rosa set out from Italy to join her husband in Wyoming, her heart was filled with love and longing to see him again. Little did she know that fate held heartbreak ahead. Suddenly a woman alone, the challenge seemed as vast as the prairies.

___ **SUNFLOWER** 0-515-10659-3/$4.95
"A winning novel!"—Publishers Weekly
Analisa was strong and independent, Caleb had a brutal heritage that challenged every feeling in her heart. Yet their love was as inevitable as the sunrise...

___ **WILDFLOWER** 0-515-10102-8/$4.95
"A delight from start to finish!"—Rendezvous
From the great peaks of the West to the lush seclusion of a Caribbean jungle, Dani and Troy discovered the deepest treasures of the heart.

For Visa, MasterCard and American Express orders ($10 minimum) call: 1-800-631-8571

FOR MAIL ORDERS: CHECK BOOK(S). FILL OUT COUPON. SEND TO:

BERKLEY PUBLISHING GROUP
390 Murray Hill Pkwy., Dept. B
East Rutherford, NJ 07073

NAME_____
ADDRESS_____
CITY_____
STATE_____ ZIP_____

PLEASE ALLOW 6 WEEKS FOR DELIVERY.
PRICES ARE SUBJECT TO CHANGE WITHOUT NOTICE.

POSTAGE AND HANDLING:
$1.50 for one book, 50¢ for each additional. Do not exceed $4.50.

BOOK TOTAL	$ _____
POSTAGE & HANDLING	$ _____
APPLICABLE SALES TAX (CA, NJ, NY, PA)	$ _____
TOTAL AMOUNT DUE	$ _____

PAYABLE IN US FUNDS.
(No cash orders accepted.)

KATHERINE SINCLAIR

__FAR HORIZONS 0-425-12482-7/$4.95
"Riveting!" — *Publishers Weekly*
A captivating novel of three women who clung to their elusive dreams of love and freedom — and never surrendered. From the bustling streets of England and the darkest corners of Australia, to the glistening shores of California, Hawaii and New Orleans, they dared to embark on a glorious journey to the ends of the earth, where every woman's dreams come true.

__A DIFFERENT EDEN 0-515-09699-7/$4.50
"A wonderful escape — I couldn't stop reading!"
— Roberta Gellis, author of *Fires of Winter*
This epic saga will sweep you away to the ends of the earth — to the magnificent estates of nobles, the exotic mysteries of Ceylon, and the untamed wilderness of the American southwest. Here is the glorious journey of a woman's heart. A soul-searching novel of love and dreams, people and places you will never forget....

__VISIONS OF TOMORROW 1-55773-276-0/$3.95
"Engrossing...an exciting journey of discovery."
— bestselling author Laurie McBain
From turn-of-the-century Cornwall to the rugged frontiers of New Mexico, this sweeping novel of love and friendship, tragedy and triumph, captures the poignant beauty of the searching heart — and the glory of golden dreams.

For Visa, MasterCard and American Express orders ($10 minimum) call: 1-800-631-8571

FOR MAIL ORDERS: CHECK BOOK(S). FILL OUT COUPON. SEND TO:

BERKLEY PUBLISHING GROUP
390 Murray Hill Pkwy., Dept. B
East Rutherford, NJ 07073

NAME_____

ADDRESS_____

CITY_____

STATE_____ZIP_____

PLEASE ALLOW 6 WEEKS FOR DELIVERY.
PRICES ARE SUBJECT TO CHANGE WITHOUT NOTICE.

POSTAGE AND HANDLING:
$1.50 for one book, 50¢ for each additional. Do not exceed $4.50.

BOOK TOTAL $ _____

POSTAGE & HANDLING $ _____

APPLICABLE SALES TAX $ _____
(CA, NJ, NY, PA)

TOTAL AMOUNT DUE $ _____

PAYABLE IN US FUNDS.
(No cash orders accepted.)